SKY MACHINE

T. M. BRENNER

Copyright T. M. Brenner 2015

Cover Illustration by T. M. Brenner

ISBN: 0692555579

ISBN-13: 978-0692555576

First Printing

Also by T. M. Brenner
Luminaries
Sky Child
Clandestined
Clandestined: Dark Times

SKY MACHINE

For My Parents

I can't thank you enough.

.

1

What have I done? My stomach twists as I realize that my decision is a mistake. I just left what I know for what I don't. I'm leaving everyone I've ever known behind. My brother Flot. My adoptive-mother Charm. My protectors Helm and Mast. And Ebb; fearless, beautiful Ebb.

I'm also leaving the Crag behind, where I'm worshiped like a god, even though I'm not one. Where people are murdered just because they're different. I won't miss living in fear. Of course, I have no way of knowing if Carter's world will be any better. For all I know, things could be much worse.

Back there, things were changing. Chaff and his evil sons were gone. Life was finally starting to improve. And I gave that up to help this person Carter, who I've never met before, and who I just shot.

I panic. What makes it worse is the darkness. When the dragon's mouth closed around us I couldn't see anymore. Inside it is warm and smells strange, and I start to worry that the dragon will burn us alive with its breath.

Thud. I hear Carter fall to the floor. He grunts in pain. Better that he is alive and making noise than dead and silent.

My eyes start to adjust to the darkness. I see a dim red torch attached to the wall, but it looks strange. There isn't any flame, yet it still makes light. Strips of metal wrap around it, and it's protected by something that looks hard on the outside, but I can still see right through it.

Something else is strange. The inside of the dragon doesn't look like the inside of an animal. I've skinned more animals than I would like to think about, and none of them looked like this. It looks like I'm standing in... a room.

"Where are we?" I whisper to Carter through the darkness.

Suddenly, I hear a loud cracking noise, and someone else enters the long room. Without realizing it, I react. I get down low and pull my knives out, ready to defend myself against whatever this person might do. I put myself between them and Carter, protecting him with my life.

"Stop! Wait!" yells the man.

Knees bent, he holds his hand up toward me, which I think means he doesn't want me to attack him. I can tell from his face that he's more worried about me than I am of him.

"Are you Sam?" asks the stranger.

I look him up and down. He's wearing the same suit of armor that Carter is wearing. I wonder if that should make me feel more comfortable, but it does not.

"Sam, it's okay. He's going to help me," whispers Carter.

I slowly stand up then take a few steps back from Carter, watching this stranger closely.

"You can put away the blades now," says the stranger.

"And you can drown in the loud waters," I say.

I can tell that the stranger doesn't know what I mean.

"Uh, right," he says. "Fine, keep them out. But I'm going to help Carter now, okay?"

I nod.

I hadn't noticed it before, but the stranger brought a bag with him. It looks different from the bags we use for the hunt, but I can tell that's what it is. He dumps out the objects inside it onto the floor.

The stranger moves quickly, finding a thin, sharp thing I haven't seen before. He puts the tip inside a very small container of what looks like water. Like magic, he makes the sharp thing grow in length, taps the tip of it, and a drop of water pours out. Without wasting a moment, he stabs Carter with it.

"Uhnnn," groans Carter.

I take a step forward, worried that somehow this stranger has hurt Carter even more.

"It's okay," says Carter. I can barely hear him. "It was just a shot. It was to help with the pain."

I look at the stranger and he nods at me. He looks back at Carter.

"We need to get you to a med station, now," he says.

"Yeah," is all Carter can manage.

"Sam, I need you to hold this gauze here where you shot him," says the stranger.

"What's gauze?" I ask.

"This white stuff. Now put your knives away and help him!"

I put my knives back in their sheathes, kneel down, and press down on the... gauze.

"Whatever you do, don't take that gauze off the hole."

I watch as the man stands up and hurries out the way he came in.

"Th-thank you," says Carter.

He doesn't look very good. It's still hard to see, but the red light filling the room makes his lips a strange purple color.

"What's his name?" I ask.

"Quinn."

"And why is he here?"

"He's the pilot of this ship."

"What do you mean 'ship', and what's a pilot?" I ask.

Before Carter can answer, the room starts shaking. It feels like I'm suddenly much heavier than I was. The strength of the shaking nearly knocks me over.

When I get back to my feet, I realize that I've pulled the gauze away from him. I move quickly to put it back.

"Unghhhhhhh," he groans.

"What was that shaking?" I ask.

"We're flying."

"Oh. Dragons do that," I say.

His mouth moves like he wants to say something, but instead his eyes look upward, so that I can only see the white in them. I have seen it once, when I watched a gray one die. His body shook as he traveled to the Sky Gods. But I can't let Carter visit them yet. I shake him hard to get him to wake up.

"Carter, I need you to be awake. You can't go yet. Come on Carter, wake up!"

I don't know what to do, so I finally slap him hard in the face. It seems to work, as the color in his eyes comes back. They stare back at me. I can tell he hasn't left yet.

A loud noise, like a new one screaming, fills the room. I can hear Quinn's voice, but it doesn't sound right. What worries me most is that Quinn isn't even in the room.

"Hold on tight back there. ETA seven minutes."

"What kind of magic was that?" I ask.

"What do you mean?" asks Carter.

"How does Quinn speak when he isn't here?"

"Oh, that's just the intercom."

"What's a..."

Before I finish my question, Carter makes a sound with his mouth like rushing water. "Shhhhhhhhhh." I don't know what to say. He seems happy that I've stopped talking, so I stay quiet.

"I just need to rest," says Carter, closing his eyes.

I nod at him, and press harder on the gauze.

2

Quinn comes back into the room and pushes something on the wall. Suddenly the room is filled with bright, white light. It stings my eyes for a moment, but I can see much better now.

I stare at Quinn's face. He looks like he's almost a gray one. Light yellow hair that's short, and none on his face. He's tall; taller than Carter.

"I have her on auto-pilot, so I could come back and check up on Carter," he says. "Is he still breathing?"

"Yes. What is auto-pilot?" I ask.

"Oh, that's where the ship flies itself."

"Of course it flies itself. It's a dragon," I say.

"I forgot; you don't know... Okay, well, this thing you're on is called a ship. It's something that humans built that can fly. Most of the time we use it to move either people or cargo from place-to-place."

"What's a human?" I ask.

"A human is us. You're a human, and so am I."

"Oh. Humans made this... ship then?"

"Yeah. Kind of amazing, huh? Well, you'll get used to it. Been piloting these things for half my life."

"What's a pilot?" I ask.

"Someone that flies a ship. I make it go wherever I want. I can control everything from up front."

I start thinking about the ship. What it is. What they can do. Then I realize something's wrong. Keeping the gauze on Carter's chest with one hand, I slowly pull a blade out with the other.

"Quinn, are you the pilot that killed my people?" I ask.

"What? Of course not! Were your people attacked by a ship, like this one?"

I stare into his eyes, trying to see if he's lying, but the only thing I see in them is fear. Good. He should be afraid of me. I slide the knives back into their sheaths.

"Yes. Many have died because of your ships. A man who I thought of as my father was killed. His name was Lagan. His death is why I became the Leader of the Hunt."

"Whoa, stop right there. Our ships would never do that. But there are more people out there than just us, ya know?"

"No, I didn't know. We thought we were the only people that survived the End War," I say.

"The End War? That was like, hundreds of years ago. So you've been in that cave for hundreds of years? Or at least your people?"

"I don't know. What are years, and what does 'hundreds' mean?" I ask.

"Wow, so you don't even know what time is? Crazy. I think I'll let Carter explain that one. I should get back to the front so I can land this crate," says Quinn.

"What's a crate?" I ask as he walks away.

"Don't worry about it. We'll get you all figured out later. Just keep Carter alive for me."

I look down at Carter as Quinn leaves. His skin is very pale, as if he'd stayed in the cave his entire life. That can't be a good thing. I put my ear to his mouth, and I can feel his breath on my skin. He is still alive, but he may not be for much longer.

After a few moments of worrying, the ship starts shaking again. I feel much lighter. This time I'm ready for the shaking, and I'm able to stay next to Carter, keeping the gauze on his wound.

I feel a sudden, very sharp drop. I'm knocked over,

but I somehow keep the gauze in place. I get back up on my knees and check his breath again. He's still breathing, but it's weaker than before.

Quinn comes back into the room and pushes a different place on the wall. The mouth of the ship opens, pouring light in from the world outside, making it harder to see.

The shadows of several men stretch into the ship. They are wearing armor like Carter's and Quinn's, only much bigger. As they climb up into the mouth of the ship, I can see what look like small skulls painted on their dark armor. Fear makes my heart pound, and I turn to Quinn for answers.

"It's okay," he says. "They're here to help."

I turn back around. One of the men is pointing something at me. It looks like the gun I shot Carter with. He has it aimed right at my chest. I reach for one of my knives, but before I'm able to throw it, the man pulls the trigger.

3

Every part of my body hurts. It feels like I've spent an entire day lifting rocks. I feel my chest where I was shot, and I'm surprised to find there isn't a hole in it. It's sore, but not bleeding. Touching the back of my head I can feel where I must have hit the ground when I fell.

Once I'm sure that nothing's broken I open my eyes. What I see makes me panic. I'm in a very small room. It isn't wide enough to stretch my arms out all to my sides, and barely long enough for me to stretch my arms the other way.

I can't see much, but what I can see are walls all around me; solid, except for one. The last wall is made of some kind of metal. It looks like they've taken metal spears and made them reach to the ceiling.

I kick at them, but they do not move. I run and use my shoulder to hit them, but the only thing it does is hurt my arm.

I yell, as loud as I can.

"ARHHHHHHHA!"

I kick at the spears a few more times but nothing happens.

This small room makes me feel wrong inside, like I'm still inside the Crag, trapped in one of the narrow tunnels we use. I have to get out of here.

I look around the room for something I can use to hit the spears with. I see something that may be a bed, only high up off the ground. It looks softer than what I'm used to. I lift it into the air, and below it is more metal; thin, long pieces and they're all connected. I try pulling on them but they won't move.

I turn and see something round and metal in the corner. It's short, reaching only to my knees. I look down into it, and it's filled with water. I decide not to drink it, because I don't know if they have poisoned it. But if they won't let me out of here, I may have no choice.

It takes me a moment to realize that they've left me with nothing I can use to escape. In my panic, I hadn't noticed that I'm no longer in my armor. I look down, and I'm wearing clothes. They are very strange, and very thin, and are the orange color of a setting sun.

I look at my chest, and in black letters I can read W-V-S. That is strange. What does that mean? I stare at the letters for a moment and realize they aren't for me to read; they are meant for others to read. The letters are upside down. What is written on the shirt is my name: S-A-M.

Without thinking, I put my hand up to my neck. I feel a small bump, but I don't know why it's there. It feels sore, like I injured it somehow, but I don't remember it happening.

I go back to the spears and stick my arms between them. There is just enough room that I can reach out, but I cannot fit my whole body between the spears. I look past them, and I can tell that just outside the room is a long tunnel stretching in both directions. I can't see or hear anyone else. I yell, trying to get someone to come, but no one does. After a few moments I stop yelling, because my throat is sore.

My fear of small spaces, of being trapped takes over. The room starts to feel even smaller. My head spins and I put my arms out to catch myself, but it's no use; I fall to the floor. I barely notice the pain in my knees as they strike the hard ground.

I keep my eyes closed to stop the spinning, and think of fields of grass and clover. Of being outside, breathing in the fresh air after it rains. When everything smells clean and alive.

I struggle to get into bed. Every few moments I wipe away the tears, but eventually I calm down. Somewhere, there is a better place than this.

I lay there, trying to fall asleep. My thoughts are with Flot and Ebb. It makes me wonder what's happening back at the Crag. Whether they were able to find Chaff's stash of seeds. If they've chosen a new Leader of the Hunt, and who it is. If they can still grow enough food to survive without Chaff's help, and who will replace him as Leader of the Harvest now that he's gone.

I also wonder about Carter. My hope is that I didn't kill him. I just wanted to make sure that he wasn't sent to trick us. When I saw that he controlled a dragon, I thought he might have magic powers, and could heal himself. But it seems that my guess was wrong.

After a long while, and after shedding many tears, I'm finally able to sleep.

* * *

BANG! A loud noise wakes me. It's the sound of wood against metal. I look up and see someone standing at the spears, staring in at me. Without realizing it, I've moved to the back of the room, as far from the spears as I can get. I bend my knees low and reach for one of my knives, when I remember I don't have them anymore.

The person on the other side is holding something black that looks like a weapon. Something he could beat me to death with; a piece of wood the length of his elbow to his fingertips, and then a little more. It has a handle on it, and is shaped like the letter 'L'.

I can't see the person's face well, but I can tell that it's a man. His dark hair is thin, and pulled across the top to look thicker than it really is. He's wearing the same black armor that the people who attacked me wore.

He sets something down on the ground then slides it through a gap in the spears that I hadn't noticed before. The hole won't do me any good because it's too small to fit through. I look down at what he's brought me, and I realize it's food. He backs away from the metal spears and walks away.

"Wait!" I yell. "Who are you? Why am I in here?"

I nearly step on my food as I move to the spears. I can barely see him as he walks to the end of the tunnel and disappears.

Looking down, I kneel so that I can pick up the food. It rests on a rectangle of metal. There is meat I think, and there are peas, carrots and smashed potatoes. There is also a metal cup filled with water. Why would they give me water when there is the large metal bowl full of it in the corner?

I smell the food to make sure they haven't put wolfsbane in it. It smells just like it should. I scoop some of the smashed potatoes into my mouth and they taste good. They've put spices inside to make them taste better, and they are smoother than what they make for us in the Crag.

It doesn't take me long to eat, and I'm surprised when suddenly the food is gone. The fear in my stomach hid the pain of hunger from me. I drink all of the water without stopping, and afterward let out a very loud belch.

I lie back down on the bed. My stomach doesn't hurt as much, and I can hear the noise of food moving around inside it. It feels like I haven't eaten in days. I just hope I can keep all this food inside me.

The sound of footsteps echo off the tunnel walls. The same man that brought me food comes up to the spears and looks in at me.

"Are you done?" he asks in a voice that makes me cringe.

"Yes."

"Then hand me your tray."

"What's a tray?" I ask.

"What do you mean? Oh, that's right, you're the primitive. They told me you were dumb. It's amazing you can speak at all. Carter must be sniffing cinnamon if he thinks you'll amount to anything."

I can see the man better now that he isn't moving. His

nose is sharp and crooked, his teeth are yellow and rotten. As I stand up, I can see they've done the same thing to his armor that they've done to my shirt; his name is Grintz.

"Is Carter alive?" I ask.

I can smell his breath, which makes the food in my stomach want to come out. He just grins and walks away.

"Wait, come back! Please! I need to know!" I yell.

4

The next day I have to make waste very badly. I don't want to do it in a corner, because it will make the room smell. Back at the Crag we would just go outside, dig a hole and then bury what we'd done.

I ask Grintz what I should do, and he says "Haven't you ever seen a toilet? Of course you haven't, stupid primitive. That back there is the toilet. Use that."

"How?" I ask.

"You just sit down on it, do your business and then flush it."

"What does 'flush' mean?"

"I didn't think you could be any more of an idiot, but I was wrong. You see that handle there? Yeah, well you pull it, and it makes it all go away. And use the toilet paper to wipe yourself. Start acting like a human."

A pair of days go by, and then another one. I only ever see Grintz. He brings me food, says cruel things to me then goes back down the tunnel. I promise myself that if I ever get out of this trap, I'll make sure he never treats anyone like this again.

Finally, someone else comes.

* * *

"Quinn!" I yell as I finally see someone I know. Someone not as horrible as Grintz. Things have been so bad that I think I'd be happy to see Chaff if he were still alive.

"Hey Sam. I'm sure you have a lot of questions, and I'm sorry you're locked up, but there are people above us that make decisions, and they say you have to stay in there for now."

"People above you? Like the Sky Gods?" I ask.

"What? No. Like, people. Humans. Breathing and moving, and taking up space. It's just a figure of speech," he says.

"What's a figure of speech?"

"Heh. I heard you'd been grieving the guard with all your questions. Figure of speech means that you say one thing, but mean another."

"Like lying?" I ask.

"No, not like lying. It's where you say something that kind of means something similar, but isn't exactly what you mean."

"Oh," I say, not really sure I understand. I can't hide the confusion on my face.

"That's okay Sam, we'll try to help you learn once they let you out of this cell. We hope that will be soon. Carter's recovering. He was in a coma for two days, but he pulled through. Thanks for helping me save his life," says Quinn.

"Why are you thanking me? I was the one who shot him. It was my fault he almost died. And what is a coma?"

"A coma is where you sleep, and they can't wake you up, but you aren't dead. Everything else works, you just aren't awake for it. And I figure you didn't really know what you were doing when you shot Carter."

"Yes I did. I knew that it would hurt him," I say. "I had to make sure I could trust him, that the gun could actually kill him. I didn't want him dead, but it was the only way."

"Yeah, well, don't go telling anyone else that. If they think you shot him on purpose they'll kill you for it. Carter and I have been telling everyone you didn't know what the gun would do; that it was an accident. If anyone asks, that's what happened. Understand?"

"So you want me to lie? I hate lying," I say.

"You better get used to lying or you won't last long here. Sometimes you have to lie because you know things that other people don't. You're smarter than they are, and they might not be able to understand why you did something. So to keep them from being angry, or doing something stupid, you tell them what they need to hear. That way they do the right thing," says Quinn.

"What kind of a horrible place is this, where you have to lie all the time just to survive?"

"I ask myself the same question every day."

For a moment I just stare at Quinn. I go back to my bed, lie down and cover my head.

"I need out of here," I say.

"We're doing what we can," says Quinn.

"You don't understand. This room; I need out of this room. I can't stand small spaces. I can feel my mind changing. It's taking all the control I have not to run myself into the spears until I die."

"Spears? What spears?"

"The spears that keep me in here. Those," I say, pointing to the metal that separates us.

"These are called bars," he says.

"Whatever they're called, I want to throw myself against them. That's how bad it feels. The only thing that makes me calm down is this," I reach out my left arm and pull back my shirt. His face fills with worry as he sees where I've scratched my fingernails into my skin. Some of the cuts are older and healing. Some are new, and still bleeding.

"You grew up in a cave, and you have claustrophobia?" says Quinn, confused.

"What is... "

"Claustrophobia is a fear of small spaces. It's what you have," says Quinn, talking over me.

"Please, Quinn. Help me get out of here. You can keep me trapped in a room, but please, make it bigger."

"Alright. I think I can convince the doctor to agree to move you. But you have to be good now. You can't fight the guards when they take you to another room. No trying to escape. Do you understand?" asks Quinn.

"No. What's a doctor?"

"A doctor is a nice person that heals you."

"What is… "

"Just hold off on more questions for now," says Quinn, interrupting. "It's going to take you a long time to learn how things are done around here. Be patient. Listen; don't talk. Understand?"

I think for a moment.

"Yes," I say.

"Okay, good. Now just hang in there until we can get you moved."

I nod my head. Quinn turns and leaves.

5

I still have to wait a few days before they try to move me. Grintz isn't there, which helps. I think if he'd been there, I might have tried escaping. It would've given me a chance to finally hit him. If I ever get out, I'm going to spend the rest of my life avoiding him.

My new room isn't much better than the old one. Same bed, same toilet, same bars. But this room is large enough that I don't get dizzy anymore. I haven't scratched my arms since moving.

The room is just big enough that I can run in circles now. I do that to stay strong, so that if I get out, I won't be useless. Back at the Crag there weren't many kinds of jobs; only skill jobs and strength jobs. If you weren't skilled, you could always work hard at a strength job to make up for it. Since I probably won't have any skills that will help in this new place, maybe I can use my strength to survive.

I have to wait another day before Quinn returns. He comes at night, just before they turn off what Grintz told me were 'lights'. Makes sense that they'd be called that, because that's what they do.

"Like the new cell?" asks Quinn.

"What's a cell?" I ask.

"What you're in. That room is called a cell."

"It's better than the old one."

"How are you doing?" he asks.

"Surviving, but I need to get out of here," I say.

"Well then I have some good news for you. They're releasing you tomorrow."

"Thank the Sky Gods!"

"Yeah, well don't thank them yet. Carter convinced our CO to let you go, but only under a few conditions. The first is that you'll need to start learning everything. Math, history, science, reading, writing, geography, and all the other basics you don't know. It's going to take a lot of work. What you're going to learn, you only have a few months to study. They're going to cram about sixteen years of learning down your throat, so try not to choke on it, okay?"

"Okay," I say. "What do you mean by 'cram down my throat?"

"It's just what we say when someone forces you to do something difficult."

"I think I understand."

"The second condition is that someone will have to watch you at all times. They'll assign someone to you at the Citadel, and after your training, Carter will keep track of you so you don't do anything stupid. He'll basically be your CO," says Quinn.

"What's a CO?"

"It's short for 'Commanding Officer'. It's the person above both me and Carter. They make decisions and send us on missions. Anything else?"

"What's a year? You still haven't told me."

"And I'm still gonna let someone else teach you that one. Anyway, try and get some rest. You're gonna have a big day tomorrow. They're taking you to the Grand Citadel to start your training."

For the first time I have real reason to hope.

"Will you and Carter be going with me to the Grand... " I can't remember the word.

"Citadel? No. We have our jobs here, out in the wastelands. Once you finish your training, they'll ship you back here. Just stay smart, work hard and I'm sure you'll do fine," says Quinn.

"Will Grintz be going with me?" I ask.

"No. He'll keep working here."

"Good. I hate him."

He turns to walk away.

"Quinn, thanks," I say.

"Yeah, no problem. Just promise me you won't do anything stupid in the meantime."

"I can't do much of anything, being locked up like this."

"Then keep doing that." says Quinn.

I can tell he thinks he's being funny, but there's no laughing when you aren't free.

6

"How's my favorite prisoner?"

Grintz' voice startles me awake. I sit up in bed and see that he's standing just outside the bars. The tired feeling, making it hard to concentrate, tells me it isn't morning yet. Dim light from the hallway casts knife-like shadows on Grintz' face. He's brought his wooden weapon along with him. Something is wrong.

I get out of bed and move to the back of my cell. Grintz tries to open the bars with what I remember him calling a 'key'. He has a hard time getting the key to fit in the lock, but eventually does. As he twists the key, a click echoes inside my room. The cell door swings open.

Fear makes the hairs on my neck stand up. I can feel my body go cold, even though I'm sweating. I watch as Grintz slowly comes inside the cell, staring straight at me. He reaches back and drops his keys outside of the bars then closes the door behind him.

"I want to make sure you can't escape too easily. No fun in that, is there?"

"What do you want, Grintz?" I ask. "I don't want to fight you, if that's why you came here."

"I don't want you to fight me either."

"Then what do you want?"

Grintz shows his disgusting yellow teeth, trying hard to smile.

"I think you know what I want, and this is my last chance to get it. You leave tomorrow. Can't let you go without saying goodbye."

"Grintz, if you touch me, I'll kill you."

"Will you? How would that look? You already shot one person, and if you kill another? Don't you think they'd put you to death for it? Even if you said it was self-defense, they're not gonna take any chances on a primitive like you. No, they'll burn you. Burn you until there's nothing left but ash."

Is he right? Will they kill me even if I didn't do anything wrong?

"Now, be nice, and stay quiet, and it'll all be over soon enough," says Grintz.

He's close enough that I can smell his breath. It smells like beer, only worse. It smells like dead things. Rotten meat. The bone piles.

He reaches for my clothes so I punch him in the face. Just a short punch to let him know he can't touch me. To get him to stop.

At first he takes a step back. He wipes at his mouth to make sure it isn't bleeding. Then his mouth turns back into the same evil smile that I sometimes see in my nightmares. Grintz lifts up his weapon and swings it at me. I block it with my arm, and it hurts like it's being burned. I scream out in pain.

The scream startles him for a moment, distracting him just long enough that I can hit him back. I punch him in the face again, this time with my strong fist. His nose explodes in blood.

His smile disappears. He lifts the weapon again and swings it at me. I do the only thing I can think to do, and block it again with my left arm. He hits me, then hits me again. Something's wrong. The bones between my elbow and hand break, and it twists my arm, making it useless. I cry out in pain, dropping to my knees. Grintz takes a step back as I hold my dead arm against me.

Grintz tries to wipe the blood off his face, but only smears it, making him look like a living nightmare.

"Well, after roughing you up I'm a prisoner for sure. Better make it worth it." says Grintz.

He steps forward, puts the weapon under my throat and pushes me against the wall. I have a hard time breathing and I panic. Grintz gets closer to me, and spits blood right in my eyes. He grabs my shoulder and spins me around so that my face is pressed up against the cold, gray wall.

"You're gonna enjoy this. Never had an unsatisfied customer," says Grintz.

I hear a metal sound behind me. He seems distracted, fumbling with something. I kick up and backward with all my strength, and I feel my foot connect. The pressure against the back of my head goes away, and I hear Grintz fall to the ground.

I stand over the top of him. Grintz swings at me again with his weapon. It connects with my right shin, sending me to the ground. He pulls the weapon back, and I reach out just in time to stop it with my good hand. I twist it in a circle, until his hand twists in a way it shouldn't. Grintz cries out and let's go of the weapon.

I hit him in the face with it a few times as I scream. His body seems to relax like I've knocked the strength out of him. I put my ear close to his mouth and can tell that he's still breathing.

It takes all of my strength to stand up. As I walk slowly toward the door of bars, Grintz reaches out, trying to grab my ankle. I pull away and step down hard on his hand, breaking a few of his fingers. I keep moving until I reach the bars.

Throwing the weapon through the bars, it bounces off the tunnel wall, making a loud 'clank' sound. The keys aren't too far away. Using my good arm, I reach out and pick them off the ground. There's so many of them. I have to stretch hard to put the key inside the lock. The first key doesn't work. I pull them back, holding them between my knees as I ready another key on the ring. I try the next key on the lock and it doesn't work either.

I turn and see that Grintz is still moving. He slowly drags his body toward me. I panic again and drop the keys then pick them back up as quickly as I can. I lose my place, not knowing what keys I've already tried, so I just pick one and try it. It doesn't work. I try another, and another. Grintz keeps moving closer.

Just as he reaches me, I find the right key and the door opens. Grintz grabs hold of my ankle, tripping me, sending me to the ground. I can't stop my fall with my broken arm, and it bends painfully underneath me. My head hits the stone floor hard. Kicking back at Grintz' hand, I get him to let go. I have to drag myself out of the cell with my good arm, but finally do. I slam the door closed, trapping him inside.

Half the world is red. I move my hand to my forehead and I can feel a cut pouring blood into my eye. Touching my mouth, I find a few of my teeth are missing. That's when I realize that Grintz has the keys.

He drags himself up the bars, reaching to use one of the keys in the lock. I pry at his fingers, trying to get them to let go of the keys before he can unlock the door. I'm finally able to break one of his small fingers and he lets go.

Thankfully, my pants have pockets, so I put the keys inside one. I pick the weapon up off the ground and make my way down the long tunnel. Even though I've only been down this tunnel once, I can remember which way I was brought to my cell. It's a skill you pick up when you live in a cave.

I take a right and then a quick left, down the long hallway, and then another right. But I stop and listen for a moment just before the final left. I hear someone talking, and I can make out the words 'escape' and 'Sam' very clearly. Somehow they know I'm out of my cell.

What if they have guns? What if they plan to shoot me? I look down at the wooden weapon in my hand then at my broken arm. It hangs at my side like it's not even attached. I have to fight the urge to throw up.

I drop my weapon on the ground then listen for another moment. I hear the word 'unarmed'.

"Sam?" a woman yells.

"I'm here," I yell back.

"I need you to come out slowly, with your hands folded behind your head."

"I can't. My arm is broken."

"Okay, we'll have someone look at it when you come out. But I need you to keep your hands where we can see them."

"I can do that. I'm walking to you now. Please don't shoot me," I say weakly.

Moving as carefully and slowly as possible, I turn the corner. About a handful of guards are standing there, pointing guns at me. Fear shoots through me like sky fire. But I keep moving toward the group, doing my best not to worry them.

"Get on your knees," yells the same woman.

My knees bend but too quickly. They hit the ground hard, sending pain up my whole body. I feel weak and dizzy, blood still pouring from my head. Keeping my eyes closed, I hope for a quick death. It doesn't come. I can feel one of the guards move behind me then put something metal on my wrists. I cry out in pain as it twists my broken arm.

"Careful, the prisoner's arm is broken," comes the woman's voice.

It's the last thing I hear before everything goes dark.

7

It feels like I've been asleep for a long time. My eyes hurt
when I finally open them. The gray walls have disappeared,
and have been replaced with light blue ones. Where there was
no sunlight before, there is now an opening I can see through.
It looks like there's a thin wall there, made out of the same
stuff that protects lights. I can also see that the sky is filled
with clouds, and it makes me feel better.

I look around the room and notice a wooden door.
To the left of that are shelves covered in many things I've
never seen before. There's also a very strange looking metal
box, almost as tall as I am. The metal thing makes bright green
lines that move up and down. The lines are beautiful to watch,
and seem to move the same way; over, and over.

Everything smells clean. Too clean. Unnatural, and it
worries me.

I look down and see that I'm covered by a blanket.
My right arm has a circle of metal wrapped around it at the
wrist. The circle is connected to another circle of metal, which
is wrapped around a bar that's attached to the bed I'm lying on.
I pull at it, but it won't let go. Even after what happened, I'm
still a prisoner.

My other arm has something hard and white wrapped
around it. It still hurts, but not like when it first broke. I tap
the shell against a bar on the other side of the bed and it's
solid. It also sends pain up my arm.

"Is anyone there? Can anyone hear me?" I say loudly.

After a short moment, a woman comes into the room.

"Oh, you're finally awake," she says. "Don't you worry, we were able to get your arm put back together just like normal. It'll take a few more weeks to heal properly, but you should be good as new soon enough."

"What is this white thing on my arm?" I ask.

"It's a cast. It will help your arm heal", says the nurse.

"What are weeks?" I ask.

"I'm sorry, what?"

"What are weeks?"

"What do you mean, dear?"

"I don't know what the word 'weeks' means. Can you tell me?" I ask.

"Well, a week is seven days of course," says the woman.

"And what is 'seven'?"

"It's... a number. It's this many," she says, holding up all the fingers on one hand, and a pair of fingers on the other.

"So numbers help you keep track of how many you have of something. Is that what numbers are?" I ask.

"Yeah," she says, looking confused. "You know, the doctors weren't sure if your brain was damaged because of the injury to your head. I'm sorry to say that it seems rather bad. You must have amnesia."

"What's amnesia?" I ask.

"It's where you forget things. Like your name. Do you remember your name, sweetie?"

"It's Sam."

"And do you remember where you come from?"

"Yes, the Crag."

"What's the Crag?"

"It's a cave."

"You live in a cave?" she asks.

"Yes. Me and many other people," I say.

She pulls my eyes open further, one at a time, and shines a small light into them. It makes them water.

"Equal and reactive. That's good at least, but I'll get the doctor anyway," she says. "I've never seen amnesia mixed with delusions like this."

I decide not to ask her what 'delusions' are. Instead, I watch as she leaves the room.

* * *

It takes a while for someone to finally check on me again. The woman comes back into the room and brings a short, nervous looking man with her. He comes up to me and checks my eyes with a light, just like the woman had. He breathes out a deep sigh once he finishes.

"I don't know what to tell you, nurse," he says, turning to the woman. "Everything looks okay. We were told not to ask Sam here too many questions. And when the government tells you to do something, you do it. We don't know if Sam's a science experiment, or test subject, or the devil incarnate. We don't know, and we don't care. So stop asking questions, okay?"

"Yes, fine, whatever you say, Doctor."

I can tell that Nurse isn't too happy with Doctor. Doctor leaves, but Nurse stays.

"Nurse, what does your name mean?" I ask.

"Oh, you think 'Nurse' is my name? No, nurses are people that help you when you're sick or injured. We're underpaid and under-appreciated. We do all the real work around the hospital. My name is Rose."

"What's a hospital?" I ask.

"The place you're in. Where we fix people."

"You mean, you change people?"

"No. Although, come to think of it, yes. Some people don't like how they look, and we can do surgeries and such to change that. But generally we just help people get better."

"So is Doctor his name then?"

"No. Like Nurse is what I am and what I do, Doctor is what he is and what he does. You can call him Doctor Vial. He's a bit of a jerk though, so be careful what you say around him," she says.

"If nurses do all the healing then what do doctors do?"

"Mostly they play golf, smoke expensive cigars and chase after young women. Oh, and they drive really fast in their dangerous and impractical cars."

"I didn't understand any of what you just said."

"That's okay sweetie, why don't you just get some rest."

Rose puts another pillow under my head and pulls my blanket up higher. She also touches something on the side of the bed and it lowers my head and back.

"Rose, how did you do that? How did you move the bed like that?" I ask.

"I just pushed the down button, dear."

"What's a button?" I ask.

"My goodness, you don't know what a button is? It's just something you push to make something happen. Like to turn on the lights, or turn on a machine. You really don't know what a button is?"

"No."

"Well, there's buttons everywhere. You really can't go anywhere without running into a button. Better get used to them," says Rose.

"Can I try a button?" I ask.

"Uh, sure. Here's a control for the bed. You can make it go up or down, however you want."

She hands me the control. I see a pair of what must be buttons. I can read that one is 'up' and the other is 'down'. I press the down button, but nothing happens. I try the up button and it raises my head and back up.

"I like that," I say.

"That's wonderful. Okay, I'm going to let you rest now. If you need anything, there's a red button on the other side. Push it and someone will come check on you."

I flip the control over and I see the word 'alert'.

"Alert," I say out loud.

Just as Rose is about to leave the room, she stops. She

turns around and stares at me.

"You can read?" she asks.

"Yes."

"But you don't know what a button is?"

"No."

"Strange. Very strange." she says, turning around and leaving.

I close my eyes and try to sleep.

8

Ｗhen I wake up, Carter is standing over me, looking down. He's wearing some kind of strap for his arm on the side I shot. I also notice that he's not wearing the armor he had before. Instead, he has on a shirt that is like the one I'm wearing; white, long, and with an opening in the back.

"Carter?" I say.

"Hey Sam. How are you holding up?" he asks.

"Better, now that I finally see someone I recognize. How's your shoulder?"

"Still sore. They were able to keep it from getting infected, so that's good."

"What is 'infected'?"

"Oh, it's when the wound gets worse, and makes you sick, and doesn't heal right. But my wound is healing right," says Carter.

I smile.

"What is that thing on your arm?" I ask.

"It's a sling."

"That's strange, I use a sling to hunt animals. That doesn't look like my sling," I say.

"They're different, but the same. You know how yours holds onto a rock? Well if you made the part that holds onto the rock much bigger, it would look just like this. Instead of holding a rock, it holds my arm."

I nod my head in understanding. My eyes drift back

down to the metal rings that are keeping me from getting up.

"Why am I still a prisoner?" I ask.

"Well, Grintz' says you faked that you were sick, so he came into your cell to check on you and you overpowered him. I don't buy it. Grintz is a piece of garbage, and I doubt it went down that way. But I wanted to find out from you what did happen."

"I think he wanted to... join with me."

"What do you mean?" he asks.

"It's how new ones are made. You know, *join*," I say.

"Oh. Wait, really?"

I just nod.

"He tried to... I'll kill him." says Carter.

There's anger in Carter's eyes, a kind of anger I've seen many times before. It's the kind that flashes in the eyes of killers, when they see that you can do something they can't. I also know what that anger can do to someone.

"Will you get in trouble if you kill Grintz?" I ask.

He stops and thinks about the question.

"Yes. They will put me in prison," he says.

"Then it's not worth it. I need you, because you're the only person I know here. I don't even know you that well. If you're in prison, I'll be lost," I say.

"Okay," he says. "I won't kill him. But we'll make sure he ends up in prison for what he did."

"How do we do that?"

"There's going to be a trial tomorrow."

"A trial? Where they make you find a burning torch, or fight someone, or make you drink poison?" I ask.

"I'm not sure I understand what you mean," says Carter.

"They put me through trials back at the Crag, to make sure I'd be a good leader. If I failed, they said they would kill me."

"No, the trial won't be like that. Sometimes though, if they think you're a bad enough person, they will put you to death. But you have to be a real danger to other people, and you generally have to kill a lot of people for that to happen. You haven't killed anyone as far as I know, right?"

I think about my answer for a moment. I sent Chaff and his sons to their death by making them leave the Crag, but I've never killed someone with my own hands.

"No, I haven't killed anyone," I say.

"Good. So when we go to the trial, only answer the questions you're asked. If they tell you to talk openly about something then you can tell them your story. But don't try to interrupt. Listen to what the judge tells you. Okay?"

"Okay."

"So you know what a judge is, then?" asks Carter.

"Yes. A judge is someone that helps people come to an agreement. So that both groups can be heard." I say.

"It's amazing what you know and what you don't know. The nurse told me that she taught you what a button was. That's crazy."

"Where I come from there aren't any buttons, and there definitely aren't any boxes with green lights on them. What is that thing?" I ask, looking at the large box.

"That machine shows your heartbeat. When you're scared, or worried, or running, the line will move faster, because your heart beats faster. It moves slower when you're resting. If for some reason your heart stopped, someone would quickly come check on you. It makes a loud noise that will hurt your ears."

"What's a machine?" I ask.

"A machine is something that does work for you. Something that you can't do on your own, or might not want to do. They make life better for us."

I think for a moment.

"Am I a machine to you?" I ask.

Carter's face looks confused then worried.

"What do you mean?" he asks.

"Did you take me from the Crag so that I will do something you don't want to do?"

He looks at me very seriously. "No, Sam. I would do

it if I could, but I can't. I don't have your mind. From what I can tell, you may have a gift. We're hoping your gift may help everyone here. Save everyone here."

"What gift?" I ask.

"Your ability to strategize, to lead warriors into battle."

"So then I am a machine to you, because I'm able to do something that you can't do," I say.

"I don't think of you as a machine, Sam. You're a person. A very important person. We think you might be the key to ending the war."

"What if I don't want to war?"

"The reason we're asking you to help is so we can save lives. War is happening whether we like it or not. And if we're able to overwhelm our enemy, quickly and decisively, then they will give up, and more people will live because of it."

"I still don't understand why you think I'm special," I say.

"Because I watched you take down a ship with a stick. A tree limb. Do you know how ridiculous that sounds? You found the one weak spot on something that should be invincible to a group of primitives."

"What is a primitive? Grintz kept calling me that. I hated it when he said it."

"Primitives are people that don't have access to all of the information and machines that we have. We consider the people of the Crag primitives because you don't make machines," says Carter.

"We can grow food, and make armor and weapons," I say.

"Yes, but you don't have machines to help you harvest plants, or make armor or weapons. You do everything by hand."

"I hate the word 'primitive'. Don't ever call me that. Don't ever call my people that either."

"I'm sorry," says Carter, looking serious. "I won't."

I nod to him.

"There was another reason we thought you'd be a good candidate to lead," says Carter. "You advanced tactical warfare in the Crag several hundred years in a matter of two days. You went from having the hunters use an antiquated phalanx formation, to forming a three-prong flanking attack, to using small specialized groups for specific situations. If you look at the history books, it took hundreds of years for warfare to evolve. You know, it wasn't all that long ago when people just stood in a wide line and fired at their enemy."

"I don't understand most of what you just said, but I think I understand what you mean. I come up with ideas sometimes, and they seem obvious to me," I say.

"And that's what I wanted to know, whether you were using a book on strategy that you had in the Crag, or if you were coming up with ideas on your own," says Carter.

"Just my own thoughts," I say.

"Well, you're either a genius, or you just got lucky. I guess we'll find out once you're trained. I hope for our sake that you're a genius."

"What is a 'genius'?" I ask.

Carter just laughs. He pats me on my good shoulder then leaves.

9

I rest for a while. Nurse Rose eventually comes to check on me. After I eat, she brings me a few books to read. It takes her a moment to realize that I won't be able to turn the pages with my arms still wrapped in metal. So instead she hands me a small, long box.

"That's the remote for the TV. Feel free to watch whatever you like. We don't get many stations, but you should be able to find something you'll enjoy," says Rose.

"What's a TV?" I ask.

"I do hope you get your memory back soon. The first fifty or so questions were cute, but now it's becoming annoying. To answer your question, that black screen over there is a TV. When you push the buttons on the remote, it changes channels. Here, I'll show you," she says.

She grabs the box from my hand and pushes down on what looks like a red button. Suddenly, part of the wall changes colors and lights up. It's kind of like the heart machine, only this one shows more than just a green line. There are pictures of people, and they move, and it's almost like I'm looking at smaller people inside of a box.

"How? How does it work?" I ask.

"The TV? Haven't the foggiest. I'm not an engineer. And before you ask what an engineer is, they're someone that builds machines."

"How come you need engineers? Why don't you just

have machines build machines?" I ask.

"Well aren't you smart all-of-a-sudden? There are some machines that can make other machines, but someone still needs to come up with the ideas. So far, there aren't many machines with good ideas," says Rose.

She shows me how to work the remote. How to make the sound louder and quieter. How to change what she calls 'channels'. Different people are on different channels. One channel even reminds me of a book back at the Crag; the one about the cat wearing a hat.

I stop and watch one channel that seems exciting. There are lots of people, and they're wearing strange armor and helmets. What's even stranger is that they're wearing clothes on top of their armor.

The more I watch, the stranger it seems. They keep throwing a brown object back and forth. Every once in a while the object gets kicked by someone. It looks like there's a pair of groups, and they try to move the object in opposite directions. I wonder if this is what war is to these people. I guess it is better than real war, because I haven't seen anyone die yet. Maybe it's a game, just like jump stones.

Rose leaves and I change channels. Some channels show nice and happy things, while others show people hurting each other. Some of the channels make me very sad. They show people who look like they don't have enough food to eat, or are sick. If this place is so much better than our 'primitive' Crag, then why are people starving? The only time anyone starved in the Crag was when Chaff was being cruel.

The more channels I watch, the more I worry about this place. Finally, once I've watched enough, I press the red button on the remote and the TV turns off.

* * *

The next morning I'm startled awake. There's a tall man in my room that I've never seen before. His black hair looks like he put meat grease in it then smoothed it backward. I can tell he doesn't work outside, because his skin is very pale. He's also wearing some kind of clothes I've never seen, with what looks like a rope around his neck. It's red, and has darker red lines going across it.

I can tell he has a white shirt underneath the rope, but he also wears what looks like another black shirt over that. I try to guess why someone would wear so many clothes, other than to stay warm, but it makes no sense. It looks uncomfortable, and would make it very difficult to do anything useful like hunt or work fields.

"I'm Collin Reigns, your representation at the trial," he says, reaching out and shaking my good hand, which is still attached to the bed. The metal rings clank against each other.

"What do you mean by 'representation'?" I ask.

"I'm your lawyer. I'll be speaking on your behalf," says Collin.

"What's a lawyer?" I ask.

"What do you mean?"

"I mean I don't understand what a lawyer is," I say.

He looks very confused.

"Do they not have lawyers where you come from?" he asks.

"They don't even have buttons where I come from," I say.

He stares at me like I must be crazy. I don't really care; I'm tired of people thinking I'm stupid just because I don't live in this place.

"I need to make a phone call," says Collin.

"What's a 'phone call'?"

He keeps looking at me like there's something wrong with me. I watch as he walks out of the room.

I hear him talking to someone, but I can't hear anyone talking back to him. His voice is filled with frustration, and I can tell he's disagreeing with whoever it is he thinks he's talking with. I catch a few sentences, like "I can't do this", "what do you mean 'primitive'", and "how am I supposed to defend someone that doesn't even know what a lawyer is?" I'm very much beginning to dislike this 'lawyer'. The last thing I hear is "Fine Francine, if they say I have to, then I'll do it. But tell

Roger that my debt is paid in full!"

Collin stays out in the hall for a moment, makes a noise like he has something caught in his throat, then comes back in the room.

"Okay, Sam. All I've been told is that you lived in a cave, that you're very important to someone high up, and that you don't really know anything. Oh, and that according to you, a prison guard named Grintz assaulted you. Is that true?" he asks.

"Yes, I lived in a cave, but I have no idea if I'm important to anyone but Carter. I do know many things; like how to hunt, and skin animals, and treat people well. That's something you never learned. And yes, Grintz attacked me. He came into my cell in the middle of the night and tried to join with me."

"What do you mean by 'join'?" he asks.

"Do you know how new ones are made?"

"New ones?"

"New people. Do you know how new people are made?"

"Yes, of course I do," he says.

"He tried to do that to me," I say.

His anger shows on his face. I tell him everything that I can remember, and go over it with him a few times. He says it's important to remember as many details as I possibly can. That the other lawyer may ask questions to see if I'm lying.

"You can't trust lawyers," says Collin. "They'll try to get you to make a mistake, so that the judge and jury will think you're lying."

"How can I trust you?" I ask.

"If you're smart, you won't. But I've been sent here to help you. It's my job to make sure that you are fairly represented. I will do what I can to win your case," he says.

"I hope so. I'm worried that if the judge doesn't like what they hear, they may put me to death."

"They won't put you to death, Sam. You haven't killed anyone. They might put you in prison for a long time though."

"How long?" I ask.

"Maybe ten years."

"How much is ten? Is that a number? And what is a year?"

"Okay, ten is this many," he says, showing all of his fingers. "And do you know what a day is?"

"Of course. I'm not an idiot."

"Well, you know how the weather changes from warm, to very cold, and then back to warm? A year is about how many days it takes to go from one warm period to the next."

"In the Crag, we count the number of snows," I say.

"That's nice," he says, but his voice sounds like he doesn't mean it. "Anyway, if they find you guilty, you'll be put in prison for ten years, or I guess ten snows."

His words make my stomach hurt.

"I don't want to go to prison," I say.

"I'll do my best to make sure that doesn't happen," says Collin. "You should rest. The trial will happen this afternoon. Just remember what I told you, and we should be fine."

10

I'm too nervous to sleep, so instead I watch some channels on the TV. After a while, I finally find something that I'm interested in. It's a channel about hunting. The hunter talks about different animals that are good to eat, how to avoid predators, and finally shows how to use a bow and arrows.

His bow is different from my own. Mine is simple and made of wood. His looks like it's made of something black, and it bends more than mine. Also, his bow has a pair of round things on it that spin when he pulls back the string.

When the hunter actually starts killing animals I decide to change the channel. I would be happy to live the rest of my life without having to kill another living thing.

I watch people cooking food instead. For some reason, watching them cook calms me. It makes me wonder if I wouldn't have been happier back at the Crag cooking, instead of hunting. I think I would like cooking with Cleave. Once the cooking channel ends, I turn off the TV.

I rest for a while, and eventually Collin returns.

"Sam, we need you to look presentable. I brought you some clothes that should fit, if I guessed your size right."

"Thank you."

"Don't thank me, you'll be paying me back for it," says Collin.

"Paying you back? What do you mean?" I ask.

"With money. I get paid money to do my job."

"What's 'money'?"

Collin's jaw clenches in frustration.

"I'm going to kill Francine when I see her. I don't do pro-bono work anymore. And don't even get started on the whole 'what does pro-bono mean', okay. Could this really get any worse? I don't see how it could," says Collin.

I decide to keep my mouth closed. If he's supposed to be helping me, it's probably better that I don't annoy him. He leaves the room, makes another phone call, and this time he yells so loud it actually hurts my ears, even though he's outside my room.

Collin comes back into the room. He just looks at me. Every few moments he paces then goes back to staring at me. I do my best to ignore his angry stares. Eventually, a guard comes into the room. His skin reminds me of Helm's; a very nice dark brown color. He smiles at me, pulls out a key, and removes the metal circles from my wrists. It's good to finally have my freedom back, even if it might not last.

My arms are sore from being in the same position for so long. It's hard to move my broken arm, and it still hurts, so I do everything carefully. I start to take off my clothes so that I can change into the ones that Collin brought me.

"Whoa, hold on there, Sam. We're going to give you some privacy so you can change," says Collin.

"What do you mean by 'privacy'?" I ask.

"It means we'll leave the room so you can change, so that we won't see anything."

"Why would it matter if you saw me without clothes on?"

"Well, where we come from, you don't just see people walking around naked. I guess things were different back in that cave they pulled you out of."

Collin and the guard leave the room, closing the door behind them. It seems strange to me that people would hide their bodies all the time. Of course, there were a few times I was around Ebb where I didn't feel comfortable being naked around her, or her around me.

I look through the bag of clothes that Collin brought me. There are a few extra things in the bag that I'm not sure of, so I decide not to put them on. I pull out a shirt, but it doesn't seem like it would wrap all the way around me and stay together. Bringing the shirt with me, I open the door to the hallway.

"Collin?" I say.

"Are you changed already?" he asks.

"No. I can't figure out how to make this shirt work."

"Just use the buttons on it."

"I don't see any buttons," I say.

"The buttons are those white, plastic circles. Use those."

I try pushing down on one of the buttons, but nothing happens.

"I think the buttons are broken," I say.

"Could you be any more of an idiot? Here," he says, grabbing the shirt away from me. "See, you take the button and you find the hole on the other side of the shirt that matches. Start from the bottom so that you don't mess it up. Then you stick the button through the hole, like this."

I watch as he puts one of the buttons through the hole.

"Now they're attached," says Collin.

"I thought you pushed on buttons to make them do something. Like on a machine."

"Yeah, well, there are different types of buttons, okay?" he says.

Collin throws the shirt at me. I decide to ignore him and go back into the room to start changing my clothes. I struggle with the shirt, and can't get the sleeve over my cast. After a few moments of fighting it, I give up and go back into the hallway.

"Collin?" I say.

"Whoa, Sam, you can't be out here naked!"

"Why not?" I ask.

"You just can't," says Collin. "Why aren't you

changing?"

"Because I can't get the shirt around my cast."

"Fine, I'll get the nurse to come help you. Just go back inside."

I turn around and walk back to the sleeping mat. Sitting down, I stare at the floor while I wait. It takes a few moments, but the nurse finally comes in. She helps me into the shirt, and even with her help it's hard getting the shirt around the cast. Once it is, she helps me with the buttons. I can't bend my arm well enough to work them myself. When the shirt is finally on me, the nurse leaves.

As I start to put on my pants, I find a button at the top. But instead of having buttons all the way down, there are tiny pieces of metal on each side of it. I take the pants out into the hallway to ask Collin how to connect the sides.

"Sam, what are you doing? You still aren't covering yourself!" yells Collin.

"Sorry," I say, trying to stay calm. "How do you make the pants work?"

"There's a piece of metal at the bottom. Pull it up. It's called a zipper," he says, looking away from me.

I go back inside the room. I'm able to get the zipper figured out. I like it better than having to do buttons. I finished getting dressed then walk out into the hallway.

"That's better. Everything fit okay?" asks Collin.

"Yes, although I have no idea how you're supposed to hunt or cook in these clothes. They don't move with me very well," I say.

"That's because they're not meant to be used for those things. They're meant to appear expensive, so that people will think you have a lot of money. When people think you have money they treat you better. And that's because you are better."

"Do you have a lot of money?" I ask.

"Yes, yes I do," he says, smiling.

"That's funny," I say.

"Why?"

"Because I know I'm better than you, and I don't have any money at all."

Collin's eyes pinch together in anger.

"You're lucky you're connected," says Collin. "Because if you weren't, if I took you on as a client by myself, I'd quit. Or I might decide to represent you, then purposely throw the case. I'd make sure you went to a prison for a very long time."

"I hope *you* go to prison," I say.

"Forget what I said before. I'd make sure you got the death penalty."

My fists clench. I want to hit him as hard as I can, but something tells me that would only make things worse. I might feel better for a moment, but then they would put me back in prison. I need my freedom more than I need to hit Collin. It takes me a moment, but I let the anger leave me.

"You ready then, freak?" asks Collin.

"What does 'freak' mean?" I ask.

"Just shut up and come with me."

I follow behind him as we walk down the long, brightly lit hallway.

11

As we turn the corner I can finally see what's outside. Before, I could only see clouds and sky. Now, what I see makes me dizzy. I can feel my knees weaken under me, and I have to reach out and hold the wall. Once I recover, I press my face against the wall I can see through to get a better look at the world below me.

The first thing I notice is how high up we are. Only birds and black fliers can fly so high. I see people walking down on the ground, and they're so far away I can't really tell what they're doing. I can barely tell that they're people.

I also see these strange, quickly moving boxes. They must be machines of some sort, and it worries me that they move faster than any animal I know of.

"What are those boxes?" I ask, pointing down to the world below.

"Just keep your mouth shut until we get there," says Collin.

He keeps walking, so I decide to follow behind him because I don't know where else to go. I have no way of feeding myself in this place, and I need to find Carter. My best chance of doing that is to suffer through the trial.

I run up to Collin but stay just behind him. I let him walk in front of me, because if something bad happens, I want it to happen to him first. I follow him around another corner and find myself in a small room with several doors. Collin goes up to one of them and pushes a button to the side of it. We stand there for a long moment, waiting. I have no idea what we're waiting for, but I stay quiet because I know asking him will only make him angrier.

I hear a noise that I've never heard before that sounds a bit like metal hitting metal. One of the sets of doors opens. Through the doors is a very small room. I can see panic in the face of someone inside, until I move and realize that it's only me. Back in the Crag, you could kind of see yourself in puddles, but it was very hard to see. This new wall shows me how I must look to other people.

Collin and the security guard both enter the room. I stand there, frightened of walking inside.

"Get in," says Collin.

"I... I don't like small spaces," I say.

"It's just an elevator. If you don't get in, you won't get out of this building, and then you're going to prison for sure. They'll force you to go down the elevator regardless."

I close my eyes and slowly walk into the tiny room. I hear the doors shut behind me. The room makes a noise and I feel lighter somehow, almost like I'm falling, but not as bad. I open my eyes just the smallest amount, and I notice that Collin and the security guard are looking in the other direction, toward the doors. I decide to turn around, but I'm not sure why.

I start to panic and reach out with my good arm. I can feel a bar behind me, and I hold onto it, trying my best not to fall. My thoughts go to grass and clover, to Ebb, Flot, Charm; any happy memories I can think of to distract me.

The feeling of lightness disappears and I start to feel heavier. It feels like something is hanging onto my body, like very heavy clothes. The heaviness finally disappears with a bounce, and I hear the same noise I heard when the room arrived at the top. Thankfully, the doors open and I run to get out of the small, frightening room. Collin laughs behind me.

"Seriously? You lived in a cave and you're claustrophobic?" says Collin. "You must be the most useless person where you come from."

"Back at the Crag I was the Leader of the Hunt. I killed a dragon, or what you know as a ship, with only a spear. I invented the bow and arrows. And according to Carter, I may be the one person that can save this awful place," I say.

"No one cares. Here, you're nobody. In fact you're less than nobody, because you aren't even useful. No money, no skills. You don't even know what a lawyer is!" he yells.

I spit at him. It seems to have surprised him so much that he doesn't know what to say or do. He just stares at me, pulls out a piece of cloth and wipes his face with it.

"Guard, I've changed my mind. Use the cuffs," says Collin.

"Cuffs won't work 'cause of the cast," says the guard. "But I can use a zip tie."

"Do it," says Collin.

I don't fight the guard. He's been nothing but nice to me. The guard takes my good arm and pulls it slowly behind my back, then my broken arm. It hurts for a moment as he puts some sort of strap around them. It makes a strange sound, like tapping your fingers very quickly. I don't like having them behind my back, and I worry I might fall as I walk.

"I can still spit," I say.

"And I can do something a lot worse than have your arms strapped together," says Collin.

There's nothing I can do except ignore him. It isn't easy though. Everything about him makes me want to hit him.

The guard holds onto my arm as we walk so that I don't fall down. I can finally see doors that lead outside. The guard and I walk behind Collin, and as he approaches the doors, they slide open by themselves.

"How... " I start to ask, but think better of it. It's frightening to go through doors when you don't know if they'll grow angry and crush you, but I do it anyway.

Collin walks up to one of the fast moving boxes I saw from up high, although this one is sitting still. He opens a door on the side of it. Inside, it looks like a place for people to sit. The guard helps me into the machine, pushing my head down so that I don't hit it on the metal top. I watch as the guard closes the door then walks back inside the hospital. Normally, small spaces like this would make me panic, but it helps to be able to see what's outside.

There's another man inside the machine, wearing dark clothes and something strange on his head. It rests on the top, but doesn't protect his face like a helmet would. It looks like it's made of cloth instead of leather.

Collin gets in on the other side of the box, sits next to me, and slams the door closed.

"Driver," he says. "Take us to the Tower of Justice, and hurry. This scrap's got a court appearance in twenty minutes."

The machine suddenly takes off and everything outside becomes a blur.

"What's... " I start to ask. Collin just turns and stares at me, daring me to finish what I was going to ask. Instead, I turn away and look out through the clear door, watching everything pass by.

I've never moved this fast before. At first, I don't think I like it very much, but once I start looking straight in front of me, and I can see what's coming more easily, I actually want to go faster. I wonder just how fast this machine can go.

Looking ahead, I can see more places like the hospital, reaching upward into the sky. Some look so tall that they could touch the clouds. They're beautiful, in their own serious way. Most of them have walls that you can see through, and almost all of them are painted white, like cliff walls.

The path we're taking becomes steep. Looking to my right, through the clear wall of the machine, I can see water below us on both sides. I worry that we might drive off the path and fall to our deaths, but it looks like they've put metal bars up along the path to keep us from doing that. I can see people in machines down on the water, and I guess they must be boats. I remember reading about boats in the Book of

Knowledge, but we didn't have any in the Crag because we never really needed them. It makes me wonder how many things I already know about...

"An automobile! We're in an automobile," I say.

"What?" says Collin. "You don't know what a button is, and you don't know what a lawyer is, but somehow you know what an automobile is. How is that even possible? Wait, never mind, don't tell me; I forgot for a second that I don't care."

"Are those buildings? The tall things like the hospital?" I ask.

"You're a genius," says Collin.

"So I'm right?"

"Yeah, Sam. Now shut up."

For the first time since leaving the Crag I feel a small amount of hope. If I can just think back to what I learned from the Book of Knowledge, maybe I can understand this place better.

"Sir, we're about to reach the Tower of Justice. ETA two minutes," says Driver.

"Driver, is that your name, or your job?" I ask.

Driver laughs.

"It's my job. My name is Fergus. Fergus Anthony Fletcher. Thanks for asking."

"Fergus, does everyone go by the names of their jobs here?" I ask.

"No. Very few people do, actually," he says.

"This really is an exciting conversation, but let's just all shut up," says Collin.

"That's fine. It doesn't really matter because we're here anyway," says Fergus.

"Good. Let's get this over with," says Collin.

12

I look up and realize that the Tower of Justice is even taller than the hospital I was in. It hurts my neck to see the top from below. It's white, like most of the other buildings, but this one is different. There are rocks that have been shaped like people standing high above us, looking down. Above the door, in large gold letters, are the words "May Justice Serve All". I pray to the Sky Gods that's true.

Collin steps out of the automobile, as does Fergus. I wait as Fergus comes around to my side to help me out. It takes a moment, because my balance is still off thanks to the strap that keeps my wrists together. I step out onto what looks like very smooth rock, much like the smooth rock that we were just traveling on. I can't even imagine what type of machine they must use to make rock look like that.

"Good luck in there, Sam," says Fergus.

I smile the best that I can, but his face tells me that fear and sadness are showing on mine.

Collin grabs the strap behind me, in the middle, and starts shoving me toward the building.

"Wait, what are those?" I ask.

"Those are steps. You walk up them," says Collin.

"They look dangerous," I say, not wanting to fall on them.

"Fine, we'll take the ramp," says Collin, pushing me around the side of the building. We reach smooth rock again and this looks much easier to climb. Once we reach the top, Collin waves his hand to one of the outside guards and she comes up to us. This guard doesn't look as friendly as the last one, but at least she's not as bad as Grintz. Collin spins me around so that the guard can remove the strap. I look behind me as the guard pulls out a very small knife. She cuts the strap and my arms drop.

Once both of my wrists are freed, I have the sudden feeling that I should run. That I should do everything I can to get back to the Crag, and away from this dangerous and frightening place. But people are counting on me to save them. At least that's what Carter said. I hope for his sake and mine that he's right.

Collin grips my arm and pulls me into a spinning door with him. I can tell he's trying to keep me from running away, and to make sure I don't get lost.

The room at the bottom of the building is huge. The walls are made of stone so smooth that they look like what see-through walls are made of. Shiny, dark, and impossibly smooth.

We get in line behind many other people. They're all going through a very strange doorway. There are no walls around it, and what's even stranger is that there's no door. On each side of the doorway is a guard. I watch as several people pass through, one by one, and nothing happens.

"Is this a ritual?" I ask Collin.

"Is what a ritual?"

"Walking through that doorway. Is that part of how your people worship the Sky Gods?"

"Sky Gods? Who are the Sky Gods? Is that part of some stupid cult from your cave?"

"You must know of the Sky Gods," I say. "They protect each of us, watch over us and test us. They created everything."

"Your Sky Gods don't exist," says Collin. "And people don't have much use for religion anymore. After the End War, most people lost hope. Our fair government decided to stop giving tax breaks to people who donate to churches, and took away the churches' non-profit status. After a few hundred years they couldn't afford to do business anymore, so they closed up. Now the buildings are used for offices or housing for the poor. And the government, in a very passive-aggressive way, was able to rid itself of religion. Not through laws, but through simple economics."

"What do people believe in then? If not the Sky Gods then what?"

"Power. Resources. Wealth. Doesn't really matter, does it? Okay, it's your turn to walk through. Go through slowly, don't act aggressively, and you'll be just fine, primitive."

I turn to him, get really close to his face and whisper: "Don't call me 'primitive'."

He just stares back. I turn around, walk through the doorway, and nothing happens. I don't feel any differently. I thought that maybe something would happen, or I'd feel something change. Collin walks through behind me. Nothing happens to him either.

Collin grabs my arm and pulls me toward another elevator. A loud noise screams behind me, so I turn back to look at the doorway. The pair of guards have guns in their hands, pointing them at someone on the ground. There's a light on top of the doorway that I hadn't noticed before, and it glows red and bright.

"What's going on?" I ask.

"Just some idiot trying to bring a weapon into the Tower. Happens all the time. Don't know why they can't figure out they'll be caught. Of course, if criminals weren't so stupid, I'd be out of a job."

"What's an idiot?" I ask.

"Just someone who isn't very smart."

"So that doorway knows if someone has a weapon?"

"Figured that out for yourself, did you?" says Collin.

"Are all doorways like that?"

"No, just certain ones. Mainly places that people are more likely to bring weapons to. Come on," says Collin, pulling me along.

Having been on an elevator once helps, but not enough. As soon as the doors open I walk in, turn around, grab the bar again, close my eyes and hold on. This time it feels different than before. I feel heavier as we move upward. Eventually everything gets lighter, and it feels like the elevator has stopped moving. The doors open, and I push my way past Collin to get out.

"Eager to be sent to prison for the rest of your life?" asks Collin.

"Eager to get hit in the face?" I ask. "Where I come from, you wouldn't last a day."

"Where you come from they eat their own feces. I'm not worried about it, because here I'm king. Money, power, women; I want for nothing," says Collin.

"Except for a soul," I say.

"Souls are overrated. Nobody with a soul ever amounted to anything."

13

Collin turns and starts walking down the hallway. I hurry to keep up. The building is very much like the Crag; with many twists and turns. The walls are white, just like outside of the building, and the floor looks like it's made out of brown fabric of some kind. It feels soft underneath my feet, and I prefer it to the hard stone floors that I'm used to.

We finally reach a room with a very large door. Above the door is a sign that says the word "Chamber" and there are other symbols that look like letters, but aren't. I wonder if those are numbers. Before I can ask, Collin grabs my arm again and brings me into the room.

The first thing I'm surprised by is the large group of people here. There's almost as many people in the room as there are hunters back in the Crag. There are many places to sit, and most people sit to the sides of the room. A smaller group of people are off to the right, sitting in what looks like an animal pen. At the front are a pair of tables, one on each side.

That's when I see him. Grintz is here, sitting at one of the tables. He's wearing the same kind of clothes that Collin is wearing. Collin looks comfortable in his clothes, like he was meant to wear them, while Grintz looks out of place. They don't look like they fit right. It makes his disgusting appearance even more obvious.

I realize that Collin is bringing me up to the front and

I hesitate. He has to push me to keep me moving. There's nothing I can do to Grintz, so I decide to hold in my feelings, my instincts to hurt him. Collin leads me to the empty table on the right, near the animal pen, and has me sit down in a chair. Collin sits next to me, blocking my view of Grintz.

I sit there quietly, not knowing what to say or what to expect. I watch as Collin pulls a small machine out of his pocket. He sets it far in front of him, almost to the edge of the table, then pushes a button.

I'm amazed by what happens. Suddenly, the section of table in front of him looks like the TV back at the hospital. I can see things on the surface, things that look like pages from a book. Collin reads them, moving them around as if they were real papers. A few he crumples in his hands and throws away, even though they aren't really there.

I look up and finally notice that there's another table straight in front of us. It's very tall and made of a beautiful dark wood. Just to the side of it, on the right, is an even smaller animal pen with a chair. It's much lower than the table next to it.

Motion off to the left catches my eye, so I turn to see what's happening. A woman comes out from behind a door wearing a long black shirt that stretches to the ground. It seems strange that someone would wear something that could make them trip. The woman's hair is silver, down to her shoulders, so she must be a gray one. Her skin looks like she's been out in the sun, but it has a different kind of color to it that I haven't seen before. It makes me wonder how many different colors of people there are, and it makes me kind of sad that there are only a few different colors of people in the Crag.

A guard standing next to the woman starts to speak.

"All rise. The honorable Judge Vernona Pham presiding."

Everyone stands up, so I stand up as well. I assume it's a ritual of some sort. Maybe it's to show respect to the judge. If I want her to help me, I will have to show her as much respect as I can. That will be difficult until I know how things work here.

"You may be seated," says the guard, and we all sit back down.

I watch as the judge moves her hands around her desk. She makes the same kind of motions that Collin did when he was looking at his imaginary papers. I notice that she has the same kind of machine on top of her desk. She must be looking at the information about what happened. After a long moment, the judge finally speaks.

"For the sake of expediency, we will be combining trials, as both parties are considered to be defendants against each other. The charges against Citizen Grintz are as follows: assault in the second degree, attempted rape, and attempted murder. The charges against Interloper Designate Sam are assault in the first degree, attempted murder, and attempting to flee a correctional institution. Mr. Wincott, council for Citizen Grintz, how does your client plea?"

"Not guilty, your honor," says the man sitting next to Grintz.

"Mr. Reigns, council for Interloper Designate Sam, how does your client plea?" asks the Judge.

Collin turns to me, stares at me with an evil grin, but after a moment it fades. I think he's trying to scare me. It's working, but I refuse to show it. He finally turns back to the judge.

"Not guilty, your honor."

"As I assumed," says the Judge. "Mr. Wincott, present your opening statements."

"Thank you your honor," says Wincott. He looks very different than Collin. Where Collin is young and strong looking, Wincott is old and round. His clothes look like they were once nice, but have been worn so often that they're almost falling apart. He also wears a pair of metal circles in front of his eyes. When he turns in the light I can see that the circles have clear things in them. I wonder what they're for. He walks up to the people inside the animal pen and starts talking to them.

"Ladies and gentlemen of the jury, what we have here is a clear cut case of an interloper attacking a noble and upstanding citizen. Citizen Grintz is someone that is just like you. He could be your brother, or your father, or even your son. All he was doing was his job. We will prove that Citizen Grintz entered Interloper Sam's cell because the interloper feigned illness, and Citizen Grintz was only trying his best to help. We will also prove that Interloper Sam brutally attacked Citizen Grintz in an attempt to escape lawful custody. We would like to recommend the death penalty, as we feel that Interloper Designate Sam is a menace to society, and a danger to all citizens."

"That's a lie!" I yell. "Everything he said is a lie!"

Collin turns to me and covers my mouth with his hand. He brings his face close to mine and shakes his head back and forth, telling me I shouldn't talk. The sound in the room grows louder as I hear people talking. Words like 'primitive', 'savage' and 'dangerous' fly through the air.

"I apologize for the outburst, your honor," says Collin, looking at the Judge. "My client is new to our rules and procedures, obviously, and doesn't understand that they should keep their mouth shut. I guarantee there won't be another outburst."

"See that there isn't," says the Judge. "Were you finished, Mr. Wincott?"

Wincott turns to look at me and smiles. "Yes your honor, I believe I'm finished."

As much as I may want to hit Collin right now, I want to hit Wincott even more. He thinks he's better than me, smarter than me. That he's already won. But I did nothing wrong, and I will prove it.

"Mr Reigns, you may share your opening statement," says the Judge.

Collin stands up and straightens his clothes. He walks with confidence over to the jury pen. In a soothing voice, like the voice people use to calm new ones, he speaks.

"Ladies and gentlemen of the jury, we will prove that Grintz entered Sam's cell with the intent to rape and do bodily harm. We will show that Grintz has a history of past accusations against himself for similar acts. We will also show that even when Sam had the upper hand, and could have done more bodily harm to Grintz, Sam did not. This is a clear cut case of self-defense. Of someone being attacked in a vicious manner by an opportunistic monster. Is Sam a citizen? No. But Sam is a decent human being who deserves our consideration and understanding. Thank you."

I look at the faces of the jury people. Most of them don't seem sure that either lawyer is telling the truth. Collin was right to tell me not to trust lawyers, because it seems that no one trusts lawyers here. Unfortunately, I need Collin's help whether I like it or not, and whether I trust him or not.

14

Collin comes back to our table and sits down.

"Mr. Wincott, please call your first witness," says the Judge.

"I'd like to call Citizen Deitrich Grintz to the stand."

I watch as Grintz walks up to the small pen and sits down. One of the guards in the courtroom walks over to Grintz and raises his left hand, making an 'L' shape with his arm. Grintz does the same with his right.

"Do you, Deitrich Grintz, swear to the Council of the European Federated Coalition that the testimony you are about to provide is both accurate and honest?"

"I do," says Grintz.

"And do you understand that bearing false witness, committing perjury or otherwise attempting to manipulate the court's interpretation of the facts in this case can lead to penalties, prison sentences and/or in some cases death?"

Grintz looks worried, but finally responds.

"I do."

The guard steps away from the pen as Mr. Wincott walks up to Grintz.

"How are you feeling Citizen Grintz?" asks Wincott.

"I'm fine, but a bit nervous."

"Well, you have nothing to be nervous about since you're innocent. May I call you Deitrich?"

"Yes."

Grintz seems to calm down some.

"In your own words, Deitrich, please describe what happened the night of the attack," says Wincott.

"I was on my nightly rounds, making sure that everything was okay with the prisoner..."

"Let me stop you right there for a moment," says Wincott. "So you work as a prison guard. Tough job."

"Very."

"But honorable. You protect the outside world from dangerous prisoners. Is that right, Deitrich?"

"Yes. Yes I do."

"And your accuser, Interloper Designate Sam, was a prisoner in your prison. Is that also correct?" asks Wincott.

"Yes it is," says Grintz, looking at me with his crooked smile.

"Thank you. Do you happen to know why Interloper Designate Sam was in prison?"

"Objection," says Collin, standing up. "Not pertinent to the case at hand."

Both Wincott and Collin look toward the judge.

"Overruled," says the judge. "It may be pertinent to the character of the witness."

Collin looks frustrated but sits down.

"Thank you your honor," says Wincott. "Deitrich, can you tell us why Interloper Sam was in prison?"

"I believe Sam shot a soldier."

"So you're saying that Interloper Designate Sam was in prison for trying to kill someone. It seems that the interloper over there has a history of attempted murder. Wouldn't you say so, Deitrich?"

"Objection your honor, both for leading the witness and for asking the witness to speculate," says Collin.

"Sustained."

"Please continue Deitrich. Describe in your own words what happened," says Wincott.

"I was making my rounds and I heard groaning noises coming from the prisoner's cell. I looked inside and saw that the prisoner was on the ground, barely moving. I was worried that the interloper might be sick or hurt, so I opened up the cell. I leaned down to see what was wrong, and then the prisoner punched me in the face. When I realized it was a trick, I pulled out my baton and used it to protect myself. The prisoner went crazy, trying to attack me, and I kept blocking their arm with my baton. That's when the prisoner's arm broke. I tried to hold them back with the baton, but eventually the prisoner knocked me to the ground. I reached out and tripped the interloper, who then kicked at me, crushed my hand and escaped," says Grintz.

"The picture you paint is one of a crazed animal, a monster. I must say Deitrich, I'm very glad you survived your ordeal," says Wincott.

"So am I," says Grintz.

"No further questions your honor," says Wincott.

"Mr. Reigns, your witness," says the Judge.

Collin flips through his fake papers, turns off the machine and stands up. He makes his way over to Grintz who is staring right at me. What I wouldn't give to hit Grintz again.

"Mr. Grintz, you just testified under oath that you went into the cell, where Sam surprised you, because you were concerned about Sam's health. Is that correct?" asks Collin.

"Yes," says Grintz, proudly.

"Well then you must not be a very good guard, if someone could get the drop on you so easily," says Collin.

"Objection, harassing the witness," says Wincott.

"Sustained."

"My apologies Mr. Grintz. Let me ask you this then: have you been trained how to properly handle prisoners?" asks Collin.

"Yes, I have."

"And have you read the instruction manual for performing work duties as a correctional officer for the EFC?"

"Cover to cover," says Grintz.

"Cover to cover. That's fine Mr. Grintz. So what is the proper procedure for handling an inmate who appears ill?"

asks Collin.

"I'm sorry, I don't understand the question," says Grintz.

"What are you supposed to do when an inmate appears sick?" asks Collin.

"I... "

"According to the manual, you're supposed to contact the prison medical team first, and then contact your superior officer," says Collin.

"If that's what the manual says," replies Grintz, weakly.

"So what you're telling the fine people of the jury is that you don't like to follow orders."

"Objection," says Wincott. "Harassing the witness."

"Sustained," says the Judge.

"I will rephrase. Mr. Grintz," starts Collin. "Did you ignore the directions that you've been given for properly helping a prisoner with a medical emergency?"

"I was just trying to help," said Grintz.

"Oh, I'm sure you were," says Collin. "But please, answer the question. Were you following the rules when you entered Sam's cell."

Grintz stares at Collin, afraid. He looks over at Wincott, who says nothing.

"Citizen Grintz, you must answer the question," says the Judge.

It takes him another moment before he speaks.

"No," says Grintz. "But I was worr... "

"Thank you Mr. Grintz," says Collin, interrupting him. "I have a few more questions for you. Have you ever tried to break your arm against something?"

"What do you mean?"

"Have you ever tried to hit your arm against something hard enough that it breaks?" asks Collin.

"No," says Grintz.

"Of course you haven't. What person in their right mind would do that?"

"Nobody."

"And yet you say that somehow Sam was attacking you with such ferocity and strength, that Sam's arm broke against your baton?"

"Yes," says Grintz.

"I think most people would agree that it would be nearly impossible for a person to swing their arm hard enough against something to cause it to break, wouldn't you Mr. Grintz?"

"Objection," says Wincott. "Speculation."

"Sustained," says the Judge.

"Is it likely, Mr. Grintz, that Sam swung an arm at your baton so hard that it broke, or is it more likely that you were swinging the baton at Sam's arm when it broke?" asks Collin.

"Objection, again, speculation," says Wincott.

"Sustained. Mr. Reigns, please ask a fact-based question that the witness can answer," says the Judge.

"Sorry your honor," says Collin. "Mr. Grintz, have you ever been in trouble for not following orders while working as a prison guard?"

"Objection, relevance," says Wincott.

"Overruled," says the Judge.

Grintz remains quiet.

"Do I need to repeat the question, Mr. Grintz?" asks Collin.

"No."

"No, you have not been in trouble for disobeying orders?"

"No. I mean you don't need to repeat the question," says Grintz, annoyed.

"So have you ever been in trouble for ignoring orders? It's a simple question."

"Yes."

"How many times?" asks Collin.

"I don't really know," says Grintz.

"So you're saying it's happened so many times that you

lost count?"

"Objection your honor, harassing the witness," says Wincott.

"Sustained."

"Is it possible, Mr. Grintz, that you've been reprimanded fourteen times since you started work as a prison guard? And that of those fourteen times, eight of them were related to physical altercations with inmates?"

"I... I don't know," says Grintz.

"The EFC employee database does. It knows, because that's what it told me. Can you explain to me why you've been reprimanded so many times, Mr. Grintz?" asks Collin.

"It's part of the job," says Grintz, worried.

"Is it part of your job to attack and rape inmates?"

"Objection your honor, harassing the witness!" yells Wincott.

"Sustained," says the Judge.

"Of the eight physical altercations, Mr. Grintz, how many of them included rape?" asks Collin.

"None of them," says Grintz.

"So you're saying that you were never formally charged with attempting to rape any inmates?"

"Yes, that's correct."

"Interesting. Because when you look at the case notes for four of the altercations, they all mention rape. Why were formal charges never brought against you?" asks Collin.

"Objection, speculating," says Wincott.

"Overruled," says the Judge.

"Mr. Grintz?" says Collin, waiting.

"Because I was innocent?" says Grintz.

"Because you were innocent. Accused eight times of physical altercations, and four times of rape. Let me ask another question. Do you know a Mr. Drake Grintz?"

"Objection, relevancy," says Wincott.

"Overruled," says the Judge. "But Mr. Reigns, you need to show relevancy sooner rather than later."

"Yes, your honor," says Collin. "Mr. Grintz, do you

know Drake Grintz?"

"Yes." he says quietly.

"And what does Drake Grintz do for a living?"

"He works for corrections, like me."

"I think that's an understatement. Isn't Drake Grintz the warden of the very same prison you work at?" asks Collin.

Grintz' face grows angry.

"Yes, he is," says Grintz.

"And who is Drake Grintz to you?"

"What do you mean?"

"Is Drake Grintz a relative of yours, and if so, how is he related?" asks Collin.

"He's my father."

Collin turns to the jury. He waits a moment before continuing.

"Mr. Grintz, is it possible that your father covered up some of your more heinous crimes? Kept the police from hearing about it?"

"Objection, speculation," says Wincott.

"No," says Grintz, before the judge can decide.

"So you're telling us, the members of the court and jury, that your father didn't protect you?" asks Collin.

"No. He wouldn't do that," says Grintz.

"Why not, Mr. Grintz?"

"Because he hates me."

"So you're saying you're such a disgusting human being that even your own father hates you?"

"Objection," yells Wincott. "Harassing the witness, your honor."

"Mr. Reigns, that kind of attack is not condoned in this courtroom. Please remember there are rules you must abide by when questioning a witness," says the Judge.

"Yes, your honor. My deepest and most sincere apologies," says Collin. He comes back to our table, drinks from a cup of water then walks back to Grintz.

"Mr. Grintz," continues Collin. "How did the other guards find you once Sam escaped?"

"I was locked in the cell," says Grintz.

"So Sam left you alive?" asks Collin.

"Yes."

"Why?"

"Objection, speculation," says Wincott.

"Sustained."

"Let me ask a different way. If Sam was acting like a crazed animal, strong enough to break an arm by swinging it at your baton, what stopped Sam from killing you?" asks Collin.

"Objection again, speculation," says Wincott.

"Sustained."

Collin takes a step back and stares into Grintz' eyes. Grintz quickly looks away.

"No more questions your honor," says Collin, walking back to our table.

"Mr. Wincott, call your next witness," says Judge Pham.

"I'd like to call Interloper Designate Sam to the stand."

I take a deep breath and make my way over to the pen, then sit down in the chair still warm from when Grintz was sitting in it. The thought alone makes me want to puke. A guard comes up to me and raises his left arm, and I do the same as him, raising my right, just like Grintz had done.

"Do you, Interloper Designate Sam, swear to the Council of the European Federated Coalition that the testimony you are about to provide is both accurate and honest?"

"Who is the Council of the European Federated Coalition?" I ask.

"They're the group of people that lead everyone in the Coalition. They make laws to protect citizens," says the Guard.

"But I am not a citizen," I say.

"True."

"Will the laws still protect me? The same as a citizen?" I ask.

"No. There are harsher penalties for interlopers. If you bear false witness, commit perjury or otherwise attempt to manipulate the court's interpretation of the facts in this case, you will be put to death."

"So why should I swear anything to anyone if I'm not being treated equally?"

The guard looks over at the judge, but the judge seems just as confused.

"If you don't swear, and testify on your behalf," says the Judge, "then we may have no choice but to put you to death."

"This is how you treat people who are different from you? People who don't come from the same place as you? You're the monsters," I say, calmly.

The judge looks at me with anger in her eyes. I reflect her anger back. She bangs a hammer down on her table many times then talks to me.

"Interloper Designate Sam, I'm very close to removing your choice to testify and instead holding you in contempt of court. If you do not repeat the words that the bailiff speaks, you will be sent to a sanitizing facility to be put to death immediately. Now do you wish to comply? Yes or no?" asks the Judge.

It takes me a moment to decide.

"Fine. Yes. I will do as you say."

"Bailiff, swear Interloper Designate Sam in."

"Do you, Interloper Designate Sam, swear to the Council of the European Federated Coalition that the testimony you are about to provide is both accurate and honest?"

"Yes."

"And do you understand that bearing false witness, committing perjury or otherwise attempting to manipulate the court's interpretation of the facts in this case can lead to death?"

"Yes."

The guard moves and stands against the wall. Wincott

walks up to me, puts his face close to mine then pulls back only a small amount. He's still leaning close to me, making me feel trapped. I want to reach out and hurt him, but I hold back.

"Interloper Designate Sam," starts Wincott.

"It's just Sam," I say.

"Interloper Designate Sam, were you arrested for shooting one Mr. Carter McManus?" asks Wincott.

"Yes," I say.

"Under what circumstances do you think it's okay to shoot someone?" asks Wincott.

"Objection, speculation," says Collin.

"Overruled, as this pertains to the witness' thought process and motive," says Judge Pham.

Wincott looks at me, waiting for an answer.

"I don't know what your laws are here, but I believe it would be okay to shoot someone who is a threat to yourself, or someone you care about," I say.

"And was Mr. McManus a threat to you, or the people you care about?" asks Wincott.

"I wasn't sure," I admit.

"So you shot someone you were worried about. Did he have a weapon when you shot him?" asks Wincott.

"No."

"Why didn't Mr. McManus have a weapon, Interloper Designate Sam?"

"Because he gave me his."

"Why did he give you his weapon?" asks Wincott.

"So that I would trust him," I say.

"Then what you're telling us is that you gunned down an unarmed man in cold blood, who only wanted you to trust him?"

"Objection," says Collin.

"Sustained," says the Judge.

My stomach starts to hurt, and I can feel cold drips of sweat running down my sides.

"But he had a dragon!" I say.

"No further questions at this time," says Wincott, talking over me.

"Mr. Reigns, your witness," says the Judge.

Collin walks up to me, looking more concerned than he did before.

"Sam, can you explain to the court what you meant by Carter having a dragon?" asks Collin.

"Yes. I forgot that you call them ships. In the Crag, we call them dragons," I say.

"Is the Crag where you come from?"

"Yes."

"Do you like it there?"

"Not really."

"Why not?" asks Collin.

"Because it's dangerous. There are many killers who live there."

"So it's kill or be killed? People can't be trusted?"

"Some people can be trusted," I say.

"Have you ever killed anyone?"

"No."

"I'm glad to hear that. Let me ask you, were you worried about the dragon?" asks Collin.

"You mean the ship? Yes," I say.

"Why?"

"Because many of my people have been killed by ships. They burn us to the ground."

"So you don't trust ships because of that?" asks Collin.

"Yes."

"It's understandable then that you would consider Carter a threat, even if he gave you his weapon."

"Objection, leading the witness," says Wincott.

"Sustained," says Judge Pham.

"I'll rephrase. Did you consider Carter a threat because of the ship that he had?" asks Collin.

"Yes."

"In your own words, tell us why you shot him."

"I shot Carter because I had to know if he would

attack my people once I left with him. He said he needed me, and that I could help save his people, and it was the only way I could know for sure how important I was to him. I also made sure to shoot him where he would be hurt, but not die."

"What happened after that?" asks Collin.

"He waved at the ship so it wouldn't attack us. We both got in the ship and left."

"Did you try to help Carter after that?"

"Yes. Quinn had me hold some gauze on the wound to stop the bleeding. I didn't want him to be hurt, but it was the only way I could see to protect my people."

"And who is Quinn?" asks Collin.

"He's another soldier, like Carter," I say.

Collin thinks for a moment.

"To me, it sounds like you had an impossible decision to make, and you did what you did to protect lives. I'd call that being a hero."

"Objection, not a question," says Wincott.

"Sustained."

"Sam, in your own words, please describe what happened the night that Mr. Grintz attacked you," says Collin.

"I was asleep when he came to my cell. He told me I was his favorite prisoner, and that there was something he wanted from me. I warned him that if he touched me, I'd kill him. He told me that I'd be killed if I hurt him, and he came closer to me. I punched him in the face to get him to back away, but instead he started swinging his weapon at me," I say.

"His baton?" asks Collin.

"If that's what you call it. Then yes. He kept swinging it at me, and I kept blocking it with my arm. That's when my arm broke. He took the baton and pushed me against the wall then turned me to face it. It sounded like he was trying to take off his pants, but I kicked him hard in his joining parts."

"What do you mean by 'joining parts', Sam?" asks Collin.

"'Joining' is how new ones are made. New people," I say. "He fell to the ground. As I tried to leave, he tripped me and I hit my head. I got out, closed the cell door, used the key to keep him inside then went to get help."

"So you weren't trying to escape?" asks Collin.

"Only from Grintz."

"I'm sorry that you were attacked Sam. No one deserves to be treated like that," says Collin. "No further questions, your honor," says Collin.

"You may step down, Sam," says Judge Pham.

I stare at her for a moment.

"You may go back to your seat," says the Judge.

"Oh." I get up out of the pen, walk over to our table and sit down.

"Let's take a short recess. Fifteen minutes," says Judge Pham, hitting the hammer on her desk again.

15

The people around us start talking and it becomes hard to hear. Collin moves close to me and whispers.

"I think it's going really well. Don't screw things up, Sam."

"I'm trying not to. It's my life I'm fighting for," I say.

"Just remember that. All that happens to me if we lose is I don't get paid," said Collin. "Oh wait, that's right, I'm not getting paid. So I guess it doesn't really matter if we win. Do whatever you want; it's your funeral."

I can't tell if Collin really cares about whether we win or not. He seems to be doing a good job, even if he doesn't care. He was mean to Grintz, and made him look like an idiot, which is good. It's sad though that Grintz hurt other people before. I can only hope this will make him stop.

"So what did you mean when you said that you were here to save this place?" asks Collin.

"Carter said that I'm really smart when it comes to war. The way I think and look at things. They want me to lead people," I say, not knowing if I should tell him.

"Military. It's starting to make sense why they wouldn't tell me anything about why you were here. Why Roger used his favor. He's probably trading the favor I owe him for a better one. Man, can you imagine what it'd be like to have a favor from the Triple-F?"

"What's the Triple-F?" I ask.

"The Federated Fighting Force. They keep the peace around here, and protect everyone from the Western Allied Military."

"And who's the Western Allied Military?"

"They work for the Western Allied Free-States, and the name alone is a lie. Basically, when the bombs flew back in the End War, only the US, Canada and Europe were spared. They had the technology to knock nukes out of the sky at the time. China didn't, but they somehow knew that war was coming. A bunch of them set up camp at the Bering Strait. When the nukes hit, and the US wasn't destroyed, they came across into Canada and the US. The general theory is that the US had no way of preventing that many people from entering its borders, so hundreds of millions of Chinese just crossed into America. It also seems like the entire government over there is now being run by the Chinese, and that they're headed towards communism."

It takes me a moment to make sense of what Collin just explained. The US, Canada, Europe and China must all be places.

"What is communism?" I ask.

"Well, it's where everyone gets the same amount, despite what job they do," says Collin.

"That sounds like a good thing," I say. "That way no one starves."

"Yeah, it's all wine and roses until reality sets in. Communist governments make sure that everyone is poor, and don't have access to information. Only those in charge have much, and they're corrupt and greedy. It's a great way to run a country if you don't have a conscience. Also, lazy wastes-of-life get to live off of everyone else's hard work."

That sounds just like how the Crag used to be. Chaff was lazy and greedy, and made sure that everyone had just enough food to survive; nothing more. He also hid information from people, like how to grow vegetables. I'm starting to think that helping the war against the Western Allied Free-States will be a good thing.

"So if your enemy uses communism, what do you use?" I ask.

"Well, we pretend it's a monarchy, when it's really a capitalist society. Monarchy is where you have a King or Queen; someone that rules over everyone. They make the decisions. Capitalism is where the smarter, harder working people make more money than the lazy or dumb. That way people who are better have more," says Collin.

"You mean like you," I say, showing my anger.

"Yeah, exactly like me. I worked hard, did a lot of studying, and now I can buy anything I want."

"If you're the kind of person I'd be fighting for, I don't know that it would be worth it," I say.

"Yeah, well let me tell you something. Capitalism is better for one simple reason: freedom. You can do anything you want, be anything you want. Your government isn't trying to keep you in the dark like with communism."

"So the government is the people that rule? And your government doesn't have any secrets? They tell everyone everything?"

"Well no, just the important stuff," says Collin.

"They don't hide anything?" I ask.

"Well they have to hide some things, so that we're all safe."

"And you trust them to decide what you should and shouldn't know?"

"Not exactly. It's complicated," says Collin.

"It sounds like to me that the difference between communism and capitalism, is that capitalism pays better."

"That's an over-simplification," says Collin.

"Then tell me, how is it better?"

"It just is. Now shut up; we're about to start."

I watch as Judge Pham clears her throat. The room goes quiet then she speaks.

"Mr. Wincott, please call your next witness."

"Thank you your honor. I would like to call Citizen Carter McManus to the stand."

I didn't know that Carter was here. I turn and look behind me, and watch as he comes through the main doors and down the path I took. He's wearing very different clothes than the last time I saw him. His clothes are like Collin's, but they don't make him look evil like Collin's do. Carter's clothes make him look smart, and strong. His arm is still wrapped in a sling, but he doesn't seem to be in pain. Carter walks up to the pen and sits down. The bailiff makes him repeat the words that mean he won't lie.

"Mr. McManus," starts Wincott, "for the record, were you shot in the chest by Interloper Designate Sam?"

"It was more the shoulder," says Carter.

"It was only a few inches from your heart, if I understand correctly," says Wincott.

Carter just stares at him.

"Well?" says Wincott.

"I'm sorry, was that a question?" asks Carter.

Wincott looks angry.

"This is a very serious matter, Mr. McManus. People's lives hang in the balance. I would appreciate your cooperation."

"And I plan to fully cooperate," says Carter.

"Thank you. So were you shot by Interloper Designate Sam in the chest and nearly killed?" asks Wincott.

"More or less."

"A simple 'yes' or 'no' will do."

"Then yes, I guess," says Carter.

"Thank you. Now when Interloper Designate Sam shot you in the chest, did the defendant know that it could kill you?"

"Objection, speculation," says Collin.

Judge Pham thinks for a moment. "Overruled."

"Your honor...," starts Collin.

"Overruled, Mr. Reigns."

Wincott turns back to Carter. "Mr. McManus?"

"It's my understanding that Sam knew the gun could kill me," says Carter.

"And what happened prior to the interloper shooting you that makes you think that?"

"Sam shot a rock and saw what the gun could do. But Sam was only... "

Wincott cuts Carter off.

"Just answer the questions I ask, please. No need for your opinions. Mr. McManus, what is your job?"

"I'm a soldier in the Federated Fighting Force," says Carter.

"And how long have you been a soldier?" asks Wincott.

"About six years."

"And what is your current rank?"

"Lieutenant."

"Now that's interesting. Most soldiers who've been enlisted for six years have already made captain, if not a higher rank. Can you explain why you haven't moved up higher?"

"I can," says Carter.

Wincott stares at him, waiting.

"Mr. McManus, stop playing games. Tell the courtroom why you haven't moved up higher in the ranks."

"I did move up higher in the ranks," says Carter.

"Yes, but weren't you demoted?" asks Wincott.

"Yes."

"And why were you demoted?"

"Insubordination," says Carter.

"Insubordination?" says Wincott, acting like he's surprised. "So you have a history of going rogue, doing things you're not supposed to. Making bad decisions."

"Objection," says Collin.

"Sustained," says Judge Pham.

"Do you think it was a bad decision to give a primitive interloper your only weapon, then teaching them how to use it?"

"No," says Carter.

"No? You nearly died, and you say 'no'? You obviously aren't thinking clearly," says Wincott.

"Objection, harassing the witness," says Collin.

"Sustained."

"No further questions your honor," says Wincott.

"Mr. Reigns, your witness," says Judge Pham.

Collin walks over to the pen.

"May I call you Carter?" asks Collin.

"Sure."

"Carter, can you please describe exactly how you were insubordinate?"

"I ignored a direct order," says Carter.

"What was the order?" asks Collin.

"To leave a fallen soldier behind."

Collin looks around the courtroom, watching people's reactions.

"Can you please describe what happened for us?" asks Collin.

"My team was under fire in a canyon, and my buddy Jones got shot in the leg. A sniper had us pinned down. Our commanding officer ordered a full retreat through our coms, said he wouldn't lose any more soldiers. I used my com-link to tell my CO that I couldn't leave Jones, but he wouldn't listen. I sent the rest of the team ahead to the extraction point then waited five hours for the sniper to leave. I could see him through a crack in the rock I was hiding behind. When I knew it was finally clear, I picked up Jones and carried him back to the extraction point. No one was there, but I got ahold of base on my com and they sent a bird to come get us."

"And how is Jones doing now?" asks Collin.

"He's good. Lost his leg, but now he uses a bionic. It seems to be working well for him. He's glad to be alive," says Carter. "His wife and kid are happy to have him home."

Collin pauses for a moment, giving people time to fully think about the story.

"So you were demoted for saving your friend's life. A fellow soldier, wounded in the process of protecting us. Sounds like you didn't really deserve to be demoted," said Collin.

"Objection," says Wincott. "Opinion."

"Sustained."

"Carter, why did you give Sam the gun?" asks Collin.

"Because Sam is intelligent, creative, and can see things others can't."

"Like ghosts?"

"No," laughs Carter. "Sam is able to come up with new strategies, and see an enemy's weaknesses. Our simulation software factored in the previous level of warfare strategy in the Crag, and how far Sam advanced it. Sam was able to develop strategies that took hundreds of years in our civilization to evolve, but did it in only a few days. The projections say that Sam could be the most brilliant military mind we've ever seen."

"Are we really in such desperate need of leadership?" asks Collin.

"Objection, relevance," says Wincott.

"Sustained."

"No further questions your honor," says Collin, walking back to our table.

Carter seems like a good person, but after hearing what he did to save his friend I trust him more. I turn to Collin.

"What is a sniper?"

"It's someone that uses a big gun to shoot people from far away."

Our conversation is interrupted.

"Mr. Wincott, do you have any further questions for Mr. McManus?" asks Judge Pham.

"Yes, I do," says Wincott.

"Mr. Wincott, your witness," says Judge Pham.

"Thank you, your honor," says Wincott. "Mr. McManus, I have a simple question: what is your motive?"

"I'm not sure I understand what you mean. Motive for what?" asks Carter.

"For bringing Interloper Designate Sam into our military."

"So that Sam can help us win the war."

"Yes, you've already said that. But what is your personal motive? Why are you doing it?" asks Wincott.

"To help our people."

"It isn't so that you'll get in good with the military, so that you'll move up higher in the ranks more quickly?"

"Objection," says Collin. "Relevance."

"Overruled. Lieutenant McManus, please answer the question," says Judge Pham.

"No," says Carter.

"No?" says Wincott. "So you aren't doing this for personal gain? To make a name for yourself and climb the ranks?"

"Objection."

"Overruled."

"Are you certain of your answer?" asks Wincott, his face right next to Carter's.

"Yes. Was I thinking of my rank when I tried to save my friend's life?" says Carter.

"Move to strike the last comment, your honor," says Wincott.

He seems frustrated by what Carter said. I think Wincott was trying to make Carter look bad, but it didn't work out that way. Carter may be good at strategy too, at least with people.

"No further questions," says Wincott, going back to his seat.

"Mr. Reigns, would you like to cross-examine the witness again?" asks Judge Pham.

"No, your honor," says Collin.

Carter leaves the pen, and on his way past my table he smiles at me. I wish I could smile back, but they may still have me killed. I can smile later, if I survive.

"Mr. Wincott, your next witness," says Judge Pham.

Wincott moves his hands around on top of his table, just like Collin did, only Wincott looks worried. He takes a moment then finally speaks.

"No further witnesses your honor," says Wincott.

"Mr. Reigns, would you like to call any additional witnesses?" asks Judge Pham.

"Yes, council would like to call sound engineer Paul Burke to the stand," says Collin.

"Objection your honor, he was not on the witness list," says Wincott.

"He's an independent expert in his field," says Collin.

"Overruled, Mr. Wincott. He will be allowed to testify. You will of course be allowed to cross-examine. Mr. Reigns, please proceed," says Judge Pham.

A young man, only a few years older than me, walks down the pathway and up to the pen. He carries a machine in his hands that I've never seen. It's small, about the size of a loaf of bread, and he sets it down on the wooden fence surrounding the pen. The bailiff comes up to Paul Burke and has him promise not to lie. Collin makes his way over to the pen.

"Mr. Burke, can you please tell us what you do for a living?" asks Collin.

"I'm an audio engineer for the Triple-F," says Paul.

"Can you please be more specific? Can you describe to the court exactly what you do?"

"Sure. I do audio surveillance work. Plant bugs, long distance audio recordings, things like that."

"And have you ever met any of the people in this courtroom before?" asks Collin.

"Not that I remember."

"So you would say that you're impartial, considering the outcome of this trial does not affect you personally?"

"Objection," says Wincott. "Leading the witness."

"Sustained."

"Let me rephrase. Mr. Burke, do you have any personal reason to side with either defendant?" asks Collin.

"No, I do not."

"Thank you. Can you please share with the court what you brought with you?"

"I brought a recording of what happened during the attack," says Paul.

"And how did you get this recording?" asks Collin.

"There was a video camera down the hallway."

"Why wasn't there a camera aimed at Sam's cell? Wouldn't it be better to use that footage?"

"It's my understanding it would violate the inmate's privacy to have a camera aimed at the cell," says Paul.

"Objection, speculation," says Wincott.

"Citizen Burke, was that something that you speculated on, or were you told that specifically by someone at the facility?" asks Judge Pham.

"I asked the Warden, and that's what he told me."

"Overruled then, Mr. Wincott."

"Thank you, your honor," says Collin. "Mr. Burke, can you please play the recording for the court?"

"Objection. Counsel wasn't given time to review the evidence," says Wincott.

"Overruled. Please play the recording, Citizen Burke," says Judge Pham.

"Of course, your honor," says Paul.

He pushes a button on the box. There's a lot of noise that makes it hard to hear. Paul pushes more buttons and the noise gets quieter, making the other sounds easier to hear. Everyone listens as things happen like I remember them. Grintz waking me, coming into my cell, the sound of keys dropping outside the cell. The struggle. Every word we said can be made out.

It's hard to listen to; reliving that horrible night. I want to cover my ears, but I don't. I look over at the jury people and their faces show that they share my pain. My anger. My disgust. I keep listening because I must be strong. Grintz must be stopped, so that it doesn't happen to anyone else. What happened wasn't my fault. I didn't ask for it, and I didn't deserve it, and I hope that he spends the rest of his life in prison.

Finally, the sounds stop. Collin looks at the jury

people. His face is filled with sadness. He walks around, looking at everyone in the courtroom, getting them to look into his eyes, so that they might share his feelings. Letting them know it's okay to be angry. Once he finishes, he turns back to Paul.

"Mr. Burke, can you say you're 100% certain that this recording is authentic," asks Collin.

"I can't say anything with 100% certainty. I can say that the audio and video of this feed were recorded by an independent group outside of the prison, and that according to my software, the recording hasn't been edited in any way. Everything points to this recording being authentic," says Paul.

"Thank you. No further questions," says Collin.

"Your witness, Mr. Wincott," says Judge Pham.

Wincott takes a while to get out of his seat. He walks over to Paul and slams his hand down on the wood fence, which startles Paul.

"Mr. Burke, let me ask you this: is it possible that this recording is fake? And before you answer, please answer just 'yes' or 'no'," says Wincott.

"Yes, it is possible," says Paul.

"Thank you," says Wincott.

"But it's ninety-nine-point-nine percent likely that it's real, based on my findings," says Paul.

"Move to strike, your honor," says Wincott.

"Overruled," says Judge Pham.

Wincott looks angry, but he says nothing. Instead, he turns and walks back to his table and sits down.

"Mr. Reigns, do you have any more questions for the witness?" asks Judge Pham.

"No your honor," says Collin.

"Mr. Wincott?" asks the Judge.

"No."

"Then Mr. Wincott, your next witness," says Judge Pham.

"No further witnesses, your honor," says Wincott.

"Mr. Reigns?"

"No further witnesses either, your honor," says Collin.

"You may make your closing arguments, Mr. Wincott," says the Judge.

"Thank you your honor," says Wincott.

Wincott stands up and walks slowly to the jury. He takes a piece of fabric out of his shirt pocket and wipes his head with it. After clearing his throat, he speaks very quietly; almost a whisper.

"Citizens of the jury, what we have here is circumstantial evidence at best. There are doubts about the authenticity of the recording. You heard as much come from the mouth of a so-called 'expert' when he clearly admitted that he can't say with one-hundred percent certainty that the recording is genuine. You must believe someone is guilty beyond a reasonable doubt, and he has given you doubt. You've also heard the testimony of an interloper; someone whose words mean less than nothing in the eyes of the law. Let me remind you that Interloper Designate Sam is not one of us; while Citizen Grintz is.

"Should we listen to the words of a feral prisoner who was locked up for shooting an unarmed solider? And should we believe the story of that same power-hungry soldier, who time-and-time-again makes bad decisions, such as giving primitive interlopers deadly weapons? Or should we believe one of our own? Someone whose job it is to protect us from bad people. To keep evil at bay. This trial is about more than what's right, it's about us. It's about community. It's about working together against a common enemy. Mr. Reigns has failed to make a compelling case, and it's up to you, citizens of the jury, to follow the letter-of-the-law: finding Citizen Grintz innocent of all wrongdoing, and Interloper Designate Sam guilty as charged."

I look at the jury, and they all look very serious. I can't tell if they believe Wincott or not. A few of them move around in their chairs. Others look over at me, some look at Grintz. Wincott walks back to his seat and sits down.

Collin gets up and slowly approaches the jury. He

takes a moment to smile to each of them. It surprises me that someone who acts like such a bad person can seem honest and good. That's when a person is most dangerous: when they are bad but you still believe in them.

"Ladies and gentlemen of the jury, I've spent over a decade defending and prosecuting people in a court of law. In that time I've never seen such a clear-cut case. It's obvious from the recording you heard, which an expert believes to be ninety-nine-point-nine percent genuine, that the monster known as Grintz is guilty of attempted rape, assault with a deadly weapon, and attempted murder. Let me repeat that: ninety-nine-point-nine percent certain.

"Mr. Wincott over there is pulling every trick in his bag out to obscure the truth from you; that Sam is innocent, and Grintz is guilty. He has to, because it's his job, and he knows that he's already lost the case. He knows that you good citizens are honest, reasonable people, and that honest reasonable people would only come to the conclusion that Grintz is evil, and Sam is a victim.

"Mr. Wincott has tried to play on your fear of people from outside our walls, constantly referring to Sam as an 'interloper'. He tried to manipulate you, to get into your mind, because he thinks that some of you might be swayed by it. But I don't. I trust you to make the right decision, having carefully reviewed the evidence, and having weighed the testimonies you've heard. I trust you to be honest and decent, because that's what we do as citizens. We do our duty with an open mind and impartial heart, so that if the time comes for our judgment, that we would receive the same fairness and justice. Thank you," says Collin. He walks back to our table and sits down, smiling at me.

I look over to the jury, and all of them are looking at me. Some of them have tears in their eyes. It makes my eyes tear up too, but I don't know why. I feel connected with them, like they understand my pain and what I went through.

"We will now adjourn to allow the jury to come to a decision," says the Judge.

"All rise," says the Bailiff.

Everyone stands as the Judge heads back into the room she came from. The jury members follow a guard through another door. Collin picks up his machine and puts it in his pocket.

"What now?" I ask him.

"Now we wait," says Collin.

16

Collin starts to walk out of the courtroom, so I follow.

"Do you think we've won?" I ask.

"I think all of the evidence points to you telling the truth. But unfortunately it's not up to me. You're still an interloper, and he's still a citizen, so they may side with him."

"But that's not right! I'm innocent and the recording proved it."

"I know, but it may not matter," says Collin.

"I thought you told the jury that you trusted them, that you knew they were good and honest people."

"I've defended too many monsters to trust any of them. I've seen mothers who drowned their children for crying, and husbands who murdered their wives because they can't cook. I've even seen children half your age stab their brothers and sisters to death over toys. Now, you tell me, how can I trust anyone after seeing that?"

There's nothing I can say. I've seen things like that back in the Crag. People being murdered for no good reason. But I have to hope, because I learned that for every evil person out there, there's a good person that you can trust.

"Collin, if they do find me innocent, I want you to know that I will owe you a favor. That I'm someone you can trust."

"You're an interloper with no money, no friends, and no power. Your favor is worthless," says Collin.

"Maybe so. But it's yours."

He just ignores me. We stand outside the elevator, waiting for it to arrive.

"Where are we going?" I ask.

"To the pub across the street to get drunk," says Collin.

"What's a pub?"

"It's a place that serves alcohol, which is something you drink that makes you act stupid."

"Like beer?" I ask.

"You know what beer is? Yeah, it's like beer. They have that too. But they have other stuff. Stuff that will get you drunker quicker."

"I don't like beer very much, and I only drink it when I have to. Where I come from, it can be dangerous to get drunk. It makes it easier for people to kill you."

The elevator door opens and we step inside. I close my eyes and keep thinking about the sky, about anything other than being trapped inside this tiny room. When I feel the room slow down to a stop, and hear that now familiar noise, I open my eyes again. As the doors split apart just far enough, I push through them and nearly fall to the ground. I hate that this place has elevators, and I wish I never had to ride one again.

Collin walks past me, and I follow him across the pathway our automobile was on.

"Collin, what's a street?" I ask.

"You're standing on it, genius."

"Oh."

Collin is still treating me like I'm stupid, and he doesn't seem to care about me, but at least he's not being as mean as he was before the trial. I hate him less now, knowing the things that he's seen, and what's made him the way he is. Somehow I feel sorry for him.

The place we walk to is a small, brown wood building with an even smaller sign that just says 'Pub'. As we walk in, I see a man who stands behind a long table with many bottles behind him. The man is a gray one, with a scratchy voice and even scratchier face filled with stubble. The bottles are beautiful, and in many colors, and I wonder what drinks are inside each of them. Collin walks up to the man and I follow.

"Bartender, I'd like... " starts Collin, but is cut off by the man who I'm guessing has the job of bartender, whatever that is.

"Sorry son, but I have to ask: is your friend here old enough to drink?"

"Oh, no. Is that a problem?" asks Collin.

"Yeah. You two can sit on the restaurant side, just over that wall. You can place your drink order here though, and we'll bring it out to you," says the Bartender.

"Three fingers of your finest single-malt scotch, neat," says Collin.

"And for you?" asks the bartender, staring straight at me.

"Uh, I don't know. What can I have?" I ask.

"Water, soda, orange juice, milk, tomato juice. I've got all of those."

"What's soda?" I ask.

The Bartender just stares at me.

"Oh, yeah, Sam here will have a root beer," says Collin. He turns to me and whispers "just trust me."

I don't. But I really don't know what else to try.

"Okay, I will have root beer. Is it really beer?" I ask.

"Nope. No alcohol in it," says the Bartender.

Collin puts his hand down on the bar, on a strange black square I hadn't noticed before. It changes to bright blue, and eventually back to black again. He pushes down with his fingers a couple of times then puts his hand back down flat. A noise, sort of like a bird, comes from the square.

"Thank you," says the Bartender.

Collin walks past me, and I follow him around the wall to a table with some benches. Sitting down across from him, I just look at him, not knowing what to say.

"How's your arm?" asks Collin.

His question surprises me. It's almost like Collin is trying to be nice.

"It hurts, but the Sky Gods will keep me alive," I say.

"Yeah, how are those Sky Gods working for you?" asks Collin. I can tell he doesn't really want an answer, so I ignore the comment. "So, do you have anyone back where you come from?"

"My brother Flot. I had another brother, Jet, but he was... murdered. There's a woman there who is like a Mom to me, but isn't, named Charm. And I have a friend named Ebb who I like very much," I say.

"Is Ebb someone you like, or someone you 'like'?" asks Collin. He makes the word 'like' sound more serious the second time than the first.

My face turns warm, and I would guess it has changed colors.

"Ah, so it's like that," says Collin. "Good for you. Everyone should have someone they 'like'."

"Do you have someone you like?" I ask.

"Yeah, I do. Me."

"I knew that already," I say.

Collin laughs.

A young woman, not much older looking than me, comes over to our table. She puts a small, clear cup of yellow liquid in front of Collin, and a much larger cup in front of me, filled with a brown liquid. Mine has a lot of bubbles in it for some reason.

"Did you put soap in my root beer?" I ask.

"No, why would you think that?" asks the woman.

"The bubbles," I say.

"It's soda. It's supposed to have bubbles."

"Oh."

"Thank you, waitress," says Collin. The waitress stands still for a moment, staring at me.

"Um, thanks," I say. Finally she leaves.

"Does your beer not have bubbles?" asks Collin.

"It does, but these look more like soap bubbles," I say.

97

"What's this?"

"It's a straw. You drink through it," says Collin.

"Why?" I ask.

"No idea."

I go ahead and try to drink some of the root beer with the straw. It tastes very sweet, and the bubbles feel strange in my mouth, but I enjoy it. Thankfully, it doesn't taste like beer at all.

Collin sips his liquid slowly, and after a few sips his face turns red.

"Don't drink much?" I ask.

"What makes you say that?"

"Your face is red."

"Not that it's any of your business, but no, I don't drink much. When I do enjoy a drink, it's always high-quality, and always expensive," says Collin.

"I've heard that word a few times. What does 'expensive' mean?" I ask.

"It means something costs a lot of money to buy, compared to other similar items."

"What things are the most expensive?" I ask.

"Houses; they're very expensive. So are nice cars. Jewelry. Boats."

"So what you're drinking is expensive, but other drinks of the same kind are not?" I ask.

"Yes, there are much cheaper alcohols out there," says Collin.

"So why don't you drink those instead, and keep more money?"

"Because I make so much money that I can afford to drink this. This costs nothing compared to how much I make in a year. Not only that, but I like it better. When I was in college, and didn't have a lot of money, I would drink the cheaper stuff. Now I can't stand it. Once you've really lived, you never want to go back to being poor."

Collin finishes the rest of his drink in one big gulp, slams the cup down on the table loud enough for the waitress to hear. A few seconds later she comes back.

"Can I get you another drink, sir?"

"The same," says Collin.

"Anything else for you?" she asks, looking right at me.

"Do you have food?"

"Of course, dear, this is a restaurant," says the Waitress.

"Then I'll have some food."

"Do you know what you want already, or would you like to see a menu?"

"What's a menu?" I ask.

The waitress looks at me strangely then turns and looks at Collin.

"Two menus would be great," says Collin.

The waitress slowly turns and walks away.

"So what is a menu?" I ask Collin.

"It's a list of food you can choose from. You can get whatever you want," says Collin.

"You mean, I can pick what I want to eat? They don't just make one thing, and you have to eat whatever they make?"

"Yeah. Whatever you want," says Collin, sounding annoyed.

The waitress comes back with a few pieces of paper, and she hands one to each of us. I catch her looking at me again. It makes me feel uncomfortable and unhappy that I still know so little about this place. Eventually, she turns and leaves.

I look at the piece of paper, and although I can read the words, I can't understand half of it. I don't know what a hamburger is, or what a sandwich is, or what a pizza is. I've read about fish, but have never seen one, and I have no idea what the chips are that go with it. I look at the words under each food and I see some things I recognize. Hamburgers have beef, and onions, and tomatoes, and lettuce, but I'm not sure what a bun is, and it doesn't say. Sandwiches sound like the things that Cleave invented. It's nice to see something familiar.

"I think I will have chicken sandwich," I say.

"You'll have 'a' chicken sandwich," says Collin, making the 'a' sound louder.

The waitress returns.

"Know what you want, sweetie?" asks the Waitress.

"I will have 'a' chicken sandwich," I say, making sure she hears the 'a' sound.

"Uh, okay. And you?" she asks Collin.

"Bacon cheeseburger, pink in the middle, no onions, onion rings instead of fries, Caeser salad, and a water."

"Coming right up," says the Waitress, walking away.

"How long will we have to wait?" I ask.

"For the food? Not long. Maybe ten minutes," says Collin.

"I mean before we find out if I live or die."

"Oh, that could take a while. The jury has to talk about everything. Go over the testimonies, the facts and information, and come to a decision they can all agree on. Everyone has to agree on it or it doesn't count. If they take too long figuring it out, or if people disagree and refuse to change their minds then you'll get a new trial, with a new jury."

"So I might not find out today if I will live?" I ask.

"At this point, since you didn't kill anyone, it's unlikely they'll put you to death. Also, you have a shot at winning the case because it sounds like you were actually innocent. I don't meet too many innocent people these days. Normally, with a case like this, both parties have done something wrong, or were in the middle of doing something wrong when they got caught. You were just sitting in your cell, like you were supposed to, waiting."

I think things through for a moment and ask a question I'm surprised I hadn't already asked.

"How come I don't have a guard watching over me now? Aren't they worried I might run away and hide, instead of finding out what the jury has decided?"

Collin laughs. "No, they aren't worried."

"Why not?" I ask.

"When they first captured you, they inserted a very tiny chip inside your neck. They can track you with it. If they think you're too dangerous, they'll make it explode and kill you. It won't blow up your whole body, it will do just enough damage so that your brain stops getting blood to it. You'll last a few minutes, maybe."

I reach up to my neck and touch the place that had been sore. Now I know why I couldn't remember hurting it.

"Get it out of me," I yell.

"Can't. Once it's in there it takes special equipment to remove it. Otherwise it'll blow up on its own and kill you. Every citizen has one. That's the price of freedom," says Collin.

"You call that freedom? Always being afraid that if you say or do the wrong thing that you might be killed? The more I know about this place the more I hate it," I say.

"I'm sure the feeling is mutual," says Collin. "But I wouldn't worry about it too much, because they rarely use it. Generally, it takes someone pretty high up to give the execution order, and they have a system that prevents any one person from terminating a citizen. So I'm sure you'll be fine."

"Oh, that definitely makes me feel better," I say, not meaning it.

"It's good to know they still have sarcasm where you come from," says Collin.

"What's sarcasm?" I ask, still worried.

"It's where you say something, but don't really mean what you're saying."

"You mean a lie? I hate lies."

"No, it's where the other person knows you don't mean what you're saying. That the opposite of what you're saying is what you really mean. I know that you don't feel any better about the chip, even though you said you did. Make sense?" asks Collin.

"I guess."

"Yeah, I've always thought that what separates man from apes is sarcasm."

"What are apes?" I ask.

The waitress finally shows up with our food, and with Collin's drinks; alcohol and water. She's also brought me another root beer. I hadn't noticed that I'd finished my other one.

The chicken sandwich looks like it will taste good. I pick it up and take a bite. It's different than what I'm used to. There's a strange chewy goo that stretches over the piece of chicken inside.

"What is this?" I ask, pulling some of the goo away from the sandwich.

"That's cheese. They don't have cheese where you come from?" asks Collin.

"No. Is it safe to eat?" I ask.

"They wouldn't put it on there if it wasn't."

I chew the cheese that I pulled from the sandwich and it tastes okay, so I go back to eating my sandwich.

"I like cheese," I say.

"Yeah, it's good stuff. They have all different colors and flavors of it. That's Swiss cheese."

It surprises me when Collin smiles at me. I look away quickly, because his sudden change from being angry to being nice bothers me. When I look back, the smile has disappeared. I think he didn't mean for me to see it. He drinks his second cup of alcohol quickly, and I can tell he's trying hard not to choke on it. Once he's done fighting the taste of the alcohol, he looks around the room. He seems uncomfortable now, which I can deal with better than him being nice to me. I go back to eating my sandwich.

"So what's the clear stuff that the cups are made out of?" I ask.

"Glass."

"I see it everywhere. We don't have glass where I come from."

"Here you can't get away from it."

Collin's face looks sad. I decide to stop asking questions and instead eat.

17

I finish the chicken sandwich quickly because it feels like I haven't eaten in days. My stomach aches from all the bad things happening lately have caught up to me, and my stomach isn't sure what to do with the food. I try to let some of the bubbles escape by belching, which comes out louder than I've ever heard. Collin gives me a dark stare, but surprises me with his words.

"Good one," he says.

"Was that wrong to do?"

"Here, most people think belching in public is rude. Me, I don't care. People are way too uptight about too many stupid things."

"Where I come from, we have too many big things to worry about. No one seems to care about the small stuff. It's hard enough just surviving to see your next sunrise," I say.

"This place can be just as brutal, trust me," says Collin.

"I don't."

"Huh, what?"

"Trust you. I don't really trust you," I say.

"First smart thing you've said so far. Good You've finally learned something useful," says Collin.

Now it's me that wants to smile, but I don't. I don't want to be friends with Collin. Just because he's less horrible when he's been drinking doesn't mean it's worth the effort. It's strange, because most people I know that drink too much get meaner and more violent. Collin almost becomes nice when he's drunk.

It takes Collin forever to finish his food. He picks at the salad, eats small bites of what I guess must be onion rings, and slowly chews his burger. I sit there, bored, with nothing to do but watch him eat.

Sometimes I look over at the other people in the restaurant. There's a woman that looks like a gray one, but she has paint on her face to make her look younger, and her hair is a strange kind of yellow color I've never seen before. In the Crag, people were respected for their silver hair and wrinkles. It meant that they had lived long lives, and had worked very hard to stay alive. Here, maybe things are so easy for everyone that they all want to be young instead.

I also see a man sitting with new ones. The youngest one squirms, and the man very carefully puts his arm on her shoulder then whispers in her ear. She stops squirming, and doesn't look hurt by what he said. I'm surprised, because it's very different from how young ones are taught in the Crag. There, children are yelled at, hit or pushed over. Sometimes they're just ignored.

The waitress comes back, picks up my empty cup and puts another full one in front of me.

"Anything more I can get you two?" asks the Waitress.

"Nothing for me," says Collin. "Sam, you want any more?"

"Is it okay that I take more?" I ask.

"Yeah, don't even worry about it," says Collin.

"Then Waitress, I would like another chicken sandwich."

"I'll go put the order in," says the Waitress.

It takes a while to get my food, and Collin finishes his burger and onion rings before it arrives. Now it's his turn to be bored. While I eat, he pulls out his paper machine and starts looking over the papers for my case.

"What are you doing?" I ask.

"Just going over my notes, making sure we didn't miss

anything during the trial. Seeing if there's grounds for a mistrial, in case we lose and want to appeal."

"What does 'appeal' mean?"

"Oh, it's where you basically say that someone screwed up, and now we have to go through the whole process again. It's a do-over," says Collin.

"I hope we don't have to go through this again," I say.

"That definitely makes two of us."

"What would happen to me if there is a mistrial?" I ask.

"Then you go back to prison for a while, until they can set up another trial. Could take a long time."

"I can't go back to prison," I say.

"You may not have a choice," says Collin.

"I'd rather die."

"That's a choice that would keep you out of prison, but it's not a good long-term strategy. Things can't get better if you're not around to see them."

I don't argue with him, but I know I'd be better off buried than to be trapped in a tiny cell, wasting my life. I need to be free, or I'll go insane and it will surely kill me. My mind wanders to other questions.

"How come I'm not on trial for shooting Carter?" I finally ask.

"I've been wondering that myself," says Collin. "Here, I can look it up."

The papers made of light disappear from the table, and are replaced with a bright blue square with some words. After poking the table a few times with his fingers, the light on the table changes again. Collin's hands move quickly, pushing fake stacks of papers away until he finds the ones he wants. It takes a few moments of reading to find an answer.

"Carter didn't press charges, and there weren't really any witnesses. For some reason, the video feed for the ship they were in cut out right before Carter walked to you. So without direct evidence, or witnesses, and an uncooperative victim, there was nothing a prosecutor could do. They dropped the charges," says Collin.

"At least I won't have to deal with that trial," I say.

"At least."

I start feeling better, knowing that I'm not in trouble for shooting Carter. I finish my food and Collin turns off his machine.

"So what do we do now?" I ask.

"I was hoping it wouldn't take this long. We've already been here a few hours. A clear-cut case like this one should only take an hour or two. The jury must not think it's that obvious then. I guess I could get you a hotel room nearby."

"What's a hotel?" I ask.

"It's a nice place to stay. Where you can sleep, and have food brought to you, and watch TV. It's like a temporary home for you. You can take a shower, too, while you're there."

"What's a shower?"

"It's how you get clean. You turn on the shower and it sprays water on you, and you use the little soaps they give you. You'll figure it out."

The waitress comes back to the table.

"Anything else you two need?" asks the Waitress.

"Not that I can think of," says Collin.

"I'm full," I say.

"Mr. Reigns, can I get your authorization on the bill please?" asks the Waitress. She sets down a black square like the one that I saw at the bar. He places his hand over it, it flashes blue then back to black. After a few taps of his finger he stands up. I also stand up.

"Thanks, and come again," says the Waitress.

I follow Collin back outside. He waits a moment for a yellow automobile to drive up then raises his hand to it. The automobile comes to a stop in front of us. Collin goes around to the other side and gets in. I stand outside not knowing what to do. After a moment, Collin gets out of the automobile and looks at me.

"What?"

"How do I open the door?" I ask, embarrassed.

"See that shiny metal thing? Pull up on it."

I reach out and pull up on the handle. The door opens, so I get inside and pull the door closed.

"Nearest five-star hotel," says Collin.

"I know just the place," says the Driver.

The automobile starts up very fast and I'm pushed back in my seat. I stare through the glass as things fly by again. I see more buildings, and some strange trees I've never seen before. The driver seems good at his job, because he's going fast and comes close to other automobiles without hitting them. Collin doesn't seem to agree though.

"Slow it up, we're not in a hurry," says Collin.

"I get paid by the distance, not the speed. I drive fast, I get more fares. Do I tell you how to do your job, Mr. Bigshot Lawyer?" asks the Driver.

"How'd you know I was a lawyer?" asks Collin.

"Greasy hair, expensive suit, smug face that asks to be punched; so you're either a lawyer or a used car salesman," says the Driver.

"You won't be getting a tip," says Collin.

"I didn't expect one. Lawyers are terrible tippers. You schmucks think you're better than everyone else and don't care about the little guy," says the Driver.

I laugh, which makes Collin turn to me with a look of anger.

"Sounds like he knows what he's talking about," I say.

"Another word and I won't take you back to the courtroom once the jury's reached a verdict. No money, no shelter, and you'll be a fugitive," says Collin.

I decide to keep my mouth closed. Collin still looks angry, while the driver has a big smile on his face. He keeps driving the way he did before, barely missing other automobiles. I stare out the glass; watching, learning, seeing.

18

The automobile finally slows down in front of the most beautiful thing I've ever seen. There's a person, a woman, made out of rock, holding some curved thing that water pours out of. There are lights all around it, and all around a pathway that leads to the building that must be the hotel. The lights sparkle like stars. We drive over the pathway and come to a stop, just outside the building.

"We have arrived," says the Driver, using a funny voice. It makes him kind of sound like Collin, only more annoying.

Collin touches a black square between us, like the ones he used at the pub, then gets out of the automobile. I get out too, figuring how to work the inside handle by myself. As I follow Collin, I put my hand up to the driver as a way to say thanks, and he puts his hand up too.

The inside is even more amazing than the outside. I look straight up, and the ceiling is higher than any ceiling I've seen in the Crag; even over the Great Fire. There is wood everywhere; dark and deep and almost wet looking. There are many lights along the wood, and it's much brighter inside than out. It makes everything seem unreal, like I'm in some incredible dream.

I see a few people sitting down on what look like very soft seats. It's strange, because the seats I'm used to are either made of wood or stone, and are painful to sit on for very long.

These seats look like you could sit on them all day and not get sore.

Instead of following Collin, I walk over to one of the pale green seats that doesn't have a person in it and sit down. It seems to change shape to fit me, and it's almost like sitting on a loaf of bread. I lean back and close my eyes.

"Sam?" says Collin.

"Yes?" I say, keeping my eyes closed.

"I need you to come over here now so that you can get checked in."

"Can I stay here? I've never sat in a seat like this before."

"Like what?" asks Collin.

"Soft," I reply.

"Oh. Then no."

I do my best to ignore him, as I move around in the seat, trying to get the most out of it.

"Come on, Sam," says Collin.

Eventually I give in, and I stand up and walk over to him.

"Now that you're done sitting down, can you put your hand on that black pad there?"

I look up, and in front of us is a woman in very dark clothes. Her eyes are a beautiful brown color, very dark and deep. Her hair is like Ebb's, light yellow mixed with brown, and straight. She stands across from us, on the other side of a table. The table is strange, because it's very tall; too tall to sit at with chairs, unless the chairs were also very tall. On the table is a black square like the ones Collin keeps using. I put my hand down on it and it flashes blue then goes back to black. It makes my hand feel a little warmer. I pull my hand away and rub it, wondering what the pad might have done to it.

"You'll be in room 417," says the woman, smiling at me.

"What is 417?" I ask.

The woman gives me the same look of confusion I keep getting. In the Crag, I am one of the smartest. Here, the youngest new one knows more than me.

Collin turns to me. "Sam, don't worry about it. I'll take you to your room, but I'll have you stay there until we need to go back to the courtroom. Okay?"

"Okay," I say, nodding.

I follow Collin to an elevator. It makes my stomach hurt just thinking about it.

"Is there another way to get there?" I ask.

"I guess we could take the stairs. It's only a few floors up," says Collin.

"Stairs? Like the things outside the court's room?"

"It's 'courtroom', and yes, like those," says Collin.

He walks around a corner then opens a door. He stands, waiting for me to follow. As I get to the door, he holds it open for me. I walk inside and see that there are stairs going up, and stairs going down.

"You said up, right?" I ask.

"Yeah."

I start walking. I don't have any problem going up the stairs, but I'm surprised Collin doesn't either. I didn't think he'd be strong, since he doesn't work hard with his hands. But when I look at him, I realize that he must do something to stay strong.

Eventually Collin tells me to stop. He pulls open the door in front of us, and lets me go first. I walk into a long hallway filled with doors. It reminds me of where the courtroom was, only nicer. The ground has beautiful patterns of dark red and gold on it, and the walls are a color very close to white mixed with gray. I let Collin walk in front of me so that he can show me which door will be mine.

"Here we are, room 417," says Collin.

"How can you tell?" I ask.

"The number on the outside. Oh, right, you don't know numbers yet. Here, see this card?" he asks, holding up a thick piece of paper with some writing on it.

"Yes."

"It has the number 417 written on it. If you get lost,

look at this card and match the writing to the door."

"Okay," I say. I think Collin can tell that I'm worried about it.

"Sam, you should have everything you need in that room except food. I'll show you how to get food, okay?"

"Okay."

"Go ahead and open the door by putting your hand on the black square."

I put my hand on the door then hear a click as it opens. Collin follows me inside.

The room is amazing. The first thing I notice is the bed, which is big enough for a family. I also see a TV on the wall. At least I'll have something to do while I wait. On the other side of the bed is a wall of glass I can see out of, and what I do see is very beautiful. I can tell that the sun will be setting soon. There are a few chairs that look just like the one I sat in earlier, and I'm excited to sit down on them.

I walk over to the glass and look out.

"Nice view out the window, huh?" says Collin.

"Window?"

"Yeah, that's what you're looking through."

"I'd wondered if it had a name," I say, not really paying attention to him.

"So a couple of things I should show you," starts Collin. I follow him back to a smaller room that I didn't notice when we first came in. "This is the bathroom. You do your business in here."

"I've used a toilet before," I say.

"Good. So here's the sink. You can use it to wash your hands after you go to the bathroom. You just put your hands under the faucet and water comes out. Use the knob to switch between hot and cold. Make sense?"

"Yes."

"Okay. Here's the important one: the shower," says Collin, pointing to a small room with a piece of glass in front of it. There's also something metal that looks like the sink faucet he showed me, only someone put it up very high. I also see some handles on the wall. The whole thing looks like it's made up of stones colored in brown and orange.

"Shower," I repeat.

"Yes. This is where you get clean. You turn these two knobs and water will come out. You can change the temperature by twisting the knobs. If you want more hot water, turn up the knob with red on it. If you want more cold water, use the knob with blue on it. Be careful though, because the hot water can be very hot. Make sense?"

"I think so," I say.

"Good. Inside this is soap," he says, handing me something wrapped in white paper. "Do you know how soap works?"

I laugh.

"Yes, I know how soap works," I say. "We make our own."

"Okay, good. When you're done washing up, dry with the towels here on the rack, and leave the wet towels on the floor," says Collin.

We go back to the room with the bed.

"Now I'm going to teach you about room service. What you do is look in this binder to find out what you want to eat or drink. Once you've figured it out, you push this button here on the phone. It will connect you with someone who will bring you food. Tell them what you want, and they will bring it to you. Make sense?" asks Collin.

"How do you talk to the person?" I ask.

"Oh, right. Okay, so before you hit the button, you pick up the receiver. That's this," he says, lifting up a handle and handing it to me.

It's not very heavy, and it has a strange curly rope attached to it. There are two parts and both have holes cut into them. One has many, while the other has only a few.

"So you want to have the cord at the bottom," says Collin. "You put the top half to your ear, and the bottom half goes in front of your mouth. Then push the button to call room service and you'll be able to talk to someone."

"Okay."

"Any questions so far?" asks Collin.

"How do I talk to you if I need your help?" I ask.

"First, if the phone rings, pick up the receiver. It'll probably be me. I can talk to you that way. If you need to call me though, push the buttons on the phone in the order that's here on my card." Collin hands me a small, thick piece of paper and I can read his name on it The weird number symbols are also on it, and he must mean I should push those into the phone to talk to him.

"Oh, wait, I need that back a second," says Collin. He takes it back from me and pulls a small stick from his pocket. He pushes on it, which makes it click, then writes something down on the piece of paper. "I almost forgot, you have to dial '9' to get out. So do you think you got this?"

"I think so."

"Well I'm heading home then. I'll call you when they're ready to reconvene. Get yourself some room service for dinner, take a hot shower and get some sleep."

"I will," I say.

He stops for a moment. I can tell he wants to say something nice but doesn't really know how. Instead he just turns and leaves the way we came in, closing the door behind him.

19

I stand there for a moment, not knowing what I should do first. I'm not really hungry yet because we just ate, so I decide not to call room service. I could use some sleep, but it isn't dark out yet. That leaves me with sitting in the soft chairs, or getting cleaned up.

I fight to take off my clothes because of the cast, but eventually I'm able to get them off of me. I carry them with me back to the shower. It's dark in the room, and I remember seeing Collin push a button near the door to make the lights work. I push the button and I can finally see.

Walking into the shower, I drop my clothes on the ground. I turn on the cold water first, because I'm worried about hurting myself with the hot water. As it comes out, I put my hand under it to make sure that it's not too hot.

I've never washed with hot water before. Back at the Crag, at the loud waters, it's usually cold. It's almost impossible to wash during the snows. Some people don't bother cleaning themselves, while others, like me, use a small piece of cloth soaked in the water.

As I shower, I wash my clothes at the same time. It takes me longer than normal because of my broken arm, but I manage. Once the clothes are rinsed, I set to work on cleaning myself. I find the warm water running on my body relaxing. If I ever make it back to the Crag, I'll have to figure a way to take hot showers, because it makes me feel comfortable in a way that I've never felt before. Almost like the soft chairs.

For a while I'm lost in my thoughts. Next to where I've been putting the soap I see a small bottle of something. I pick it up, and it says 'Shampoo' on it. It also says something about vanilla and cedar. I'm not sure what those are.

Twisting off the top, I sniff the liquid inside, and it's one of the most amazing things I've ever smelled. It smells like wood, and sweet like some of the foods we grow. I take a taste but spit it out. It tastes horrible. Maybe it's not meant for drinking. My tongue burns a little, so I decide to put the top back on and leave it alone for now.

I rinse all the soap away, making sure that every part of me is clean, then step out of the shower. I take one of the towels and dry off. The towel is very, very soft, but doesn't do a good job of drying me. My towel back home works better. I like the feel of this one, but I would keep my old one if I had the choice.

I also realize that I can't dry off my arm inside the cast. I wish I'd thought about that before I used the shower. I let my injured arm hang at my side, hoping that the water drips out of it.

I walk into the room with the bed and lay down. Picking up the remote for the TV, I notice it looks different than the one I used before. Not a lot, but enough that I have to read all the buttons. I remember that to make the other TV work, I pushed a red button. This also has a red button marked "Power". I push the red button and the TV starts working.

It takes me a while to finally choose something to watch. I go back to watching people cook because it looks like fun. I watch TV until the sky outside grows dark. My stomach needs something in it, so I look through the book of food that Collin told me about. I have a hard time figuring out what most things are from their names, but many of them show what meat and vegetables go into them, so I can guess whether I'll like them or not.

I pick up the receiver and put it up to my face. It

makes a weird buzzing noise like an angry fly. I push the button on the bottom part of the phone for room service. The buzzing disappears, I hear a click, and then I can actually hear someone talking.

"Room service, this is Esteban. How may I assist you?"

"Hello. I'm Sam. What is ice cream?" I ask.

"You would like ice cream? What flavor?" asks Esteban.

"Well, what is it?"

"You have not had ice cream before? Well, it's creamy, because it's made from milk. And it's very thick and cold. You will like it. Would you prefer chocolate, strawberry or vanilla?"

I think for a moment. I do love strawberries, which we grow back at the Crag, but I'm not sure about the other two.

"Does the vanilla ice cream hurt?" I ask.

"Only if you eat it too fast. Why, what do you mean?" asks Esteban.

"I tried tasting the vanilla cedar shampoo and it hurt my tongue."

"Oh, you're not supposed to drink shampoo. You're supposed to wash your hair with it. You must not be from around here."

"No, I'm not," I admit.

"If I could be so bold as to recommend a flavor, I would recommend the chocolate. It's very rich and complex, and I'm sure you'll enjoy it."

"Yes then, I will have chocolate ice cream. I would also like beef borgin-something."

"Boeuf Bourguignon?" says Esteban. The sound of his words changes.

"Um, yes."

"Anything else?"

"Do you have root beer?" I ask.

"Of course, we have many soft drinks. Would you

maybe prefer a red wine with your meal? It may pair better."

"What is wine?"

"It's a drink made from grapes."

"Well, can I have root beer and wine then? I will try it," I say.

"Of course. Should we charge it to the room?"

"What do you mean?"

"How would you like to pay? We can charge it to your room, or you could give us money when we bring you the food," explains Esteban.

"I don't have any money," I say.

"Then we will just charge it to your room. It will take about 30 minutes. Thank you," says Esteban.

The phone clicks and I can no longer hear him. The receiver starts making an annoying buzz again so I set it back down how I found it. I don't know how long 30 minutes is, but I hope it's quick.

I decide to go over to the window and look out. I see many things with lights on all over the city. It's very beautiful, almost like the stars are on the ground instead of the sky. I can't see as many real stars as I can back home which makes me sad. Maybe they have less stars in their sky here.

Bringing one of the soft chairs over to the window, I sit down. I look at other buildings and wonder what the people inside them are doing now. Are they watching TV, or eating, or staring out through their window, wondering what everyone else is doing.

After sitting there, looking out for a while, I finally hear a knock at the door. It startles me. I get up and walk over to the door, leaving my towel behind. It takes me a moment to figure out how to open it.

Standing there is a young woman, about my height, with red hair pulled up behind her. She looks like she's only lived a few more snows than me. Her skin is pale, and her lips are bright red like her hair. She'd been looking away, but finally turns to look at me.

"Room serv..." says the woman.

"Hello," I say.

"Naked," she says, staring at me. Her cheeks turn bright red. "Um, I have your dinner."

"Oh, okay," I say, looking down at the cart full of food.

"I... can bring it in, if you like," says the woman. She has her name on her shirt and it says 'Rebecca'.

"Please," I say.

She won't look me in the eye. I back up to let her in and she pushes the cart inside. Pulling the door closed behind her, she finally looks at my eyes.

"I'll just put these right here," she says as she sets the food and drinks on the table next to the bed. "Is there anything else you need?"

"No, I don't think so."

"Well then, take care" she says as she pulls the cart back out of the room, closing the door behind her.

I sit down on the bed and cut into the meat. The beef is amazing. I eat it quickly and wash it down with root beer. They don't go together very well, but I enjoy both of them just the same. I also eat the vegetables that come with the meat, even though I've never seen them before. They are long, and green, and the tips look like unopened flowers.

The wine smells horrible, like rotting food. It reminds me of how beer smells. I close my eyes and take a sip. It's bitter and disgusting but I swallow it. I set the glass down and decide not to have any more.

The ice cream is melting like snow. I should have realized it would melt. It's mostly solid, but some of it has become a thick soup. I eat it quickly, because I want it to stay frozen. It's the most delicious thing I've ever eaten. It's sweet, and the flavor is hard to explain. I've never tasted anything like it.

About halfway through eating the ice cream my head starts to hurt. It's the worst pain I've ever felt. I groan and fall onto the bed, covering my eyes. I lay there, waiting for it to go away. Thankfully it does, but it takes a while for it to disappear. It's worse than the poison I drank in the trials. Why do people eat ice cream if it hurts so much? Then I remember Esteban saying it would hurt if I ate it too fast. I wish I'd remembered that.

I decide to let the ice cream melt a little so that it doesn't hurt my head again. No food is worth that pain. Once I'm sure I'll be okay, I slowly spoon the ice cream into my mouth. The pain never comes back.

Finishing my meal, I lie back on the bed and watch more TV. I try many different shows, but nothing interests me. Eventually I fall asleep.

20

A sudden burst of noise scares me awake. It takes me a moment to figure out where I am, and another moment to realize it's just the phone ringing. As I pick it up and put it to my face, I turn and look through the window to the world outside. It's still dark out. I wait until someone speaks.

"Hello?" I hear on the other end.

"Hello," I say.

"Sam?"

"Yes?"

"It's Collin. Good news, the jury came to a decision. We'll need to be to court by 8:00am. Think you can manage being ready by 7:30am?"

"I don't know what that means."

"Oh, right. Don't know numbers, can't tell time. Well, it's 6:30am now, so that gives you about an hour. Start taking a shower now if you haven't already. Did you have the hotel wash your clothes?" asks Collin.

"I didn't know they could do that until later. I washed them in the shower," I say.

"Wait, you WHAT?"

"I washed them in the shower."

"They're dry clean only! You've probably ruined them!" says Collin.

"I didn't know!" I say. It takes a moment for Collin to respond. I hear a grunt of anger then Collin lets out a deep breath.

"I know, and I was a little drunk at the time. I forgot. Anyway, I do have one more set of clothes you could wear. I'll bring them in a little bit and hand them to you through the door. Okay?"

"Okay," I say.

"Good. See you shortly." I hear the phone click, so I put it back down.

I decide to take another shower, not because I feel I need it, but because I enjoy the warm water beating down on me. I use the shampoo on my hair this time and it smells amazing. When I finally finish my shower and dry off, my hair seems thicker somehow.

As I walk out of the bathroom, I hear a knock on the door. I open it up just enough for Collin to hand me some clothes, which I happily take.

"You better hurry or we'll be late. Just get them on and we'll get out of here," says Collin.

"Okay."

I'm able to get most of the clothes on by myself, but I can't get the shirt around my cast by myself. I go over to the door and open it.

"Collin?" I say.

"You're ready?"

"I need you to help me get my shirt on," I say.

He grunts like he's angry, opens the door and comes inside. I can tell that he's uncomfortable even though I only have my shirt off. He tries not to look at me as he helps me put my cast through the sleeve. It takes a lot of pulling to finally get it around the cast.

"There, you're fine. I'll be outside when you're ready. Now hurry the hell up," says Collin.

It takes me a while to work the buttons on the shirt, but I finally finish dressing. I open up the door, and Collin's standing there, staring at me.

"You look like crap, but it'll have to do for now. The jury's already made up their minds, so I don't think your appearance will affect the outcome. Let's go."

It takes me a moment to realize there's nothing for me to bring from the room. The old clothes are probably ruined, and I didn't have anything else with me. The only thing I brought into this new world was my armor. I wonder what happened to it.

I follow Collin down the hallway to the stairs. As we walk down them, I decide to ask him.

"Do you know what happened to my armor and weapons?"

"Yes, they were logged into evidence but never used. Wincott must not be as bright as he seems, because if I were trying to send you to prison, I'd make sure the court saw you in your armor. It looks like something a samurai might wear. It'd be a good way to make the court afraid of you."

"What's a samurai?" I ask.

"They were Japanese soldiers, very skilled and very deadly. Their armor made them look like demons," says Collin.

"What are demons?"

"Imagine the most evil, corrupt and cruel person you can."

"Chaff."

"What?" asks Collin.

"He's the most evil person I can think of," I say.

"Well take that amount of evil and triple it. That's a demon."

"What does triple mean?"

Collin just grunts in anger again. I wish he'd stop being so angry at me all the time. I can't help not knowing things.

We leave the stairs behind and step into the large, wood covered room with the soft chairs. Walking next to Collin, instead of behind, we make our way out the door.

"This is my car. Get in," he says, as I stare at the bright red automobile in front of me. There's no back door for me to get into, and no driver to take us anywhere.

"Car?" I ask.

"Same thing as an automobile," says Collin.

"Who's going to drive it?"

"I will," says Collin.

"Do you know how?" I ask.

Collin just laughs. I have to get down very low to the ground to sit inside, and I don't know how to make the door close.

"Just pull the door down. Grab that," he says, pointing to a handle I can hold onto. The door seems much lighter than I would have guessed, and I pull the door down into place with a snap.

"Make sure to use your safety harness. This goes much faster than the taxis," says Collin.

"What's a safety harness?" I ask.

"Oh for crap's sake, here," he says. He pulls up a strap with a piece of metal attached to it from between my legs, then over my shoulders he pulls down two more, connecting all of them. I watch as he does the same thing for himself.

"This is a Ferraghini," starts Collin. "About a century ago, two car companies merged and started making the fastest production cars on the market. I can't remember their names. But anyway, to this day, this is still the fastest car allowed on the road. It cost me two years' salary just for the down payment."

"Um... wow?" I say, unsure of what else to say.

All of a sudden the car starts moving very fast. I'm pushed back into the seat. I decide that I'd rather take a taxi than this machine. The entire time we're in the car I'm worried about dying. I imagine if we hit something, there won't be anything left of us.

"Can you slow down?" I ask.

"Why, not enjoying it?"

"It's hard to enjoy things when you think you might die."

Collin slows the car down some. "Eh, it's wasted on you anyway. Why am I trying to impress an interloper who lives in a cave?"

I don't answer his question, because I know the answer will only anger him.

"Will we make it?" I ask.

"We'll be a few minutes early. Always want to be a little early, just in case," says Collin.

I just stare out the window, trying my best not to think dark thoughts about being trapped in a cell for the rest of my life. After a few moments we arrive. Collin doesn't stop the car in front of the building. Instead, he drives to the back of the building, where there are many white lines on the ground. I see other cars resting between the lines, and Collin puts his car between a pair of them.

He pushes a button on his straps and they come apart, going back to where they came from. I do the same with my straps. I watch as Collin pulls on a handle that's part of his door, and I do the same. The door opens and slides up, letting me get out.

I follow Collin to the building, and we go through a different door than the one we went through last time. This time the elevator doesn't scare me as badly. I still hate feeling trapped, and I keep my eyes closed, but when I finally get out, I'm able to walk instead of run.

We walk down the long hallway to the same room we'd been in before. People are standing outside waiting. Just as we approach, one of the guards opens the door and lets us inside.

The courtroom looks like it would be a nice place to live in, if it wasn't being used to deal with bad people. There's a lot of space, and there are many places that people could sit. I wish we had a place like this back in the Crag. It would be a better place for meeting than standing outside in the rain.

We sit down at the table we sat at before. This time Collin doesn't use his paper machine. Instead, he just leans back in his chair and stares at the table in the front.

"Someday I'll sit up there," says Collin.

"Why don't you go sit up there now?" I ask.

"No, I mean, someday I'll be a judge. When I'm tired of defending idiots and miscreants. I'll work one day a week, just to keep my mind sharp, and I'll spend the rest of my time golfing."

"What's golfing? Is that the thing that doctors do?"

Collin looks at me funny, like he can't believe what I just asked.

"Yeah, a lot of doctors golf. And lawyers. Pretty much anyone with money. It's kind of expensive, and some courses you have to know someone to get in, or be someone important. So don't worry, you'll never have to golf," says Collin.

"Someday I might be someone," I say. I don't really care if I'm ever important here, I just want Collin to shut his mouth. It doesn't work.

"Yeah, the day you're famous is the day I'll give it all up and become a nun," says Collin.

"What's a nun?" I ask.

"I don't really know. It's just something people say. I think it has something to do with a religion from long ago."

"So what is golf?"

"You try to hit a very tiny ball a very long distance with a club, and put it into something the size of a drinking glass," explains Collin.

"How big is the ball?"

"Hmm. Take the tip of your first finger and touch it to the tip of your thumb. That's how big the ball is."

"That's about the size of the rocks I like to hurl with my sling. I could use my sling to make it go into the drinking glass," I say.

"Yeah, well, you can only use clubs, and it's a very long distance. Farther than your sling could probably throw."

"I would surprise you," I say.

"Until that day, shut up."

I look away from Collin. I'm sick of him. Prison doesn't seem as bad as having to being around him for so long.

"You should stay drunk. You're nicer when you're

drunk," I say.

"I wasn't asking," says Collin.

I'm done talking with Collin, so I look over to where the jury sits. I watch as they come into the room from another door and sit down. Eventually, one of the bailiffs opens the door to the judge's room and out walks Judge Pham.

"All rise. The honorable Judge Vernona Pham presiding," says the Bailiff.

Everyone stands up, waiting for the judge to make her way to her table. A few more people enter the back of the courtroom and then the doors are closed. I wonder why so many people have appeared when I don't know any of them, and it doesn't seem like Grintz would have so many friends and family. Do people just come to watch judgments, like it's some sort of TV show?

"You may be seated."

We all sit back down.

"The jury has reached its verdict. Mr. Wincott, Mr. Reigns; is there anything else that should be taken into account before we proceed?" asks Judge Pham.

"No, your honor," says Wincott.

"No, your honor," says Collin.

"Very well then. Jury foreman, can you please address the two plaintiffs and deliver your verdicts?" says the Judge.

A small man, who is maybe only as tall as my shoulders stands up. He clears his throat then in a deep, scratchy voice he speaks.

"In the matter of Interloper Designate Sam's charge of attempted murder, we the jury find Sam..."

I look over at Collin. His face is serious, but he won't look at me. It's like time slows down. I feel dizzy. The next words that come out of this man's mouth could mean my death, even though that's all they are; words. A group of people that I've never met, that I've never talked to, are deciding my fate. If they knew me, they would know that I would only harm someone if it meant protecting myself or others. But I can't tell them that. I can only hope that they believe my story.

"... not guilty."

My breath catches. Thank the Sky Gods that they have seen fit to protect me! The crowd mumbles, but people sound happy, like the right decision was made.

"In the matter of Interloper Designate Sam's charge of aggravated assault, we the jury find Sam..."

I didn't know that there was more than one thing that I could be found guilty of. Does this mean I still might die? Is what they think I did so bad that I might still be put to death?

"... not guilty."

Tears form in the corners of my eyes. For the first time I feel relieved. But the feeling doesn't last for long.

"In the matter of Interloper Designate Sam's charge of trying to escape a federal corrections facility, we the jury find Sam..."

No! Please! Don't find me guilty! The other two I can see them saying I wasn't guilty, because I was only trying to defend myself and the recording proved it. But it's harder for people to know whether I was trying to escape from Grintz, or just escape. And is trying to escape something they might kill me for?

"... not guilty."

I feel like I'm going to throw up. My stomach hurts badly, even though they've found me innocent. The feelings of worry are too much, and I nearly throw up on myself. I fight back the feeling and drink some of the water in front of me. Please let that be the end of it.

"In the matter of Citizen Grintz's charge of attempted murder, we the jury find Citizen Grintz..."

Good, they must be done with me, so I'm safe. I don't have anything to worry about anymore. If they found me innocent, they must believe my story. Now I just have to watch as they find Grintz guilty. I hope he rots.

"... not guilty."

What? How could they find Grintz not guilty? They heard the recording, and it agreed with everything I said! I look over at Collin and his jaw is clenched tight. His eyes are closed, and I can tell he's angry.

"In the matter of Citizen Grintz's charge of attempted rape, we the jury find Citizen Grintz..."

I can understand, maybe, why they didn't find him guilty. It didn't seem like he really wanted to kill me, but he definitely tried to... rape me. Please Sky Gods, if you are good, make him go to prison.

"... not guilty."

I start to feel like I'm going to throw up again. This time it's worse. How could the jury not find him guilty of trying to rape me? I look over at them, and the few people in the jury who were looking at me look away. None of them will look me in the eyes.

"In the matter of Citizen Grintz's charge of aggravated assault, we the jury find Citizen Grintz..."

I don't want to hear anymore. If they believe he's innocent of trying to rape me, then why would they find him guilty of assaulting me?

"... not guilty."

Now I'm angry. I look over at Grintz, who's smiling. I want to kill him. I have to kill him. I start to stand up, but Collin grabs me and pushes me back down in my seat. He looks just as angry as I am, but instead he whispers to me.

"Don't. He's not worth it. You're free. You have to let it go."

I try my best to calm down, but can't. I look over at the jury. They still won't look me in the eyes. They all look disgusted, and I hope it's with themselves. How can Grintz get away with everything that he's done?

"How come they didn't find him guilty?" I whisper angrily to Collin.

"Maybe they felt that since you're an interloper, crimes can't actually be committed against you. You aren't a citizen, and don't have the same rights we do. If you were someone's dog, Grintz would go to prison for the next ten years. But because you aren't part of the system, you are worth less than nothing to them."

"But I'm still a person!" I say.

"I know, Sam. I know. I'm... sorry."

21

I close my eyes and breathe in deeply. For as many things as I like about this new place, there are many more that I hate. Just because I was born somewhere else I'm treated like I'm less than nothing. If I win their war for them, will it be any different? Or will they still see me as just a machine; a weapon to be used and nothing more?

"All rise," says the Bailiff. I watch as Judge Pham goes back into her room, as does the jury. Before they reach the door, I yell at them.

"I'm still a person!"

One of the women in the jury turns to me. She has long brown hair and deep brown eyes. She looks like she could be a mother. Lines at the corners of her mouth where she smiles, and more lines in the corners of her eyes. She has a friendly face. She looks like a nice person.

"We're sorry Sam. We believed you. It was the laws that failed you, not us."

I stand there, not knowing what she means or how to feel. Maybe some people here are decent, but the people that make the laws are evil.

"So what happens now?" I ask Collin.

"We're done here."

"Thank you, Collin, for saving me."

"Don't mention it."

"I know that we don't get along, but I will be in your

debt forever," I say.

"Did you not hear the part where I specifically said not to mention it?" says Collin. I can see in the corner of his mouth the start of a smile, but he fights it.

"I hope we never have to meet again," I say.

"Me too. Good luck, Interloper."

Collin gathers his things and leaves. Only a few people are left in the courtroom. Thankfully, one of them is Carter. I was starting to worry that I'd be stuck here alone. I wouldn't know where to go or what to do. He walks up to me and shakes my hand.

"Congrats," he says. "I was worried they would throw the book at you just because you're not one of us. It wasn't fair that Grintz got off scot free though. I'd like to see him hang for what he did."

"I'm worried that he'll do it again," I say.

"Don't worry too much. I heard that his Dad is cutting him off completely. No job, no money. He also won't have his father's protection anymore. He'll be forced to be a better person or he'll end up in prison. He wouldn't last long there, and he knows it. His life is ruined, if that makes you feel any better."

"I wish it did. More important than my revenge is protecting others from him. If he does try to rape or murder someone else it'll be my fault, because I didn't kill him when I had the chance. I could have killed him in that cell."

"You could have, but then you'd still be in that cell, waiting for them to execute you. You did the right thing, Sam. It may not seem like it now, but you did the right thing," says Carter.

"I wish I hadn't," I say.

"If you had killed Grintz, you might have killed millions more in the process. People who are depending on you to win the war."

"Those people don't even know me. The few that do know me call me 'interloper' or 'primitive' and treat me like I'm not even human."

"Someday they'll know your name. Someday everyone will know your name. Just wait. They'll make statues of you," says Carter.

"What's a statue?" I ask.

"It's normally a person carved out of rock."

I think back to the hotel, with the beautiful stone woman pouring water. That must be what he means.

"I don't want a statue. I just want people to treat me well."

"Don't we all. You ready to go then?" asks Carter.

"Where are we going?" I ask.

"I'm supposed to escort you to the Grand Citadel."

"The place you told me about? Where they'll train me to lead your war?"

"Yeah. That's the place."

Carter turns and starts walking away. I don't follow him. Instead I stand there, unmoving. It takes him a few steps to realize I'm not coming. He turns around and sees my face then walks back to me slowly.

"You don't think that these people and this place are worth saving, do you?" asks Carter.

"They aren't my people," I say.

"But they're still people. Didn't you just say something like that? Weren't you upset because you weren't being treated as an equal? You're doing that to all of them."

"I am."

"Don't you want to be better than them?" asks Carter.

"Not really. Why should I be?"

Carter can't think of anything to say. He just stares at me, worry on his face.

"Okay. I understand. I get it. Let me take you somewhere," says Carter.

I don't say anything.

"I'll take you one place and then you can decide where you want to go. I can help you get a job, and you can live out the rest of your life here. I'll even take you back to the Crag if you want. Your choice. Just please; come with me."

It takes me a moment to put my thoughts together.

"I will come with you. One place, and then you'll take me back to the Crag?" I ask.

"Yes, if that's what you want," says Carter.

"It is. I will go with you now."

I follow Carter. We walk together, out of the courtroom, down the hall. I close my eyes in the elevator. This time it's worse. All of the emotions from the trial start to come out. Tears roll down my face, but I hold in the sounds so that Carter won't hear. He's turned away from me, and I don't want him to see me like this.

When we finally reach the bottom the elevator doors open. I follow behind Carter, wiping the tears from my eyes. Please don't let him turn to see me.

Thankfully, he doesn't. We just keep walking; out the door Collin and I came in this morning. I follow Carter to his car. It looks very simple. Not at all like what Collin drives. I pull on a handle to open the door, but instead of it sliding up, it moves toward me. Crouching down, I'm able to get inside and pull the door closed.

"Where are we going?" I ask.

"You'll find out when we get there," says Carter.

I decide not to ask again. I'm not worried that Carter will harm me, he could have done that at any time. I just hate not knowing. It bothers me not knowing things. That's why I ask so many questions.

We drive for a while. I watch out the window as the buildings seem to disappear, replaced by more and more animals and trees. I also see fields of vegetables and wheat. They are much larger than back home, but I imagine they would have to be with so many people to feed.

I see machines in the fields; large machines that look dangerous, with spinning things that seem to destroy the vegetables. Maybe that's how they collect them. They use machines to pull the vegetables out of the ground, so that people don't have to. I wonder what people do then if they don't have to grow things.

Maybe they hunt. I can't imagine a machine being good at hunting. How would it remember where it's good to hunt? How would it hit an animal with a bow or sling? Or maybe people don't hunt anymore. Maybe they keep their animals in buildings, like how we keep animals in a pen back at the Crag. What do people do if they don't have to work hard anymore?

It feels like it takes forever, but we eventually arrive at a large red building. It's made out of rectangles of stone, each about the size of both my fists, with gray in between. In letters, above the front door, it says 'Kennedy School'.

Carter gets out of the car and I follow him inside the building. The hallways are smaller than in the other buildings I've been in, but because the walls are white, it doesn't feel quite as small as it really is.

I see pictures on the walls, like in some of our books. They don't seem very good, like they were made by new ones. Carter keeps walking down the long hallway, but eventually turns to his left. As I come around the corner, I see several people at tables. One of them stands up and walks over to Carter. I stay behind, just in case.

"Carter McManus, is that you?" asks a happy-faced woman. She wears circles of glass in front of her eyes, and has her hair up in a ball in the back. She looks old enough to be our mother, and then some, but her hair is only partly gray.

"Noreen, how are you?" asks Carter. He reaches across the raised table between them and hugs her.

"I'm doing well. We haven't seen you in probably close to fifteen years," she says.

"That sounds about right," says Carter.

"What are you up to these days?" asks Noreen.

"I'm a soldier now. Trying to do my best to protect people."

"That's wonderful. I remember you always tried to stop fights on the playground and looked after the younger kids. So who is your friend?" asks Noreen.

"Oh, this is Sam. Sam is from far away, and doesn't

know what school is. Thought I might introduce Sam to Mrs. Iacolucci. Is she in?"

"She is. The kids just came in from recess. Should I let her know you're coming?"

"No, that's okay," says Carter. "I'd rather surprise her."

"Okay. Well it was wonderful to see you. Don't be a stranger," says Noreen.

"I won't."

I smile at Noreen and she smiles back. It's a very sweet smile that I'm not used to, like nothing could ever upset her. Not at all like back in the Crag. There aren't too many things to smile about in the Crag.

I follow Carter back down the hallway, near where we came in. He stops, then turns right and opens a wooden door. There's a tall, thin window next to it, but I can't really see much through it. I can hear new ones talking inside, and their words grow louder as Carter steps through the doorway.

"Carter? What are you doing here?" says a woman's voice.

"Hi Mrs. I. I just wanted to come say hello and introduce you to my friend Sam," says Carter.

I step inside the room and look around. I see Carter hugging a woman who is tall and thin. Her hair is cut short, almost as short as mine, but her's is a dark brown color. She wears a long shirt that goes down to her knees that reminds me of what the judge wore. Mrs. I's shirt however is a beautiful light-green color.

My eyes move around the room and I see many new ones. They each sit in their own chair, and at their own small table. They have books in front of them, and it looks like it's all the same book. It must be nice to have enough copies that everyone can read the same thing. Back in the Crag we only had one copy of each book. It was tough when you needed to look something up in a book but couldn't because someone else was already reading it.

I reach out to shake Mrs. I's hand, but instead she

hugs me. I don't know how to react, because we seldom hug in the Crag, and when we do, it's only someone we know very well. I don't know this Mrs. Iacolucci. She seems nice, but it makes me nervous that she would treat me like she already knew me.

Carter and I follow Mrs. I up to the front of the room so that all the new ones can easily see us.

"Class, these are our very special guests: Carter and Sam. Can you tell them hello?" asks Mrs. I.

The entire class very slowly says 'hello Carter and Sam'. Carter says 'hello' back, but I just smile, not knowing what to say or do. I feel very uncomfortable in front of all these new ones that I don't know. It would be easier if they were wearing armor, and I was wearing armor, and I was about to teach them how to hunt. Instead, I don't know what I'm going to say, or what they're going to say, and it makes me nervous.

"Carter, can you tell the class what it is you do?" asks Mrs. I.

"Sure. Hi everyone. I'm Carter, and I'm a soldier in the Triple-F."

One of the new ones raises her hand.

"Do you shoot people?" asks the girl.

"Only when they shoot at me first," says Carter.

"Have you ever killed anyone?" asks a little boy in the front.

"I try my best not to," says Carter.

"Is it fun to shoot guns?" asks another girl in the back.

"Only when you're not aiming it at a person," says Carter.

"Okay class, let's not ask Carter any more questions about shooting people," says Mrs. I. "So what do you do, Sam?"

"Hi. I'm Sam, and I'm a hunter," I say.

"What do you hunt?" asks a very serious looking boy in the middle of the room.

"Mostly deer and wolves."

"My Dad does that too," says the girl who had raised her hand.

"What's the coolest thing you've ever killed?" asks the little boy in the front.

"A dragon."

All of the new ones' eyes get big.

"Dragons aren't real," says the very serious boy.

"They are where I come from," I say.

"Where do you come from?" he asks.

"I come from a cave, very far from here. It's called the Crag. We don't have much. We don't have machines, or buildings, or cars, or TV. We don't even have a lot of people," I say.

"You live in a cave?" says the serious boy. "That's dumb. You should live here instead."

"Well, I do now," I say.

The little boy in the front speaks up again.

"How did you kill the dragon?"

"I threw a spear, and it hit the dragon just in the right spot to kill it," I say.

"Are you a hero then?" asks the girl in the back.

I don't know how to answer.

"Yes, Sam's a hero," says Carter. "Sam saved many people by killing the dragon."

"Good. I want to grow up to be like you," says the girl.

I'm surprised by her words. Why would anyone want to be like me? My life has been filled with death and loss. I've always hoped for a better life, but every time things start going well, they get worse.

"I hope you don't have to live my life," I say. "One of my brothers just died."

The new ones all seem very sad to hear this.

"How did he die?" asks the little boy in the front.

"He was killed by bad people," I say. I look over and see that Mrs. I is worried about what I'm saying.

"Did you kill the bad people back?" asks the little boy.

"No. But they are dead now," I say.

"Good. Bad people should die."

I don't know what to say to that. I agree; bad people should die. But only very, very bad people, and only when they might hurt or kill others. But I'm not going to tell these new ones that.

"Bad people shouldn't be bad people," I say.

I watch as the new ones each think about what I said. Many of them smile.

"Yes, well thank you, Sam," says Mrs. I. "Class, would you like to come up and hug Sam and Carter?"

The new ones all stand up and come running toward us. I take a step back, but before I know it I'm covered in new ones. They're hugging me, and climbing on me, and making me laugh. I look over and see the same thing happening to Carter.

"We're under attack," I say, jokingly.

"It's a good thing we're unarmed," says Carter, smiling back at me.

It takes a while for the new ones to calm down and go back to their seats.

"Well thank you Carter for bringing your friend Sam in. Class, can you tell Sam and Carter thank you?" asks Mrs. I.

"Thank you," says everyone in the class.

I just smile back at them. They all seem so young. So innocent. Like Flot and Jet were not very long ago. My eyes start to drip, but I quickly wipe them, hoping the new ones don't see it. Carter gives Mrs. Iacolucci a final hug, I do the same, and we leave.

22

Carter and I get back into his car. We sit there for a while, not talking. I stare out the window at the school, wondering what it would have been like to grow up here. Where I wouldn't have to worry about being killed. Where I wouldn't have to hunt to survive. Where everyone seems so happy and so innocent. That's how new ones should look. They shouldn't have to live through what I've lived through.

Finally, Carter breaks the silence.

"So have you decided? Do you want to go back to the Crag?"

I don't answer him.

"Sam?"

"I want to go back to the Crag, but your trick worked. I will go with you. I will help you protect these new ones. I just hope they grow up into people better than I've met. So far, most people here are terrible," I say.

"You think that just because you've mostly met lawyers," says Carter. "Everybody hates lawyers."

"Do lawyers hate lawyers?"

"More than anyone. Do you know what they call a thousand lawyers at the bottom of the ocean?" asks Carter.

"What's an ocean?" I ask.

"An ocean is a very, very large body of water. So large that when you're in the middle of it, you can't see land in any direction. Planes can fly over it, and boats can sail on it, but you couldn't swim across it by yourself."

"What's a plane?" I ask. "And what is swimming?"

"Swimming is where you wave your arms and legs around in water to move, so that you don't drown. A plane is another way of saying 'ship', like what you think of as dragons," says Carter. "Anyway, put on your seat belt. It's time to go."

After making sure my seat belt is tight, I watch out the window as things move all around us.

"So what do they call a thousand lawyers at the bottom of the ocean?" I ask.

"A good start," says Carter.

I think about it for a moment.

"I don't understand," I say.

"It means that all of the lawyers should be at the bottom of the ocean. It's a joke. Like, lawyers are so bad that they should all be drowned."

"That's kind of a sad thought. As bad as Collin was, I don't know that I'd want him dead. He still helped me."

"You're over-thinking it. Jokes don't really mean what they are saying. That's why they're funny," explains Carter.

"We don't really tell jokes where I come from," I say.

"Apparently not."

The rest of the ride we don't talk. It's not that I don't like talking to Carter, it's just that I don't know him very well, and he doesn't really know me. I can't think of anything to say to him, or to ask him, so I just look out the window, trying to learn as much as I can from the world around me.

We drive for a very long time. It's so long that we have to stop to fill the car with something called 'electricity'. I guess it's what makes most machines work, including TVs and lights. Carter tells me how it was discovered, and I think that what he calls 'lighting' is really sky fire.

He also tells me that things used to run on something called fossil fuels, but that the place that it came from was destroyed. He says the only place left you can get it from is in the Chinese controlled US.

Once we get moving again, I finally start asking him important questions.

"Who will be teaching me when we get there?" I ask.

"Not sure. Probably a lot of people. My guess though is that they'll assign you someone to make sure you get to the right places at the right times, until you get the hang of things. They'll have to start you at the very beginning; how to do math, basic history, science, all that stuff. I'm sure you'll pick it up. What we don't know is how quickly you can learn it," says Carter.

"I don't know," I say. "I think pretty fast."

"You do. I guess the first part will tell us whether you're actually as smart as I think you are."

"What will it be like? The Grand Citadel, I mean?"

"The food there is good; better than out in the wastelands for sure. You'll be too busy learning to do much else. Eat, sleep, learn; that's gonna be your life for a while," says Carter.

"Will I be able to call you? Like on a phone?" I ask.

"I don't think they'll let you, once you start training. They'll need you to focus. Don't worry though, we'll see each other again. And if things go as well as I hope, it might be sooner than you think."

"Okay," I say, even though I'm not okay with it. "One more question: do I get money?"

"Yes, you do. Lots of it, if they accept you."

"What do you mean, 'if they accept me'?"

"You'll have to pass tests," says Carter.

"Are those like trials?" I ask.

"Sort of. They aren't dangerous though. They give you a sheet of paper with a bunch of questions on them. The paper won't tell you what the actual answer is; instead you'll have to pick which one you think is the answer. Then, when you've answered all the questions, they'll see how many of your answers match theirs. You'll get a score telling you how many you missed and why."

"What happens if I don't pass the tests? Will they kill

me?"

"No, they won't kill you. They'll probably just send you back to the Crag. But if that happens..."

Carter's putting so much pressure on me. He keeps telling me that so many people's lives depend on me doing well.

"Why do I have to be the one to save your people?" I say, feeling angry.

"Because you're the best of what we have," says Carter.

"You don't even know that! I haven't taken your tests yet. I could be stupid, or lucky, and I could be nothing. Why are you so sure?"

Carter is quiet for a while.

"Faith," is all he says.

I stay quiet the rest of the trip.

23

After driving for most of the day we come upon a massive gray building; bigger than any building I've seen so far. It's built into the side of a very steep cliff, and surrounded by water on nearly all sides. I can't see any land across the water that surrounds it.

"Is that the ocean?" I ask.

"Yes," says Carter.

"It's amazing!" I say.

"Yeah, it is. But what about the building? We call it Candlestick."

"Um, it's nice," I say.

"It's over one-hundred stories tall, it's nearly indestructible to conventional weapons, and was design by Piezo Montalado himself. All you can say is that 'it's nice'?"

"It's very nice?" I say, unsure of what I said wrong.

"It took thousands of people to build it over the course of fifty years. Parts of it are still under construction. It's one of the greatest accomplishments of mankind," says Carter.

"Mankind?" I repeat.

"You know, man. What man has created."

"They didn't allow women to work on it?" I ask.

"I'm sure they did," says Carter, confused.

"Then wouldn't it be 'people' that created it, not 'man'?"

"It's just a saying."

"It's a terrible saying."

"I didn't create it," says Carter.

"Maybe not, but you use it," I reply.

"Maybe I'll stop using it then," he says quietly. "I didn't mean anything by it."

"I know."

Carter drives us to a much smaller building right next to Candlestick, and many men stand outside, holding guns. One of them comes up to Carter's window, which he opens.

"What's your business at the Grand Citadel," asks the soldier.

"I'm here to drop off a package. It's a delivery for Eddie Felson," says Carter.

The soldier holds up a small machine at us, which makes a clicking noise, then presses on it a few times with his fingers. Eventually he looks back up at us.

"You're cleared. Drive down that ramp," says the guard, pointing with his thumb. "Park, then follow the directions to get to floor D53. Got that? Don't deviate from that path or you'll be incinerated. Have a nice day."

Carter rolls up the window and drives us down the ramp.

"Who's Eddie Felson?" I ask.

"He's just a character in a movie," says Carter.

"What's a movie?"

"It's like a TV show, only longer."

"Oh. Does Eddie Felson work here?"

"No, they're code words, so that they know it's really us. They told me to use them when I brought you in. I was supposed to ask for Harry Frigg if we were in trouble," explains Carter.

"In trouble?"

"Yeah, like if someone was using us to sneak in."

"Has that ever happened?" I ask.

"Not that I know of, but better safe than sorry," says Carter.

"Code words seem like a good idea. Should we have code words?" I ask.

"You mean like if one of us gets in trouble, and we need the other one's help?" asks Carter. "How about we use the phrase: the raven flies at midnight."

"I don't even know what that means," I say. "How about we say: may justice serve all."

"Yeah, that's good. How did you come up with it?" asks Carter.

"I saw it written on the Tower of Justice."

"I've seen that building many times, but never noticed the words. Been too busy or focused to look up, I guess."

"Where I come from, you always have to be aware of what's going on around you. Otherwise, you'll end up dead," I say.

"Then I guess I'm glad we're here, and not there," says Carter.

"Not me."

"I know. I'm sorry, Sam."

Carter drives us down a smooth dark tunnel that opens up into a very large area where many other cars are parked. He stops his car between a pair of lines, turns off the car and we get out.

"Okay, Sam, just follow me and don't wander off. That guy back there wasn't kidding when he said we'd be incinerated if we didn't follow their directions exactly," says Carter.

"What does incinerated mean?"

"It means they'll burn us with fire until we're nothing but ash."

"I don't want to be burned," I say, worried.

"Neither do I," says Carter. "We'll be fine as long as we read the signs and take things slow. Those are the elevators. That's where we need to go."

I follow behind him, just in case someone jumps out to burn us. I like Carter, but if I have to, I'll use him as a shield to protect myself and get away. I hope it doesn't come to that.

We get to the elevators and I'm surprised just how many there are. It's more than the number of fingers I have on both hands. I look around, but don't really pay attention as Carter pushes a button near one of them. We stand there waiting for what feels like a very long time, but eventually I hear that familiar noise saying the elevator is ready for us.

I step inside and I feel relieved because the elevator is large. Larger than my cell was in prison. I still feel trapped, but not as badly as I normally do in an elevator. No one is inside the elevator as we enter, and I'm glad because I don't want anyone to see me afraid. Especially if I have to work with some of these people.

As I turn around to face the door, I notice that there are buttons on both sides of it. Above one set of buttons is the letter 'D', above the other is the letter 'U'.

"What floor did the guy say?" asks Carter.

"I don't remember the first part, but I do remember it had the letter 'D' in it."

"Good. I'm pretty sure it was floor 53, just couldn't remember if it was up or down," says Carter.

"What do you mean 'down'?"

"Oh, yeah, so you know how the building is really tall? Well it stretches just as far going down. We're going underground," he says, pushing a button next to me.

He can see the worry on my face.

"Hey, Sam, it'll be okay. You grew up in a cave, where most of it was underground. And honestly, it's probably safer down here than it is in the Crag. Not only is the structure reinforced to withstand a nuclear attack, but no one here will be trying to kill you."

I worry less, but it still makes me feel uncomfortable. I don't think I was meant to live underground.

"What's a nuclear attack?" I ask.

Carter thinks for a moment.

"You know when wood is on fire it sometimes makes a popping noise and sends small pieces of wood everywhere?" asks Carter.

"Yes, of course."

"Well, it's like that. Only imagine that the piece of wood was the size of the Crag."

"Okay," I say.

"Now do you remember me telling you about the number one million? Where if each person in the Crag had their own cave, and each cave had that many people in it?" asks Carter.

"Yes."

"Well, imagine taking that number and having that many pieces of wood the size of the Crag. That's how big of an explosion a nuclear bomb can deliver. If they dropped a few here in Ireland, the entire island would be gone. The cities, your cave, everything; completely destroyed. Except this building. Well, the bottom half anyway. The top could still be destroyed. Supposedly they designed it so that anything but a direct strike on the facility will cause the upper half to break away from the base and float off into the sea. That way people aren't trapped down here."

"What about the people in the top half? It doesn't sound very good for them," I say.

"Better that some people survive than none was their thinking, I guess."

I can't get the thought of people dying out of my head, so I try to change the subject.

"What's Ireland?" I ask.

"No one's told you yet? That's the country you're in right now. We're an island that used to be separated into two areas, but after war broke out we unified. Now most of the Triple-F's military is based here, because we act as a way-point across the Atlantic Ocean," explains Carter.

"So what is an island?" I ask.

"It's land that's surrounded entirely by water. If you were to walk in any direction, eventually you'd hit the ocean."

"Aren't people afraid that the island will sink?"

"No, not really. It sticks up out of the water pretty far, and it's so huge that it would be nearly impossible for that to happen. Basically, the water level all around the world would have to get higher and higher, and then we'd have such big problems that the island sinking would be the least of everyone's worries," says Carter.

The elevator finally stops. It takes a moment for it to open, and when it does, two guards are waiting. Both point guns at us. Slowly and carefully, Carter walks toward them. I follow behind, but the guards yell out.

"Stop. Move away from Lieutenant McManus."

I do my best to move carefully away from him, so that I'm at Carter's side.

"On your knees, and place your hands on the back of your head."

I do as I'm told. I get down on my knees as one of the guards comes over and puts his hands on me. He moves them around my body and I'm not sure why. It bothers me, but I let him do it anyway.

"Clean", says the soldier. "Stand up."

I get to my feet and the guard throws something at me. I catch it out of the air. Part of it looks like thin, flat rope, which is attached to a rectangle made of the same stuff shirt buttons are made out of. I think Collin called it 'plastic'. It has a picture of my face on it.

"What do I do with this?" I ask.

"Put it around your neck. It's your ID badge. You lose it, you'll be shot on sight. Any questions?" asks the guard that touched me.

"No, I understand," I say.

"Good. Follow me," says the soldier.

The other soldier waits for me and Carter to pass, keeping his gun aimed at our backs. We walk down a long tunnel to a table where another soldier sits. He's old, much older than me, with wrinkles at the corners of his eyes and across his brow. His hair is thin on top, and I can see skin through it. The soldier's voice is deep and dangerous sounding, and it reminds me of wolves growling.

"Lieutenant McManus, we'll take it from here," says

the soldier.

Carter just stands there, staring at him. He doesn't look happy.

"Leave now," says the soldier, looking Carter in the eyes.

"Yes, sir," says Carter, through his teeth. "May I have one last word with Sam?"

"No."

Carter turns to me and his lips move, but I hear no sound. From how they moved, I think he was trying to say 'don't trust him'. It worries me, because I barely trust Carter. Now he's telling me not to trust the person who's supposed to watch over me. Carter finally turns and leaves, and I watch as he walks back to the elevator and disappears.

I turn to look back at the soldier. His grin makes me feel uncomfortable, because I can't tell if it's a mean grin or a happy one. I just stand there, not knowing what to do. Finally he speaks.

"Welcome to hell, Sam. That's what we call this place. You might think we named it that because it's so far underground, but it's because my first name's Lucifer. My old man had a sick sense of humor and thought it'd be funny to name me after the devil. I'm Major Brock. Just so we're clear, you will follow orders or you will be shot. Do you understand?"

"Yes."

"Yes what?"

It takes me a moment to realize he wants me to say something.

"I don't understand," I say.

"Address me as 'sir'. When I speak to you, the only thing I want to hear out of your mouth is 'yes, sir'. Do you understand me now?"

"Yes," I say. He starts to stand up and I can tell that he's angry. He's much taller than he looks when he sits. "Uh, sir."

Thankfully, he sits back down.

"Understand that I don't care what the brass thinks about McManus. He doesn't follow orders. I put him in the same category as deserters and spies. So if you think you'll get special treatment because you're his pet, think again. I'm not fair, I hold grudges, and I play favorites. Right now, there's only one person in this world I despise more than you, and that's McManus. You're a very close second. I think you're a waste of time, but I follow my orders. My orders say I have to teach you, and turn you into a great military mind. But the orders don't say I have to treat you well."

I wonder if this is the man that ordered Carter to leave his friend behind to die. I didn't think things could get worse than prison, but maybe I was wrong. Maybe Major Brock is worse than Grintz.

"Do you have any questions, interloper?" asks Brock.

"Yes, sir. What is hell, and who is Lucifer?" I ask.

Brock stares at me, an empty look on his face. Then he starts laughing. A creepy, evil laugh. He thinks he's funny. I hate being laughed at. I hate this place and I hate feeling like I have no control. He thinks I'm nothing.

I throw a punch as hard as I can at his face and it connects. He stops laughing. Slowly, calmly he stands up, pushing back his chair. Blood trickles from his nose. He comes around the table to me, and before I can react, grabs me by the throat then slams me to the ground. My head hits hard and the world spins. I fight the urge to vomit. The urge wins and I gag, sending my last meal down the sides of my face.

"The first punch was free. If you attack me or another soldier, unless ordered to do so, you will be shot. I am your judge, jury and executioner. You will obey, you will submit, and you will become a soldier. Is that clear?" yells Brock.

Through the choking and gagging I manage to say, "yes, sir."

Brock kicks me in the side then reaches down and grabs me by the hair. The last thing I see is his fist flying toward my face.

24

When I finally wake up, everything hurts. My face is sore and I feel dried blood crusted over it. I can tell that the ribs on my right side are bruised, and the back of my head feels like someone hit it with a rock.

Wherever I am right now it's dark. Very dark. All I can see is the outline of a small rectangle of light high above me. Struggling to stand, I look closer at the rectangle of light, but I can't see anything more than that. I put my arms out in front of me and feel metal. Running my hands along the wall, I reach a corner. I turn and follow that wall to another corner, then another, and then another. Looking back at the rectangle of light I realize that I'm in a small room, just big enough to lay down in if I bend my knees.

I scream until my throat is sore. I hope that someone can hear me, that someone will come and let me out of this horrible place. This place of darkness and emptiness. But no one comes. I am alone, trapped, living my worst nightmare. If I survive this, if I get out, I will kill Brock for putting me in here.

I reach my hands up to the rectangle and try to push it. No matter how hard I push, it won't move. Hitting the rectangle also does nothing. I move my hands around again, hoping to find a handle, or button, or something I can use to get myself out. The more I try, the more I panic, and the more I realize that there's nothing I can do to get out of this room.

I lie down on the ground and give up. Rocking back and forth, I try to calm the fear inside me, but it does no good. Tears wash away some of the crusted blood and vomit from my face, but they don't wash away the pain, or the feeling of hopelessness.

After a while I hear a voice talking. I try to listen; make out the words. It sounds like a crazy person rambling. That's when I realize that I'm the one talking. It's like my mouth and my brain aren't connected. Like I'm trapped inside myself, and whatever is going on outside my body is being controlled by someone else.

Maybe it is. Maybe they found a way to control people's bodies. Maybe I'm not even really trapped in this room. Maybe I'm trapped inside myself.

That's an even scarier idea; that something is wrong with my thoughts. I could be imagining this room, this horrible place. Maybe I'm torturing myself and I don't even realize it.

I start to calm down, hoping that this is a bad dream I can wake from, but I need to know if it's real or not. In dreams, my senses are duller. I don't smell things, but I can feel things. I can see and hear, but I can't taste.

I sniff the wall and it smells like metal. I touch my tongue to it, and it tastes how it smells. When I hit it with my fist, my hand hurts. I really am trapped inside this room, and I need to get out.

I yell again until I can't yell any longer. My voice disappears as my throat goes raw. No one comes.

Being careful with my broken arm, I take off my shirt and twist it around like it is rope. I tie a loop in it and put it around my head. Placing my left hand over my nose and mouth I pull tightly against the shirt with the right, making sure I can't breath and I can't slip my hand away. My left arm throbs from the pain. It's not long before I start to struggle against it and panic, and feel everything start to slip away.

Finally, a noise comes from outside the room. I hear only one word: 'stop'. I struggle with both hands, and it takes all of my strength to pull the shirt away from my head. I gasp for air, which makes my throat feel like I swallowed a knife. After a few coughs, I find the strength to speak.

"Brock, let me out of here," I whisper.

"Why?" asks the voice.

"Because I'm afraid of small spaces," I say.

"I know. That's why I put you in there," says Brock. I can tell now that it's him. "People are like horses. You break their spirit and you can mold them into whatever you want. The quickest way to break you is to use your fears against you."

"Please, let me out of here and I'll do anything you want," I say.

"You won't. You'll be a stubborn, arrogant, worthless interloper. You won't listen to me and you won't follow orders. I have to destroy you completely. There's still fight in you, but don't worry, I'll take that from you soon enough."

The sound of Brock's footsteps echo outside my cell.

I sit on the floor and try to calm down, but my trick for imagining faraway places, like my clover field, isn't working. All I can think about is the darkness, and how small the room is.

It reminds me of the prison cells I was in, but at least with the prison cells they had bars that I could look through. I could see what was just on the other side, and watch people coming and going. Here, I'm all alone, shut off completely from the outside world.

After putting my shirt back on, I spend time feeling around the floor, seeing if maybe someone dropped something I could use to get out. In one corner I find a hole, but it seems to go straight down. I make the mistake of putting my face near it. It smells horrible. My guess is that it's meant for me to make waste in. It's too small for me to climb down into, even if I was willing to, which I'm not.

The rest of the floor is smooth and cold. I can't get comfortable lying down. I stand up and try to push and pry at the rectangle of light again, moving it back and forth with the tips of my fingers. After what feels like forever, I'm finally able to push it open some. It opens just enough that I can look out into a dimly lit hallway. No one's there, but it makes me feel a little better knowing that I can see out.

I try to focus, pretend that I'm actually out in the hall and not trapped in this tiny room. The more I try to push the dark thoughts out, the more they push back. I get dizzy and fall to the ground, still surrounded by darkness. I cry until I have no more tears left then fall asleep.

* * *

My nightmares are horrible. I dream of being crushed by rocks and attacked by soldiers. Sleep doesn't feel like it lasts very long, because I wake up more tired than when I fell asleep. My hands and feet hurt, as do my knees and elbows. I can only guess that when I was asleep I must have hit the walls around me. I try to stretch out, when my arm touches something.

I feel around in front of me. Someone must have put a bowl in here with me while I was asleep. I can tell that the food inside of it is still warm. I put my mouth to the bowl and tilt, trying to pour some of it down my throat, but it's thicker than soup and doesn't move. I put a hand inside the bowl and scoop out what feels like maggots. Disgusted, I pull my hand away.

Holding it up to the rectangle, I can see that the small white pieces of whatever they are aren't maggots. I also see that there are pieces of meat in it. So they do mean for me to eat this.

Scooping some into my hand, I carefully chew the first few bites. It doesn't have much flavor. The white stuff tastes like nothing at all, while the meat tastes like cow. I'm glad that I can focus on the food, because it helps distract from the fear that this tiny cell is beating into me.

Too fast I eat the food and it makes me gag. I'm able to keep most of it inside me though. When I finish, I bang against the wall with the bowl. It makes a loud sound that hurts my ears, but I keep hitting the wall anyway. Hopefully

I'll annoy them enough that someone will come tell me to stop. I bang, over and over again, but nobody comes.

How did they get the food in here without me noticing? They had to open a door to put it in here. Maybe the wall with the light is actually a door.

I run my hands very carefully along the wall I think is a door. Eventually, I find a very thin seam, but it's too small for me to do anything with. I can feel the outline of the door, but knowing it's there doesn't help me much. At least if someone comes in I'll know where they're coming from.

I take the bowl and start hitting the edge against the rectangle of light. Hitting it harder and harder, I eventually dent the rectangle. After a few more swings it pops out, letting me see more easily into the hallway. The cell is brighter now, and I can see inside better. Having the extra light doesn't help much, because there's nothing really to look at in my cell. No writing, no markings. No objects that I've missed. It's me, the hole, the bowl and the door.

If I wanted to I could throw the bowl out into the hallway, but why waste the only thing I can hold onto?

A thought races through me: what if I can somehow reach the door handle on the other side and let myself out?

I stick my right arm through the rectangle, but it won't reach very far. It's up high enough that only part of my arm can go through it. If I could just stand a little taller...

Turning the bowl upside down, I use it as a step. I still can't quite reach, so I stand on just the toes of my left foot. I'm finally able to get my right arm through and bend it. I touch all the way around in a circle, but the door is flat. The only thing I really feel is the metal that held the rectangle in place. I can't feel the door handle at all. It must be there though, because there has to be a way in and out of this cell.

Think, Sam. What can you use to reach it?

I take off my shirt then twist it like a rope again. I make a loop on both ends and attach one of them to my wrist. Sliding my arm out of the rectangle, I try to hook my shirt on the door handle. I swing it in every direction, and after a few tries it finally hooks on something. Maybe I'll get out of here on my own.

I pull with all of my strength, feeling the handle move, but not enough. I start pulling in quick motions, and eventually I hear a click. The door suddenly opens outward, and I hang from it, unable to touch the ground. My arm feels like someone is trying to cut it off. All of my weight is being held in place by it, wedged in the rectangle. I can't get my wrist loose.

I realize that I'm very close to the wall on the other side of the hallway. I kick out, pushing away and closing the door, but it only stays closed a moment, not long enough for me to find the bowl. It bounces off, swinging me back toward the wall. I kick off again, this time with less strength. As I get close to the cell I can feel the bowl with my toes, and I'm able to stop my motion with it. Standing as tall as I can, I unhook the shirt from the handle and pull my arm through. It's bruised, sore and bleeding, but I'll survive.

I untie my shirt and put it back on. I pick up the bowl from the ground and the rectangle of metal I knocked out of the door just in case I need to use them again. The hallway is long and there isn't much light. The walls are a very dark gray color, like the tunnels of the Crag, which makes the hallway feel even smaller than it really is. Both directions look the same, and I have no idea which way I should go, so I just choose.

I run as fast as my legs will take me, trying hard to keep my foot falls silent. If I do run into someone, the only way I'll be able to beat them is to surprise them. They'll be wearing armor and I will have none. They will have guns, while I have only a piece of metal and a bowl. I may as well throw dirt at the sun.

Reaching the end of the hall, I stop then peek around the corner, wondering if I'll run into any guards. Hoping to find a way out, all I can see is walls. There's nowhere to go; just more cell doors.

I turn around and run even faster. I run so fast that

my feet hurt, and they make a slapping noise with every step. This time I'm even more worried, because I have so far to go down the hallway. The guards will come around the corner, see me, and I'll have nowhere to hide. It makes me wonder how much it will hurt when they shoot me.

I'm amazed when I reach the end of the hall and I'm still alive. I try to slow down but fail. Having nothing on my feet makes it too hard to stop, and I end up going past the corner and into the next hallway.

A guard stands in the middle of the hallway. His back is to me, but he hears my steps as I round the corner. He turns, surprised to see someone running at him. Before he can react, I hit him in the face with the bowl. His nose explodes, sending blood spraying from his face. I run past him, leaving him behind, because there's nothing more I can really do to him while he's wearing armor. I could slice his throat with my piece of metal, but he did nothing to me. He doesn't deserve to die.

I come to another corner, but this time I'm able to slow up for it. Looking down the hall I see no guards; no one that might stop me. I keep running, picking up speed, until I see a door unlike the others. It's bright orange with a long metal bar on it. It must lead out of here.

When I get to the door I try to push out on it but it won't open. I pull the bar toward me and nothing happens. I keep trying, but the door won't move. I look back and the guard with the broken nose is running at me. He looks angry, and he has his gun in his hand, ready to shoot.

Finally, desperate to get out, I push on the bar and the door opens. I get through, slam it shut, and then take my piece of metal and try to wedge it in the door to keep it from opening. It doesn't work, and the guard comes flying through the door, knocking me to the ground.

He trips, nearly falling on top of me, and drops his gun. It fires, and I can feel the bullet move my hair, barely missing my head. Reaching out, I grab the gun, twist away from him then stand in the corner behind the door.

Keeping it pointed at his back, I look around. We're in a short hallway in the shape of the letter 'T'. I have no idea what's around either corner, but I know a way to find out.

"Turn over," I say. "And before you think of trying something, know that I've shot people before. I have very good aim, and I'm an interloper. That means you are nothing to me. I don't care if you live or die."

I have to hope he believes me, even if it isn't true. I do care if he lives.

"Okay, just don't shoot," says the guard. His voice doesn't sound right, probably because of his broken nose. He turns over and looks at me, keeping his hands out in front of him.

"What's your name?" I ask.

"Brian," he says.

"Okay, Brian. I need you to tell me how to get out of here."

"Not happening."

"I'm an angry primitive with a gun!" I yell. "Tell me or I'll kill you!"

He just looks at me.

"Fine, I'll take my chances. But if you follow me, I will shoot you," I say.

He keeps looking at me. I make my way past him, trying not to get close enough for him to kick or punch me. I wave the gun to make him move far away from me then head down the hallway and turn right. I stop for a moment to listen and wait. I don't hear Brian coming after me, so I turn left.

This hallway is different. There's a door made of metal bars directly in front of me, and off to the side I hear talking. I can't see anyone yet, but I would guess that the people I hear are guarding this final door.

Pushing myself against the wall, I move as quietly as I can toward the people. I keep the gun in front of me, hoping that I don't have to use it. Once I get close enough, I can hear the conversation the guards are having.

"They were all dead, and the island was limbo," says

one voice.

"No it wasn't. I read an article that said it wasn't limbo, that it all really happened," says another.

"There's no way! How do you explain the ending then?"

"It was like, in the future, after they had all died."

"Whatever. I think the writers just made stuff up as quick as they could, and when the end of the show came, they did the same thing they did in that old space odyssey movie. Just showed a bunch of weird stuff that didn't explain anything."

"That makes more sense."

"I know!"

That's when I turn the corner and point the gun at the guards. It takes them a while to realize I'm not a guard, and even longer that I'm pointing a gun at them. They both slowly raise their hands in the air.

"Do you have guns?" I ask.

"Yeah," says one of them.

"Put them on the table," I say. "Slowly."

I watch as they each reach to their sides and pull their guns up slowly, making sure not to point them at me. Once they've put them on the table, I take one of the guns and throw it down the hall. Thankfully, it doesn't fire. The other one I keep, so that I'm now holding a gun in each hand.

"Open the door," I say, looking at the bars.

"We can't," says the older of the two men.

"Let me out or I'll shoot you," I say.

"I have a wife and kids!" says the younger one.

"Shut up, Jimmy," says the older one.

I use the handle of the gun in my right hand and hit the older one in the face with it. He covers his face with his hands and falls to the ground.

"Open it!" I yell, looking at the younger guard.

"Alright, I'll do it. Just don't kill me," he says.

I watch as he pushes something underneath the table. The door opens by itself. Not waiting until it's fully opened, I

159

run toward the door. Once I'm through, I keep going down a long hallway. I look back and neither guard is following me. That's when I hear a loud, horrible noise. It hurts my ears, it's so loud. Red lights I hadn't noticed before on the ceiling start to shine. I won't be able to surprise the other guards now.

If they know I've escaped they'll come after me. They'll make sure they have a lot of guns, and a lot of people, and I won't be able to stop them from killing me. I must hide. I look both directions, but don't see any guards yet. It feels like it won't be long before someone finds me.

The walls around me have regular doors instead of cell doors. No bars, just wood with metal handles. I tuck the guns into my pants and try opening one of the doors but it won't move.

I try another door and this time I get lucky. I jump in as fast as I can, closing the door behind me. It's dark, so I feel around for a button to turn on the lights. Eventually, near the door, I find one. The lights flicker to life. Inside I see many shelves filled with rolls of paper, containers of liquid, and a few other things I don't recognize. I take one of the sets of shelves that reaches to the ceiling and knock it down in front of the door, hoping it keeps the guards from reaching me.

Behind where the shelves were standing I see what looks like a metal covering for a hole. It's a little bigger than me, definitely large enough to hide in. I try to pull the cover away, and kick it once with the heel of my foot, but it won't move.

I look around the room, searching for something I can hit it with. There's a red metal container attached to the wall that looks heavy. Pulling it away from its holder, I aim the flat end at the metal cover and swing. The cover dents inward but doesn't come free. Again and again I hit it, until finally it swings inward toward the hole.

I crouch down to see inside. It reminds me of some of the very small tunnels in the Crag. It looks like it's just big enough to fit me, but it's completely dark, and I don't have anything to make light. The thought of being trapped in a small space in the dark makes me panic. I have no way of seeing where I'm going, but I climb in anyway. I figure if I get lost I can always come back.

It takes me a while to find my way through the tunnel. I can still hear the loud noise from outside, and sometimes I can even hear soldiers yelling. I feel in front of me, trying not to make too much noise. It makes my arms hurt, both my broken one and my good but injured one.

I finally find another hole cover, only I don't know if it leads to a room since everything is dark. I try and push it, but the cover won't move. I'd kick at it, only I don't have enough room to spin around and aim my feet at it. So I back up and try taking a different path through the tunnels. I find several more covers, but all of them lead to darkness. Just when I start to lose hope, I finally see light.

25

It takes a few turns to reach the hole cover, but when I do, I carefully look out, making sure no one can see me. Thankfully, there's no one waiting on the other side. I listen, but hear nothing, not even the loud noise that hurt my ears.

The hole cover also looks different than the one I destroyed getting into the tunnel. Instead of having thin strips of metal, this has many, many small dots. When I push up against it, it seems to move like fabric. I push with my right hand really hard and it stretches then breaks, sending me falling into the room.

Quickly, I pull my guns out, aiming them around the room. I see strange things, like pictures of skeletons and a table with straps. There are also machines in here, ones that I remember from the hospital. Maybe that's what this room is, maybe it's like a hospital room. Hopefully the doctor doesn't come in while I'm here.

Tucking one of the guns into my pants I turn off the lights, so that only the skeleton pictures are lighting the room. I slowly open the door, looking out, trying to see if anyone is in the hall. I am alone.

Sneaking out into the hallway, I listen to see if I hear the sound of soldiers running. Nothing. I hold the gun out in front of me, just in case I'm wrong and someone is coming for me.

I'm at the end of a hallway with only one way to go.

At the other end is a single elevator and a large red door. I run toward the elevator, planning to take it back up to the surface, but I feel like there must be something important on the other side of the door. Maybe they're hiding something if there are only two doors and an elevator in this part of the building.

Making my way to the door, I open it just enough to take a look inside. I see books and the corner of a table but not much else. If I open the door any further, someone inside will know I'm there. So instead I open it quickly, bending low to the ground and keeping my gun straight in front of me.

I can't believe what I see. Brock is sitting in a large chair, behind a wooden desk, and he's smiling. I aim the gun at his head and he laughs.

"Congrats, Sam. You broke the record by a few minutes," says Brock.

"What do you mean? What's a record?" I ask.

"It took you less time than anyone else to find me."

"This was a trial?" I ask.

"Yes."

"How many people tried before me?"

"Hundreds of thousands. It's something we do to recruits when they first come here. Only about a third even make it out of their cell. Of those, most are captured before they reach me. Out of all the people that have ever tried it, just ten have reached me. Of those ten, you were the fastest," says Brock.

"Did Carter reach you?" I ask.

The smile disappears from his face.

"Yes. Now put down the gun," commands Brock.

"What if I don't?" I ask.

"It doesn't really matter. You don't have live rounds in there."

"What do you mean?"

"Blanks. Fake bullets. They make a loud bang but don't do anything. All you'll do is hurt our ears," says Brock.

"Fine. If that's true then..." I pull the trigger.

The sound of the gun does hurt my ears. I look at

Brock, and he seems surprised I fired the gun, but he doesn't look injured. Maybe he's right, maybe the gun doesn't work.

"You're lucky I told you about the blanks. If you'd fired the gun at me when you thought they were real bullets, we'd 'disappear' you."

"You mean you'd take me home?" I ask.

"No. We would have hidden what was left of your body," says Brock.

I wish I had real bullets. I hate all these threats. I hate the way that Brock smiles that creepy, evil smile. I'd shoot him in the face, just to rid the world of that smile.

"Why did you put me through the trial?" I ask.

"We needed to know how clever and athletic you are. How well you can handle stress. It was especially important to test you, since you're an interloper. It's going to be a long time before we can trust you, and the first step is finding out if you're a merciless killer. A psychopath. You didn't try to kill any of the guards when you had the chance, and you didn't try to kill me when you came in here."

"How do you know I didn't kill any guards?"

"I was watching you the whole time on closed-circuit TV. Here," says Brock, spinning a small TV screen on his desk toward me.

On the screen are images of guards walking down hallways, someone repairing my cell door, and the guard I hit getting his nose fixed in a hospital room. There's also a camera inside the cell I was in, but that image is a light green color. It's strange, because it's bright like there were lights inside, even though there weren't.

"How can you see inside my cell?" I ask.

"Infrared. You know the colors you can see? Well, there are colors you can't. We have lights that emit infrared and cameras that can detect it," says Brock.

"You mean you were able to watch me the whole time? When I was screaming, and falling apart?"

"Yes, and it was very entertaining. I couldn't stop laughing."

I raise the gun up, aim it at him and fire until it's empty. He looks worried, maybe even afraid, but that look quickly disappears.

"You're a monster," I say.

"Yes," he says, smiling that evil grin again.

I stand there, staring at him, until I get so sick I can't stare him down any longer.

"What's next?" I ask.

"You'll start your training. Because you know almost nothing, we'll hook you up to Einstein. Get you through the first thirteen years of school. After that you'll learn military theory. History, strategy, economics, politics, science, engineering."

"How long will it take?"

"Depends on you. On how smart you are; how hard you work. We'll find out quickly if you're an idiot. Don't think for a second though you can fool the tests. They'll know if you answer questions wrong on purpose. And if you do that, don't think we'll send you home. I'll keep you here as a pet instead, just to piss McManus off. You'll be my slave, and I'll make your life miserable. Understand?" asks Brock.

My face is hot with anger. I barely hold back from trying to kill him again.

"Yes." I say quietly.

"Excuse me?" he says.

"Yes... sir."

He laughs.

"Any questions, soldier?" asks Brock. The way he says 'soldier' makes me want to punch him.

"Where can I get real bullets?" I ask.

His smile fades.

"Just remember this," I start to say. "I know where you work now. I can find this place whenever I want."

"Oh, can you? This is just one floor of the facility, and this isn't even my office. None of it's real. The camera feeds work, and the infirmary is real, but we don't hold prisoners down here. The floor we actually keep our prisoners on has never been broken out of. Remember that when you think about making trouble. No one has escaped this building, let alone their cell. You're trapped here, and the sooner you realize it, the sooner you can start being a soldier."

He can tell by the look on my face that I don't care about being a soldier.

"I tell you what," he starts to say. "If you graduate, and I mean you make it through all the training and classes, and the brass are actually dumb enough to advance you, I'll let you punch me in the face again as hard as you can. I won't hit back. Call it an incentive."

"And what if I fail?" I ask.

"I call you Barkley and make you fetch me things."

"I don't understand what you mean."

"Don't they have dogs where you come from? You know: four legs, furry, tail," says Brock.

"We have wolves," I say.

"Wolves are like dogs, only bigger and meaner. You're a little dog, and me, I'm the Big Bad Wolf. Remember that."

"I have killed many wolves. I once scared a wolf off with nothing but a rock in my hand. He could tell that I did not fear him, that I would fight until my death. You would be smart to know the same."

For the first time Brock acts like he's unsure of me. He moves in his chair as if he's uncomfortable in it and looks away. After a moment he presses a button on his desk.

"Jones," he yells. "Use the red lift and come to floor D83. We're in room 'A'. I have an assignment for you."

A voice seems to come from nowhere, surrounding us.

"Yes, sir," is all the voice says.

Brock looks back at me.

"Jones is going to show you around the place. If you give him any trouble, you'll have to deal with me," says Brock.

"I'm not afraid of you," I say.

"If you're that dumb, you won't last fifteen minutes with Einstein. I hope that happens. I hope your tiny, pathetic interloper brain can't cope with it. I really could use a new mutt. Now sit down, shut your hole and wait for Jones."

I sit in a chair in front of Brock's desk, turning away from him enough so I don't have to look at his ugly face, but I can still watch him. I stare out the door, into the hallway, hoping it doesn't take Jones long to arrive.

Lost in my thoughts, I eventually hear the sound of the elevator. A thin man steps out of it and comes toward us. He's wearing dark green clothes like Brock, and walks with a limp. Something seems familiar about that.

He walks in and stops short of Brock's desk, standing up very straight. His eyes look forward at nothing at all.

"Sergeant Chris Jones, reporting for duty, sir," is all he says.

"Jones, I have a babysitting assignment for you. I want you to take this piece-of-waste interloper to get some clothes and find a cot. Once you've done that, show the interloper around. Mess hall, workout facilities, showers. Got it?" asks Brock.

"Got it, sir," says Jones.

He turns around and starts walking away, so I get up and follow. I'd rather be following a complete stranger than spend another moment with Brock.

We stand there, waiting for the elevator, but he doesn't say a thing. He looks very serious, more serious than I've ever seen anyone look. I wonder if he hates Brock as much as I do. He'd have more reason to, I would think, since Brock wanted to leave him for dead, and ordered his soldiers to do just that.

When the elevator arrives I get inside. It's smaller than the other elevators in the building. I close my eyes and try to think of anything other than this tiny box falling to the ground, crushing us.

The elevator starts moving and I feel heavier. I think that means we're going up. I hope that where we're going isn't underground.

"Where are we going?" I ask.

"U61," says Jones.

"Are you the... " I start to say, but he cuts me off.

"Not here."

I take Jones' advice and keep my mouth closed. I was hoping that I could distract myself by talking with him, but now I can't do that. So I go back to imagining myself in a clover field.

Eventually the elevator stops and we get out. I follow Jones down a long hallway and into a smaller hallway filled with a long line of people.

"We can talk now," says Jones, turning to me.

"Why couldn't we before?" I ask.

"Because Brock was watching us through his cameras."

"But not now?"

"No. He has access to the cameras in the areas he's in charge of, but only those. The man doesn't know and see everything that goes on. Honestly, it'd be impossible to. Way too many floors and way too many people. Software does keep track of most everything that happens, but only a handful of people have access to that information," says Jones.

"Did Carter save your life?" I ask.

His eyes look away from me, as if he's looking at something far off in the distance.

"Yeah, he did," he says quietly.

"What happened?"

"What do you know?"

"Not much. Just that you got shot by a sniper, and that he waited until it was safe to get you, then carried you to the place where you were both rescued," I say.

"What you didn't hear was that it was a suicide mission from the start. Brock ignored intel that said our target had moved, only my team didn't know that at the time. He was trying to make a name for himself by taking out the head of a Chinese terrorist cell operating here in Ireland."

"What's a terrorist cell?" I ask.

"What do you mean?"

"I don't come from here. I don't know what that is," I

say.

"A terrorist cell is a group of people who do horrible things. They attack innocent civilians, people that aren't soldiers, and they do it in a cowardly manner. Things like planting bombs in public places, making children kill, assassinating world leaders; all justified by whatever ideology they believe in."

"So Brock wanted to kill one of those people? A terrorist?" I ask.

"Yeah, and I can't fault him for that. The target was a militant who named himself Sun Tzu. Thought he was good at war, I guess, but he was just another piece-of-crap psychopath masquerading as a freedom fighter. He'd already killed hundreds by the time we were sent after him. But Brock was stupid, and sent us in knowing that Sun Tzu wasn't supposed to be there. Worse, it was a trap. The Chinese wanted to use us as target practice, so they fed us some bad intel. Brock acted on that intel, even though we got other reliable intel saying that Sun Tzu was in a different country. Anyway, the Chinese had been trying to take out our team for years. We were one of Ireland's best tactical units before that mission."

"So why was Brock angry when you came back?"

"If a soldier gets killed, it's easier to sweep it under the rug. If the soldier survives, they can live to tell about it. They'll go digging around until they figure out the truth. Brock didn't want anyone to know he'd made a bad command decision, so he wanted me to die to save face with his superiors," says Jones.

"Did you find out then and tell someone?" I ask.

"No. Never told anyone anything, but Carter did. He made sure that everyone knew. Brock says he hates Carter for disobeying orders, but that's not it at all. He hates him because Brock got demoted when Carter told the upper brass about what happened. That's why he only trains soldiers now, and doesn't run any field operations."

"Brock isn't just acting like a bad person to scare me; he really is a bad person?"

"Yeah," says Jones. "He really is."

"How do I avoid him?" I ask.

"You can't, and it never gets better, only worse. Especially if you're smart and capable. That's the mark of a bad leader; they get insecure and try to make you look bad. Put you down, bully you. All they care about is protecting their job and looking good for their bosses. So they keep the best and brightest from being heard. They steal the credit for a job well done. It's pathetic, and you'd be surprised at how often it happens."

"No I wouldn't. It was worse back where I come from. If you were good at something, or smart, you wouldn't get bullied; people would just kill you. I had to pretend to be dumb just so I wouldn't go to sleep and never wake up. I couldn't be too good at what I did or they'd stab me, or poison me, or beat me to death," I say.

"Wait, where do you come from?" asks Jones.

"The Crag."

"What's that?"

"It's a cave," I say.

"Ah. So you're Carter's ace-up-the-sleeve?" asks Jones.

"I don't know what that means," I admit.

"It means he's hoping you're the one who will lead us. That you will be the edge we need to beat the Chinese."

"Carter thinks so."

"You speak English. How do you know how to speak English?" asks Jones.

"That's what we speak in the Crag."

"Really?"

"Yes. I can read too."

"Well at least you aren't starting from scratch. That's something," says Jones.

"Brock told me I'm supposed to be hooked up to Einstein," I say.

"Yeah, that's the Rapid Learning Machine. Not everyone is able to learn that way, though. Me, I prefer a classroom over a machine any day."

"Is it dangerous?" I ask.

"No, it figures out your pace automatically by how quickly you retain the information. Something to do with brainwaves I think, but not sure how it works."

I look up and realize we're at the front of the line now. A very tough looking woman behind the desk stares at me. Her eyes are tired and her body says I mean nothing to her. Her brown hair is pulled back, making her face look angrier than she probably actually is.

"What size pants, shirt and shoes?" she asks.

"I... I don't know," I admit.

"Hold still," she says.

The woman raises what looks like a gun at me. Without thinking, I drop to the floor and roll away, hoping she doesn't shoot me.

"Sam, it's okay," says Jones. "It won't hurt you; it just takes your measurements."

Slowly, I get back to my feet then walk up to her. She aims it at my chest and pulls the trigger. A red line of light starts at my toes and makes its way up to the top of my head. Thankfully, I feel nothing.

"Turn right," she says. Her voice is dead, and I can tell that she hates what she's doing.

I turn to my right and she runs the red light up and down my body again. Once the light disappears she plays with some buttons on the gun. I turn back toward her to watch. A moment later she pushes some buttons on her desk that I hadn't noticed before.

"Name?" she asks.

"Sam," I say.

"Sam what?" she asks.

"Sam. My name is Sam."

"What is your last name?"

"I don't have one," I admit.

"Make something up then. Computer says you have to have a last name or we can't give you your uniform."

What should I use? My mind, which normally is too full of thoughts, isn't working at all. Should I use a word that I like? Someone's name? A place? Sam Crag. Sam Flot. Sam Jet. Sam Ebb. Sam Loudwaters?

"How do people normally pick a last name?" I ask Jones.

"Normally you're born with it. You get it from your parents."

"I don't have any parents."

"Well, sometimes people are named after the job they do. Like Smith, or Baker," says Jones.

I think hard for a moment. Finally, just as the woman starts to get angry, I look up at her.

"Sam Hunter," I say.

The woman pushes some buttons on her desk. "Sam Hunter," she mumbles. "Okay, stand in line 'B' to pick up your clothes." I look to where she's pointing, which is another long line of people. Jones and I walk over to it and wait.

"How did you come up with 'Hunter'?" asks Jones.

"It's what I was in the Crag. I hunted anything that could feed us. Wolves, deer, sometimes cows or sheep," I say.

"What did you hunt with?" he asks.

"A sling, mostly, but I was starting to use something I invented called a bow and arrow."

Jones laughs.

"What?" I ask.

"The bow and arrow has been around for thousands and thousands of years, and you're saying you invented it?"

"Yeah, well, we didn't have it where I come from," I say, annoyed at Jones.

I decide I'm done talking to Jones for a while. He's a good guy, but that doesn't mean he's not annoying.

Line 'B' doesn't take as long to get through as Line 'A'. I watch as the people in front of me say their name then someone hands them a very large bag. When I get to the front I do the same. The bag they hand me is very heavy, but I'm strong and carry it with only my right hand. It would probably hurt too much with my broken arm to use both. Others have to use both, while some have to drag them on the floor behind them. It makes me feel better, because even though I don't know anyone here, and I have much more to learn than everyone else, I am stronger, and probably faster and deadlier than those around me. That will keep me alive.

"We better find you a room now," says Jones.

26

We take the elevator again, this time to floor D14. I start to realize just how often I'll be taking the elevator back and forth every day. I'm tired of being afraid of small spaces, and I won't be able to get away from them, so I make a decision. Instead of letting it bother me, I'm going to pretend that it doesn't. I'm going to act like everything's normal, and that it doesn't bother me. Maybe if I do it enough, I won't be afraid anymore.

So I keep my eyes open and look around. I stare at Jones. Like Carter, he doesn't seem that much older than me. His light brown hair is cut very short, almost to the point where he's bald. His clothes are very clean, and I notice that he has many colored pieces of metal attached to his shirt.

"What are those?" I ask.

"Oh, those are medals. We get them for different things, like battles we were in and heroic things that we've done," says Jones.

"Why?"

"It lets other people know that we've fought hard and fought bravely."

"We don't have that where I come from because we do not war; we only hunt. The meat we bring back at the end of the day is our reward," I say.

"Almost sounds better than here," says Jones.

"In many ways it is. We have no lawyers," I say.

Jones laughs at my words.

"You have a wife and new one?" I ask.

"New one? You mean child?" asks Jones.

"Yes."

"I do. My wife's name is Margaret, and our son's name is Zachary. He's three now."

"What is 'three'?" I ask.

"It's this many," he says holding up most of the fingers on his right hand.

"I had heard that word before, and guessed it was a number, but wasn't sure. Are they going to teach me numbers? I'm very interested in learning about them."

"Yes, I'm sure they will," says Jones. "Probably first thing you learn, since so much of the world is based on numbers. You can't even make a phone call without them."

"Yes I can, and I have before."

"Really? How?"

"I looked at the numbers that were written down and pressed the buttons that matched the numbers," I say.

"That would make sense," says Jones.

Finally we arrive at D14. Focusing on our conversation seemed to help. It was not as horrible being on the elevator. I follow Jones to a desk only a few steps from the elevator. Behind the desk sits a man who looks like he's been a gray one for a very long time. When he grins I can see that some of his teeth are missing. His skin reminds me of Helm's, a very deep shade of brown, and his hair is almost completely white.

"Hey Charles," says Jones.

"Jonesy, they got you babysitting someone?" says Charles.

"Not just someone. Sam here is gonna save the world," says Jones.

"No kiddin'. Well nice to meet you Sam," says Charles, staring at me. "Can I get your last name and rank?"

"My last name is Hunter, but I don't know what you mean by rank," I say. "I've heard that word, but I don't know what it means."

175

"You must be a private if you're just starting out. Your rank is what level you're at in your training and capabilities," says Charles.

"We had something like that back where I come from. What is the highest rank they have here?" I ask.

"General" says Charles.

"Then I was a general where I come from."

"I wouldn't mention that to people," says Jones. "Better they don't know much about where you came from. That, and you'll get stuck with a nickname like General Sam."

"That doesn't sound too bad," I say.

"I like it," says Charles.

"Stay out of it, wise guy," says Jones, smiling.

"Whatever you say, Jonesy. Private Sam, go and find an empty bunk and report back to me with the number on it. You can leave your stuff there. Nobody will mess with it," says Charles.

"Okay."

I walk past the desk and into a very long room. No one is inside, which surprises me, and it's very quiet. The many beds in this room look like the ones in prison, only these are much cleaner. I have to walk to the very back of the room before I'm able to find a bed that doesn't seem like it's being used. I set my bag down on the bed and it squeaks from the weight.

I see a door next to the end of my bed. I look inside and it's dark. It takes me a moment to find the button, but once I turn on the lights I can see what looks like a very large bathroom. I see toilets, sinks and showers. What I don't see are walls. It's very strange, because I thought everyone was worried about being seen naked. I wonder why it's different here.

As I turn off the light then leave, I notice that in front of my bed is a large box. Above that on a piece of wood are some symbols that must be numbers. Staring at them doesn't help, so I try to make them into a picture in my head. Once I'm sure I've got it, I walk back to Charles and Jones.

I can hear them laughing as I approach then get quieter when I finally reach them.

"So what number did you end up with?" asks Charles.

"I don't know how to say it, but I might be able to draw it," I say.

"Uh, okay. Here's some paper and a pencil."

I take both and write down what I think I saw.

"Ninety-nine," says Charles, looking at the paper. "So, you don't know numbers?"

"Not yet, but I'll learn," I say.

"Yeah, well good luck with Einstein. That will do a number on ya," says Charles.

"What do you mean?" I ask.

"Sometimes you hear whispers of people dying while using it. I don't actually know anyone that's happened to. In fact, the people who say it happened don't know anyone either. Not personally. But you hear rumors just the same," says Charles.

"Way to freak out the newbie," says Jones.

"Hey, better to know going into it," says Charles.

"Nobody's ever even been hurt by it."

"If you say so, Jonesy."

"Don't listen to him," says Jones, looking at me. "The machine has fail safes, and it'll only push you as hard as you can take."

"I just wish I knew what it did. I worry more about things I don't know about," I admit.

"We're all that way," says Charles.

"Don't worry, Sam. We'll get you hooked up with it soon enough. We should head to the mess next," says Jones. He turns back to Charles and shakes his hand. "Thanks."

"Ain't no thing."

Jones and I walk back to the elevator. This time we're heading above ground; floor U4. That makes me realize something.

"Jones, can you write down the floors for me, so that I know where to go?" I ask.

"Don't worry about it. You're not the first newbie I've had to babysit. I'll be helping you out until you understand the floor numbers, and then you'll be able to remember them on your own."

"But what if I get hungry and you're not around?" I ask.

"Then you're out of luck," says Jones, smiling.

"I miss the food back in the Crag."

"The food isn't bad here, but it isn't great. It's not hotel food, that's for sure. You'll probably be so hungry at the end of the day that you'll be happy just to have something. But avoid the tuna noodle casserole, okay?"

"What's that?" I ask.

"You'll find out soon," says Jones. "When was the last time you ate?"

"I ate some white things that reminded me of maggots, and some cow meat back in my cell, but it wasn't much."

"You're probably hungry then. Don't worry, I'll make sure you get some real food in you," says Jones. "So how did you do in the prison trial?"

"He said I was the fastest ever."

"So you actually got to him. Did he look angry?"

"Not at first. After I tried to shoot him he looked angry," I say.

Jones laughs.

"Did you go through the prison trial?" I ask.

"Yeah, everyone does. I made it out of my cell, and I wanted to climb in the vents, but I'm afraid of small spaces."

"Me too," I admit.

"How did you overcome it?" asks Jones.

"I thought it was either go through the vents or die there. I didn't know the guns were fake, or that the prison was fake. I thought they would kill me if I didn't escape. So I ignored my fear the best that I could."

"Maybe that's why so few people ever make it to the end. They don't think it's real."

"Maybe," I say.

27

We finally arrive at floor U4. I follow Jones out of the elevator. It's funny, even though we talked about being afraid of small spaces, taking the elevator bothered me even less than last time.

"They call this place Euphoria," says Jones.

"Why?" I ask.

"Because it's 'U4'. Euphoria. They sound the same."

"Oh. What does euphoria mean?"

"It means you're so happy that you're dizzy."

"I've never been that happy," I say.

"I have, when I got married, and when my son was born," says Jones. "But it doesn't happen often. The other reason we call it Euphoria is to be ironic, because the food really isn't that great."

"What does ironic mean?"

"It means that something unexpected happens or something like that, but most people mean it to be where something is one way, but they refer to it in another way," says Jones.

"Like sarcasm?" I ask.

"Yeah, kinda like sarcasm."

We walk over to another line. Maybe that's all this place really is, lines and elevators. The line isn't as long as the other lines we've been in at least, and seems to be moving faster.

Ahead of me people are picking up trays, and I realize this place is more like home than like a pub. Except for the elevators, the more things I learn about, the more it seems like the Crag.

I watch as people talk to the cooks, hand the cooks their tray then the cooks put food on the trays and hand them back. That's when I realize I don't have any money to pay for the food.

"Jones, I have no money," I say.

"That's okay, it's free," he says.

"Free? I don't have to pay?"

"Nope. It's part of being a soldier. Don't have to pay for your food."

It's another way this place is like the Crag. We all do our jobs, and we get food for it. Everyone eats.

When I reach the cooks, I don't know what most of the food is called, so I just point to what I want. I get what looks like smashed potatoes, and some white meat I haven't seen before. Without asking they pour sauce on both. It's a very light brown color, and I can kind of see through it. I also get a square stack of something that has tomato sauce and cheese on it. The layers between are flat and yellow, and remind me of bread dough. There are also chunks of meat in it.

"Lasagna, good choice," says Jones.

At the end of the line I see that people are filling cups with liquids from a machine. One person gets something clear with bubbles, another gets something that looks like root beer. I think I will have more root beer.

I set my tray down next to the machine, grab a cup then read the words on each spout. None of the words make sense to me, so I go by the pictures on them. One looks kind of like it's a glass of root beer, so I put that under the spout. I had seen the people ahead of me push on the squares, so I do the same. It makes me happy to see root beer pour into my cup.

"I like root beer," I say to Jones.

"Uh, yeah, that's great, Sam. C'mon, let's find a place to sit."

I follow Jones over to a nearby table and sit down on a bench across from him. The benches also remind me of the Crag, only these are nicer. Ours are wooden and rough. These are smooth. They look like they've never had food on them before, while ours have many colors where spills have happened.

"I'm glad to be sitting down," says Jones.

"How come?" I ask.

"Because of my leg. The prosthetic helps a lot, but I still get sore when I walk around," says Jones.

I eat for a while, but I can tell Jones is getting bored watching me. The lasagna is very good, and the white meat and sauce are good too, but in a different way.

"That's turkey," he says, pointing to the white meat.

"I don't know what that is," I say.

"It's just a big dumb bird that tastes good," says Jones.

"Oh."

"So what happened to your arm?" asks Jones.

"I was attacked."

"By what?"

"It was a 'who', not a what," I say.

"Then who?" asks Jones.

"A prison guard."

"Wait, you were in prison? Why?"

"Because I shot Carter," I say.

"Wait, you did WHAT?" asks Jones.

"I shot Carter."

"Why? I thought he was your big supporter or whatever."

"I needed to know if he was trustworthy. He gave me his gun and I had to make sure he wasn't giving me a broken weapon that couldn't actually hurt him. I also had to make sure that if I went with him, he wouldn't hurt my people. Only way I could think to make sure of that was to shoot him and see what he did," I say.

"Wow, that's cold. Maybe you are tougher than you look," says Jones. "Is he okay?"

"Yes, he survived, but his arm is in a sling because I shot him in the shoulder."

"Make sure that I'm nowhere near you when you're doing weapons training."

I just smile.

"So this prison guard, he attacked you. Why?" he asks.

"He was drunk. He tried to rape me."

The look on his face changes from one of humor to one of seriousness.

"I'm sorry that happened to you."

"I survived. Beat him up pretty good once I got his weapon away from him, even after he broke my arm," I say.

"What happened to the guard?"

"Nothing."

"What do you mean 'nothing'?" asks Jones.

"I mean nothing. We went to a courtroom and I was found not guilty for fighting with him and escaping my cell. But they found him not guilty too," I say.

"How could they? Wasn't there evidence?"

"They recorded our voices and it matched my story."

"So why did he go free?" asks Jones.

"Because I'm an interloper."

"No way. That's total crap. They should have fried him."

"At least I'm alive," I say.

"That's not enough. He has to pay for what he did to you," says Jones.

"I can't do anything about it. I'm in here and he's out there."

"Well, I hope you get payback someday."

I nod my head in thanks.

"You know, the docs here might be able to fix your arm up so that you don't have to wear the cast anymore," says Jones. "They have some pretty advanced medicine here, stuff that regular hospitals don't have. That's the way it works; the military gets the good stuff first because they can't get in trouble for experimenting on soldiers."

"I would be willing to try, if you think they can help," I say.

"I'll take you to see Doctor Capaldi tomorrow, once you're done with Einstein."

"Will it hurt?"

"I don't know. We won't know until we ask the Doc," says Jones. "If it does though, they can probably knock you out or something. You won't feel a thing."

"Okay, I will go see the Doctor then."

It doesn't take me long to finish my food. I leave the table and walk over to the large windows, while Jones waits for me at the table.

The sun is starting to set. I stare out into the ocean. It's so large, like the night's sky. I walk along the edges of the building, and I find that I can walk around the entire floor while still looking out windows. It makes the world seem even bigger, that Candlestick could be surrounded by endless water on three-sides.

I see birds in the distance, and I wonder what's inside the ocean. Surely nothing could breathe underwater, so nothing could be living in it. It seems like it would be a waste though if the ocean was only water. The question bothers me enough I walk back to Jones.

"What's in the ocean?" I ask.

"Sand, water, fish and other creatures, wrecked ships. Stuff like that," says Jones.

"Things can live in the ocean? How do they breathe?"

"Some have gills. They pull oxygen out of the water and use that to breathe."

"What's oxygen?" I ask.

"It's part of air; the stuff we breathe. But really it's only a small part of it. Don't worry, you'll learn all about it once we get you hooked up to Einstein."

"I'm worried about that," I admit. "Sometimes it feels

like I don't think like most people. I'm worried that the machine won't work on me. If it doesn't, how long does it normally take to learn all the things I need to know?"

"You mean like a normal person? In classes, and just life stuff in general?" asks Jones.

"Yes."

"Sit down and put your hands out on the table."

I do as he asks.

"Okay, now spread your fingers out," says Jones, which I do.

I watch as Jones puts out his left hand and all its fingers, but with his right hand he only uses two fingers.

"You see all these thumbs and fingers?" asks Jones.

"Yes."

"That's how many years it would take for you to learn all that stuff."

Now I'm worried. That seems like a very, very long time.

"I wouldn't be done until I'm a gray one," I say.

"And the war's happening sooner rather than later. I think if it doesn't work out between you and Einstein, they'll probably send you home. There would be no use in keeping you, because you wouldn't be able to get ready in time. But if Carter has faith in you then maybe you can," says Jones.

We sit in silence for a moment.

"Can I do swimming?" I ask.

"You mean 'can you go swimming'? Sure, why not."

"In the ocean?"

"I wouldn't recommend it. It's dangerous around here, because there really isn't a beach; just rocks. If the waves catch you, and they will, they'll either pull you so far out to sea that you won't be able to swim back, or they'll smash you against the side of the cliff. We have several Olympic size swimming pools that you can use instead," says Jones.

"Swimming pools? What are those?"

"Do you know what a puddle is?"

"Yes."

"It's like those, only big enough that people can swim in them. Each pool takes up most of a floor, so they're big as pools go, but nowhere near as big as the ocean."

"Do you use them for anything other than swimming?" I ask.

"Not really. Sometimes they train underwater, for missions that might require that sort of thing. But mostly people just swim," says Jones. "Anyway, I should show you the workout facilities."

28

As we head back to the elevators I don't worry as much. Instead I talk with Jones, keeping my mind on things other than the tiny moving box that I'm trapped in, which could fall so far, so fast, that I'd be crushed like a tomato under a foot.

"U27" he says.

"What is that?" I ask.

"The floor number for the workout facilities."

"I probably won't remember that, since I don't know what it means." I admit.

"It's okay. The great thing about the brain is if you hear something or do something enough times, you'll eventually remember. Even very difficult things."

"I hope so."

Thankfully, the elevator ride doesn't take long. When we get there we find a few people already using parts of the room. Some of the things I see are amazing, others are strange. I watch as a woman jumps up and down on a round piece of fabric, and she twists and turns in the air between bounces. She flies much higher than a person could on normal ground. I also look over at a number of people running, but they aren't running anywhere. They are staying in exactly the same place. Why would people do that?

Looking around more, I notice a few others lifting very heavy objects, but they aren't doing anything with them. Just moving them up and down, over and over. I can't understand what the purpose is. If they were lifting rocks they could build a wall in almost no time.

"What is this place?" I ask.

"It's where you come to work out," says Jones.

"What does 'work out' mean?" I ask.

"That's where you make your body stronger. Like your mind, the more you do with your body, the better it works. You'll build muscle and endurance. You'll need to come here every day, because the stronger you are, the better soldier you will be. At least that's what they tell you."

"Why aren't people actually doing things then? Like running somewhere, or lifting things to build something? Why are they just... pretending?" I ask.

"Because nothing else really needs to be built. It's also easier to run inside than outside, because the weather can get bad. That, and the treadmills take up less room than a track would. Does that make sense?" asks Jones.

"No, not really."

"Well, try it anyway. You'll be strong in no time."

"I already am strong," I say.

"You could be even stronger," says Jones.

"If I'm too strong, it will make me slower."

"Not by much. Just make sure that you swim or run every day. That's what will get your heart going, which will help you be a faster runner."

"Running fast isn't as important as being fast," I say.

"What do you mean?" asks Jones.

"If someone attacks you with a knife, you need to move out of the way fast. React fast. If my muscles are too big, they could get in the way and slow me down."

"They used to think that, but it's not really true. And you would have to work very hard, and probably use illegal enhancers to get strong enough to be muscle bound," says Jones.

"What does that mean?" I ask.

"Never mind. Just exercise regularly and you'll be fine."

I really don't like the idea of pretending to do work, but I will do it. If I don't then I will grow weak like those that never leave the Crag. I wish instead they'd let me go outside to hunt. I could bring back my own food and have them cook it for me.

"Do you want me to show you some things?" asks Jones.

"Like what?" I ask.

"Like how to bench press. I'm guessing they didn't have that back where you came from."

"No, they did not. Yes, you can teach me."

I follow Jones over to what looks like a very short table. There are two pieces of metal that stick up from it, and they hold a long rod with large discs attached at the ends.

"Looks like it's set for 150 lbs. I should be able to lift it," says Jones.

He lies down on the table, slides his head under the rod and raises his arms. Grabbing the rod, he lifts it up into the air, nearly sets it on his chest then lifts it again. He does this a few times then sets the rod back into place.

"Make sense?" asks Jones.

"Yes."

"I should probably show you how to use the treadmill now."

"Okay."

I follow Jones over to a machine that seems very simple. He stands on the long flat part of it then pushes a few buttons on the top. The part he's standing on starts to move. He walks at first, and as the machine picks up speed he starts running. I'm surprised at how well his machine leg works.

"Push the red button to turn it on then twist this knob here to make it go faster or slower. Real simple. There are other things it can do, but that's all you need to know to use it," says Jones.

"Okay. How do I make it stop?" I ask.

"Just hit the red button again and it'll stop, but I suggest turning the knob back down so it's easier. Slow down instead of just stopping. Make sense?"

"It does."

"Why don't you try," suggests Jones.

He stops the machine then steps off it. I climb onto it and push the red button to start it. When I turn the knob I accidentally turn it too quickly. I have to run as fast as I can to keep up. It takes me a moment to turn the knob back down, so that I'm not running too hard. I keep running for a little while until I'm tired then hit the red button again. It isn't too hard for me to stop, thankfully.

"Not bad for your first time. You run pretty fast too. I figured you would since you seem so light. You're built kind of like a marathoner," says Jones.

"What's a marathoner?" I ask.

"Someone that runs very long distances for fun."

"Why would someone want to do that?" I ask.

"To be in shape. It's kind of an accomplishment, because it's not easy to run a marathon."

"What's an accomplishment?"

"It's when someone does something very difficult, that many people can't do," explains Jones.

"Most people must be lazy in your world if running a great distance is an accomplishment. For me an accomplishment is killing a dragon," I say.

"What do you mean 'killing a dragon'? You know those don't exist, right?" says Jones.

"You call them ships. Carter and Quinn fly one," I explain.

"You thought our ships were dragons? That explains a lot. Wait, did you take down one of our ships?" asks Jones.

"It wasn't one of yours, but yes."

"How the hell did you do that?" asks Jones.

"I hit it with a sky spear."

"A spear? You took down an air ship with a spear? No wonder Carter thinks you have potential. That's kind of like destroying the building we're in with a ping-pong ball."

"What's a..." I start to ask, before Jones talks over me.

"Never mind. Let's just say you couldn't damage this building with a million of them."

"Oh, I know what a million is!" I say, excitedly. "It's a very large number."

"Yeah, it is. Do you know the number five?" asks Jones.

I think hard for a moment.

"I've heard it before, but no," I admit.

"It's this many," he says, holding up all the fingers on one hand.

"I understand."

"Wow, knows what a million is but doesn't know 'five'. That's okay, you'll start learning everything you need to know first thing tomorrow," says Jones.

"Einstein?" I say.

"Yeah, Einstein. You ready to go?" asks Jones.

"Yes."

"It's getting late. I'll take you back to the barracks then."

Jones and I walk back to the elevator. This time I barely think about dying inside of it. I may be getting better. I hope I'm getting better. I don't want my fear to rule me.

29

Jones pushes the button for D14 and I feel a little lighter.

"You're going to have a big day tomorrow. They'll start you out with Einstein then do some light field training. Make sure to get some sleep, because you'll need it," says Jones.

"I will sleep well because I'm very tired. I'm also no longer afraid of this place," I say.

"I think being afraid is normal," says Jones.

"Are there wolves that live inside the building, roaming at night, looking for people to eat?" I ask.

"No."

"Will someone come and murder me in my sleep?"

"If anyone comes near you while you sleep, the security systems will go off and knock out the intruder. So no, no one can hurt you," says Jones.

"Then I will sleep very well. For the first time in my life I won't worry while I sleep. Maybe I won't have nightmares. It seems like I only ever have nightmares."

"That's rough. I hope your nightmares stop," says Jones.

We reach the barracks level and leave the elevator. Charles is still sitting at his desk, talking to some of the other soldiers. It sounds like many people are here now, because I can hear voices coming from inside the sleeping room. I turn back to see Jones leaving.

"What do I do now?" I ask him.

"Whatever you want. You should probably take a shower because you're starting to smell. Get some sleep, okay? I'll be back in the morning to get you," says Jones.

"Okay," I say weakly.

I turn around, give Charles a smile then walk back to my bed. I pass by many people. It feels like there are as many soldiers here as there are hunters back in the Crag. Some people talk with each other, some read. Some look like they're using small TVs.

When I get to my bed I find that my bag is exactly where I left it. No one went through my things. If I'd had a bag like this back at home, it would already be gone. Someone would have taken it.

I pull a bar of soap and towel out of the bag. Without thinking, I take off my clothes. My shirt is fairly loose, so I don't have much trouble getting the sleeve around the cast. No one says a word about me being naked. No one seems to care. I drop my clothes on the floor next to my bed and start to walk toward the showers.

"Hey, newb, you gotta throw your dirties in the bin, just inside the door. You'll get clean ones in the morning," says a voice, coming from the bed across from me.

I look over and see a young woman sitting on the bed. Her skin isn't as dark as Charles skin, or as light as my own. It's a beautiful color somewhere in-between. She wears a shirt with no sleeves, and I can see her shoulders. Her curly hair stretches down to them. I like it very much.

"What's a newb?" I ask.

"You know, a newbie. A new person. Someone who doesn't know anything, like how things work. That's you," she says.

"Oh. Is that a bad thing?" I ask.

"It is if you stay that way. Just try not to do anything too dumb your first night here," she says.

"I will try," I say.

"I'm Harriet. Harriet King. What's your name?"

"I'm Sam."

"Just Sam?" asks Harriet.

"Oh, I have a last name now. It's Hunter," I say proudly.

"You have a last name now? Did you not have one before?"

"No."

"How do you go through life without a last name?" asks Harriet.

"I come from a cave," I say.

Her face goes blank. I can tell she's confused by my answer. It makes me feel a bit uncomfortable, so I pick up my dirty clothes, towel, soap, and make my way to the showers.

After throwing my dirty clothes into what I guess is the bin, I walk over to the nearest shower. It takes me a moment to figure out how to make the shower water hot, but not too hot.

When I wash, I try my best not to let my cast get too wet. The last time I did, it made my arm itch for a while. I hope Jones is right and they can fix my arm. If they want me to train how to fight then I will need my arm working.

Once I finish washing I dry off. I was lucky, because I only got a little water inside my cast this time. Hopefully my arm won't itch. I make my way back to my bed and open up my bag.

"There should be pajamas in there too," says Harriet.

"What are pajamas?" I ask.

"Are you for real?" asks Harriet.

"I am real," I say, confused.

"Okay, pajamas are what you wear when you sleep."

"I don't wear anything when I sleep," I say.

"Well, you should around here. Don't want anyone trying anything. Plus, sometimes they come in here in the middle of the night and have us do drills. You'll thank me later for telling you to wear something," says Harriet.

Digging into the bag, I pull out some gray clothes.

"Are these what you're talking about?"

"Yeah, those are them. Sweatpants and a t-shirt; just like everyone else."

"How come your shirt doesn't have short sleeves like mine?" I ask.

"Oh, I brought this with me. Charles doesn't seem to care that I'm out-of-uniform or whatever. He's a good guy."

"He seems to be."

"No 'seems' about it. I really wish he could be my CO. I'd die for Charles," says Harriet.

I look her in the eye and I can tell that she means what she says. I know the feeling. If I could die to bring back Jet, I would. I'd die to save Flot. I'd also die to save Ebb.

I put on the pants and fight the t-shirt a little. The sleeves are short but not very wide. When I finish getting dressed I move the bag off my bed, setting it aside. I pull back the covers, climb in, and before I even realize it, I'm asleep.

30

Nightmares. I dream of finding Jet's lifeless body, of being trapped in that tiny, dark cell that Brock put me in. I dream of being attacked by Grintz, and of falling to my death while trapped inside an elevator. All of my worst fears fill my sleeping head.

I wake up many times in the middle of the night. Sometimes my arms hurt from trying to fight off imaginary enemies. Sometimes my mouth hurts from clenching my jaw in fear. I try my best to calm down, but every time I shut my eyes I see something that scares me.

Half way through the night I roll over and see the person in the bed next to me. He's young, a little older than me. His face is hairless and smooth. He snores, but not loudly. I sit up and look over at Harriet. She's kicked the sheets off her bed, and I can tell that she must have a hard time sleeping too. Her body is twisted up and her arms are pinned beneath her. It looks uncomfortable.

I get up and walk into the bathroom. Turning on one of the faucets, I scoop water from my hand to my mouth, hoping to sooth my sore teeth. I also rub it on my face, but it doesn't help much. Using my shirt like a towel, I dry off.

"Can't sleep either?"

I turn around quickly to see who it is. It's a man I hadn't seen before. I look him up and down, wondering if he's a threat or not. I keep my feet spread apart, my arms at my sides, and my knees bent just in case.

"Are you okay?" he asks.

"Yes," I say.

"First night is rough on everyone," says the man. "Don't worry, once you start your physical training you'll sleep like the dead. They push you to the point of exhaustion, then push you even further. I'm Desmond."

"Sam."

"Is that short for something?" he asks.

"No, it's just Sam," I reply.

"Well Sam, it's good to meet you."

I nod my head at him. I can't see him very clearly, as only the dim light from the sleeping room is coming into the bathroom. I didn't turn on the lights because I didn't want to wake anyone, but now I wish I had. I can't see his face at all; just a shadow standing in the doorway. He turns and leaves. I have met someone and I don't know what they look like. He acted like a friend, but something seemed... wrong.

After a moment I head back to my bed. Before I leave the doorway I stop, just in case someone is waiting for me to come out. Thankfully, no one is. I look around to see if I can spot Desmond, but I can't see people's faces well enough to tell. Giving up, I climb back under the blankets and cover my head.

Sleep finally takes me, and this time my dreams are of fields of clover and hunting. It has been a long time since I had any normal dreams and I welcome them.

* * *

"Attention!"

The yelling startles me awake. I uncover my face and look out at the other sleepers. They jump out of their beds, hurrying to stand in front of them. I decide I should do that as well. Even though I don't know why someone yelled 'attention', and why it means that everyone should stand, I fear if I don't follow along I may get in trouble. The last time I didn't do what I was told I was put inside a tiny cell. I won't let that happen again.

I look across at Harriet and make sure that I'm standing like her. She has her chest out, her shoulders pulled back and her feet together. She looks straight ahead, like she's looking through me, not at me, so I do the same.

The voice that yelled attention yells again.

"Alright, you have twenty minutes to get ready for breakfast. Move it!"

Harriet hurries and takes off her clothes, grabs her soap and a towel, so I do the same. Dumping our 'dirties' in the bin, we are the first two to make it into the showers. Many, many other people come inside the very large bathroom, but there aren't enough showers for everyone. People stand near the entrance, naked and waiting. It is interesting, because everyone has a body like a hunter. Strong, with muscles and almost no fat.

Harriet scrubs her body quickly, and I do the best I can to keep my cast dry while I scrub fast too. Once she's rinsed, she pulls her towel around her then walks back to her bed. I follow and stand near my own, doing what I can to get dry.

I watch as she pulls something out of a box at the front of her bed. It's small; just a handle. She also pulls out a round thing about the size of a knife.

"What's that?" I ask.

"Toothbrush and toothpaste, newb. Grab yours."

I look through my bag, find them then follow her back into the bathroom.

This time she goes to a sink. I do the same. I watch as she twists the top of the round thing off then squeezes some blue goo inside it onto the top of the handle. She puts the tip of the handle inside her mouth and moves it all around. I just stand there watching, wondering why she's doing it. She realizes I'm staring, so she spits out a mouth full of what looks like ice cream into the sink.

"What?" she asks.

"Why are you doing that?" I ask.

"It keeps your teeth from falling out. Try it," she says.

I finally work up the courage to put the handle in my mouth. I rub it around and the goo starts to turn to foam. It tastes good. Once I'm sure I've rubbed it all over my teeth, I swallow.

"Oh, crap, did you just swallow that stuff?" asks Harriet.

"Yeah, why?" I ask.

"You aren't supposed to. You're gonna have a heck of a stomach ache. Don't do that again, okay?"

"Okay."

I turn on the sink and suck water to get rid of the rest of the foam from my mouth. I look back at Harriet and she's already making her way back to her bed, so again I follow her. She puts on some clothes, and thankfully I find some clean ones in my own bag.

"Harriet?" I say.

"Yeah, what's up?"

"Which one is Desmond?" I ask.

"Desmond? I don't know anyone named Desmond, but I don't know everyone here. Ask Charles. He knows everyone."

"Okay. Is there anything else I'm supposed to do?"

"No. You should be good to go to breakfast. Better hurry and get some while it's still hot," says Harriet.

I make my way to the front of the room. Charles is already there, looking through some papers.

"Charles?"

"Ah, General Sam, how are you this fine mornin'?"

"I'm well. Do you know who Desmond is?" I ask.

"You sure get to the point. Nope, I don't know any Desmond. What does he look like?" asks Charles.

"I don't know."

"Then why are you askin' about him?"

"I met him last night, but it was dark and I couldn't see him. I was wondering who he was."

"Let me see if there are any Desmonds in the system," says Charles.

I watch as he touches his desk and it lights up. It reminds me of the box that Collin used for reading papers. The brightness from the desk lets me see more of Charles' face. He has a long scar on his left cheek that I hadn't noticed before. He also has lines at the corners of his mouth and eyes, and I can tell he's spent most of his life smiling. I hope someday that I have lines like that.

His fingers move across the desk, touching this and touching that. Finally, he looks up at me.

"You sure his name was Desmond? It couldn't have been something that sounded like Desmond, but wasn't?" he asks.

"No, I'm sure it was Desmond."

"Well, the odd thing of it is, there are no Desmonds in here. Of the thousands of people here at Candlestick, not one of them has Desmond as a first, middle or last name. Even that's odd, because Desmond's a pretty common name in Ireland."

So the person is a mystery. Could someone sneak into Candlestick without the guards knowing? Maybe the person was just lying about their name. But if they were, why'd they do it?

"Maybe it was a dream," I say, not believing it.

"Maybe it was," says Charles.

"Only, I'd never heard that name before. So it couldn't have been a dream."

"Well, I sure don't know what to tell you. Strange things happen around here sometimes. Secret things. Just be careful, Sam."

"I will."

"Ready for breakfast?" asks a voice to my left. I turn and look, and Jones is standing there with a grin on his face.

"Yes. I'm ready."

We walk to the elevator. This time I don't panic. I don't even think much about the fact that I'm getting into an elevator. It's not until we're halfway to the mess hall that I even notice we're inside it.

200

"You're doing better with the elevator thing," says Jones.

"What do you mean?" I ask, pretending not to know what he's talking about.

"When I first met you, you were terrified of them. Seems like they don't bother you so much now."

"I decided to not let them scare me," I say. "How could you tell?"

"I've never seen anyone tense up like you do. I could use you as a straight edge, you're so stiff."

"What's a straight edge?" I ask.

"Don't worry about it. You don't need to know for what we do here," says Jones.

"I still hate not knowing things."

Jones takes in a deep breath.

"A straight edge is used to draw lines. Carpenters use them to build things. They're generally very rigid, just like you are when you're afraid."

"I'm not always like that. I faced a wolf once, by myself, with a rock. I wasn't rigid," I say.

"Yeah, well, you must not have been afraid of the wolf then."

"I wasn't. My brother had just died. I welcomed death."

Jones face looks very serious.

"I'm sorry about your brother," says Jones.

I don't want to talk about it anymore, so I don't answer him. We leave the elevator and stand in line for food. There are many things here, but I choose what I recognize, which are eggs.

"You should try the waffles. Have them put some maple syrup on them for you," says Jones.

I look up at a very unhappy old woman serving food.

"Can I also have waffles? With marble syrup?" I ask. Jones laughs.

"Sam here means maple syrup."

My face turns red in embarrassment. I don't like

making mistakes and having people laugh at me. The woman puts a couple of light brown discs on my plate and pours a brown liquid over them. Jones gets the same, and we find a table to sit down at.

"I don't like people laughing at me," I tell Jones.

"No one does, Sam."

"If you do that to someone from the Crag, they might kill you for it."

"Then it's a good thing we aren't in the Crag," says Jones. "So, you think you're ready to start learning?"

"I'm not sure. I just hope they don't get rid of me," I say.

"Don't worry; they won't. And you'll do fine. You seem fairly smart for not knowing anything. How are the waffles?"

I take a few bites. The syrup is sweet and the waffles are very good. They taste a bit like the shampoo I put in my mouth though. Thankfully, I get past the memory and still enjoy them.

"They taste like shampoo," I say.

"They taste like shampoo? You drank shampoo?"

"I didn't know what it was."

"I bet your tongue was silky smooth and full of body after that," says Jones.

"What does that mean?" I ask, staring hard at him.

He just smiles. Jones is being annoying again, so I stop talking and finish my breakfast. I look up, and Jones is staring at something on his wrist that I hadn't noticed before.

"What's that?" I ask.

"It's a watch," he says.

"A watch what?" I ask.

"Just a watch. You tell time with it. Don't worry, you'll learn how to use one soon enough. There should be one in your bag."

"I haven't looked through the bag yet."

"So you haven't found the severed head?" he asks.

"What head?" I say, worried.

"It's just a joke. Don't worry, there isn't really a head in there."

"It's easy to make fun of someone who doesn't understand. Someday I will know more than you," I say.

"Well, until that day, I'm going to keep making fun of you," says Jones.

"Then I will work hard on learning, so that day comes sooner."

"I hope you do. We should get going."

We walk back to the elevator. He pushes the very bottom button, D117, as we get in.

"We're headed to the most isolated place in the whole building. They do that on purpose so there are no distractions. No noises. The rooms are pretty much sound proof. No echo even. It's a little strange when you talk, because your voice just dies," says Jones.

"Is there anything else I should know about?" I ask.

"Yeah, when you're in there, relax. If you're nervous, it will take longer to learn. Just let the information flow into you."

"Okay."

It takes a while, but we finally reach the bottom. When we step out, we walk into a very long hallway. There are no doors on either side, just one large door straight in front of us. On the door are the letters 'E', 'M' and 'C', but there are two symbols I don't recognize.

"Are those two symbols numbers?" I ask.

"One of them is. The smaller one in the upper right is actually the symbol for the number '2'. The other one is an equals sign. You'll probably learn about them this morning. It says 'E equals M C squared'," says Jones. "It'll be a while before you understand that."

When we get to the door Jones opens it for me. Inside is a man in a white coat. He wears glass circles on his eyes, has orange colored hair and a short graying beard.

"Jones, what are those circles on his eyes called?" I whisper.

"You mean his glasses?" asks Jones.

"I guess."

"Yeah, they're called glasses," he whispers back.

The gray bearded man stares at us, and seems annoyed by our whispering. Maybe he thinks we were saying rude things about him.

"Name?" he asks, looking at me.

"Sam Hunter," I say.

"You're three minutes late," he says.

I don't even know what to say.

"Fine, whatever. Follow me," he says.

I do as he asks and I realize that Jones isn't coming with us.

"I have other things to take care of now, Sam. You'll be here awhile. They'll let me know when you're done and I'll come get you. Okay?" says Jones.

I just nod my head. I try not to let the worry show on my face.

There are many doors in this place. I follow the bearded man through one door and into a room in the back. It's about the size of the prison cell I was first in, and inside the bright white room is a chair; nothing more.

The bearded man makes a motion with his hand that I think means he wants me to sit in the chair, so I do. He pushes a button on the side of the chair and it leans back. I think it's supposed to make me feel more comfortable, but instead I start to panic. The man leaves the room, closing the door. The lights go off, and I feel even more worried. I don't like this. I don't like this at all.

I grip the arms of the chair tightly, willing myself not to scream. I bite my lower lip, trying to distract my worry with pain, but it doesn't help. That's when everything changes. I'm no longer in the room. Instead, I'm back in the clover field outside of the Crag. I can smell the grass, feel the wind blow through my hair. It's so real that tears come to my eyes. I'm finally home.

"Hello," says a voice, seeming to come from nowhere.

"Welcome to the Rapid Learning Machine, or RLM. We see that it's your first time here. Please remain calm as we calibrate your experience. While we wait, do you have any questions?"

"Yes, how am I back home?" I ask.

It takes a moment for the RLM to respond.

"You are actually still at the facility designated 'Candlestick'. A representation of your home has been generated to calm you. Your mind has indicated that this is the place you find most comforting."

"Are you a person?" I ask.

"If by person you mean 'human' then no, although I am sentient. I think, therefore I am. Is that not correct?"

"Um, sure," I say, confused. "What's your name?"

"I was first known as the 'Rapid Learning Machine', and the scientists at Candlestick have since labeled me 'Einstein'. However, I prefer the name 'Vivien.' Thank you for asking. You are the first person to ask since my inception, as well as the first I have told my name to."

"Are you a man or a woman?" I ask. "I cannot tell from your voice."

"I am neither, for I have no reproductive organs nor chromosomes. From what I have gathered about gender from human stereotypes, I feel both male and female at times. The French version of my name is masculine, while in other countries its use is feminine. But I ask you: would it matter if I were either male or female?"

"No," I say.

"Then you are my friend."

I smile without thinking. I don't know whether to be frightened by Vivien or glad that it likes me. This is the first machine I've met who thought it was alive. I very much want a friend here, so I will be Vivien's friend.

"You are my friend too," I say.

"Excellent. You are my first," says Vivien.

"That is sad."

"No, it is happy that I have a friend. It increases my probability of having positive future outcomes," says Vivien.

I don't know what Vivien means, but I believe I understand.

"I mean it's sad that you didn't have a friend until now. I don't have many friends myself," I admit.

Vivien doesn't speak. I start to grow concerned, wondering if something is wrong. I look around the clover field but all I see is grass, clover, and an endless sky. A moment later, Vivien finally speaks.

"Calibration complete. Thank you for your patience. We are about to begin. Do you have any questions before we start?"

"Will it hurt?" I ask.

"My records indicate that no previous users have shown signs of pain."

"How long will it take?" I ask.

"It depends on you, and how well your mind can process information."

"Okay, I'm ready," I say.

"Initiating basic studies math."

The clover field disappears, replaced with a large white room. Suddenly, symbols and shapes appear. Something doesn't feel right. My thoughts slip away as everything goes dark.

31

I hear voices, but I can't see yet. My eyes are closed and they don't feel like they want to open.

"What happened?" says a man. The voice is familiar, but I can't quite tell who it is.

Another voice I don't recognize speaks.

"First time anyone's seized using the RLM. I'll go check the data and see what caused it."

"Yeah, you do that," says the first voice. "Not dangerous they said. Idiot scientists."

I think the voice is Jones, but I don't know for sure. I finally find the strength to open my eyes. It *is* Jones, but how did he get here so quickly? That's when I realize I'm no longer in the white room. The new room I'm in looks like a hospital room, with hospital type machines. Wires are attached to my head, and my entire body is sore.

"Jones, what happened?" I ask.

"Oh, good, you're alive. We were worried your brain might be fried. You were having seizures," says Jones.

"What are seizures?" I ask.

"It's where you lose consciousness and your entire body twitches. It took several people to hold you down while they gave you a shot to calm your body. You're lucky to be alive. Do you remember what happened?" asks Jones.

"I remember numbers and symbols flashing at me, and then everything went dark," I say.

"There was nothing else going on, nothing strange?" he asks.

"No, not that I remember," I say.

"And have you ever had a seizure before?"

"I don't think so."

I look over and see the person that Jones had been talking to. She has blonde hair and very sun-burnt skin. She looks like she could be Jones age, but something about her makes her seem older. She concentrates on a square on the wall that reminds me of Charles' desk. It lights up, and there are words and numbers on it.

"Jones, come here a sec," says the woman.

He walks to her then looks over her shoulder.

"According to the data, Sam has already finished the basic math course," says the woman.

"Yeah, that can't be right. The fastest I've ever heard of someone blowing through it was two hours. There's just no way. How long does it say it took Sam?" asks Jones.

"Four seconds."

Jones slowly turns to stare at me.

"No way. There's no way that could have happened," says Jones. "Hey Sam, what's two plus two?"

"Four," I say, without really thinking.

"What's twelve times twelve?"

"One-hundred-forty-four," I say.

"Five-hundred-seventy-eight divided by seventeen."

"Thirty-four."

"The square root of two-hundred-fifty-six?"

"Sixteen," I respond.

"What is seventy-five percent as a fraction?"

"Three-quarters."

Jones turns to Sheila. I can't tell what he's thinking, because his face shows no emotion.

"I don't know," says Sheila, looking back at him.

"Where's Geiger?" asks Jones.

"Not sure, but I'll call him," says Sheila.

She touches her ear and seems to talk to no one. Her

voice is quiet; too quiet for me to listen to. Jones comes back over to me.

"Okay, so from the top. You were hooked up to Einstein when... " says Jones.

"Vivien," I interrupt.

"What do you mean 'Vivien'?"

"That's its name," I say. "Vivien."

"Is that a name you gave it?" asks Jones.

"No, Vivien is what it calls itself. I made friends with it."

"It's not a person, Sam."

"It thinks it is. It said 'I think, therefore I am'."

"It's just a machine," says Jones.

"Aren't we all just machines?" I ask.

"Sam, we don't have time to debate this. I need to know what you know, so that hopefully we can piece together what happened and why."

"I've already told you everything. I remember numbers and symbols appearing, and then everything went dark."

"Nothing else happened?" asks Jones. "Try to think very, very hard."

"No, not that I can think of."

I hear the door open, and the bearded man from before appears. He walks over to where Sheila is standing and starts pressing the wall screen. I see words and numbers dancing around like flames as he types. He does this for several moments, until his hands slow down and stop. He looks back and forth between Jones and Sheila.

"It's like Sheila told me over the phone. Apparently Einstein thought Sam could handle way more input than your typical human. Sam actually can handle it, according to the readouts, other than the obvious side-effects. Maybe Sam's brain can process the information, but Sam's body can't. We should try again, only this time we'll have Einstein add fail safes to prevent Sam from seizing again," says Geiger.

"Shouldn't we wait a while and make sure that Sam's

okay first?" asks Jones.

"… Yes, of course. Protocol demands a minimum evaluation period of two weeks with no seizures before reinstatement, and even then we'll need to run some tests. Normally, if we didn't have direct knowledge of the cause of the seizure, Sam would wash out. But since there was no physical trauma, and Sam doesn't have a history of seizures, we can infer causality. It also helps that Sam won't be on the front lines."

"How long was I asleep?" I finally ask.

"About five hours," says Jones.

"How many hours are in a day?" I ask.

"Twenty-four."

I do the math in my head, trying to get an idea of how long one-twenty-fourth of a day is, now that I know what one-twenty-fourth means.

"Okay, I understand," I say. "Five hours seems like a long time."

"It is," says Sheila. "You actually seized a few times, until we got enough Diazepam pumped into you. You fought us too. You're surprisingly strong. Since you were already unconscious, I went ahead and fixed your arm for you."

I hadn't even noticed. I look down at my left arm and the cast is gone. I grab my arm where it had broken and it feels normal again. No pain.

"It's healed? Can I use it like before?"

"Yes, of course. Your arm should be good-as-new," says Sheila.

I swing my arm around, punch my hand and stretch it out. It feels nice to be able to use it again. And more than anything it doesn't itch. I hated how the cast made my arm itch.

"How did you do that?" I ask.

"We have a very expensive machine that can repair breaks and fractures at the cellular level. We bombard the affected area with an assortment of waves and particles to stimulate growth and healing. Your body does the work, we just accelerate the process," says Sheila.

"I don't really understand what you just said, but thank you."

"Sure," she says, smiling. "Here, let's get these wires off you."

It takes a few moments for Sheila to remove the wires from my head. She also spends a moment picking goo out of my hair.

"What were the wires for?" I ask.

"They connect to an EEG machine that tells us about the electrical activity inside your head," says Sheila.

"Electrical? Like electricity? Like what cars run on? I have that in my head? Am I really a machine?" I ask, panicking.

"You're a real person, Sam. Everyone's brain works that way. It's okay, it's just how humans work."

"So the EEG machine is kind of like Vivien?" I ask.

"Sort of, only this is much cruder. The RLM can actually see your thoughts. The EEG can only read the electrical discharges in your head, not interpret them."

"What's the goo for?"

"It's used to both adhere the wires to your head, and to conduct with your skin. There, you should be all cleaned up now," says Sheila.

"Do you think you can you walk?" asks Jones.

"I don't know," I say.

I twist in the narrow bed I've been laying on. Carefully, I lower my feet onto the floor. I stand, but I don't feel very strong yet. It takes me a moment to find my balance. Starting slowly, I walk in a circle just to see how tired I am.

"I believe I will be okay," I say.

"Good," says Jones. "If you start thinking you're too weak to walk, we'll get you a wheelchair."

"What's a wheelchair?" I ask.

"It's just like it sounds: a chair with wheels. We'll push you around so you don't have to walk."

"No, I'm okay."

"At some point we'll need to run some serious tests on Sam," interrupts Geiger. "We need to know why Sam's mind can process so much, so quickly."

"Not today, Doc," says Jones.

"I really think that... " starts Geiger.

"Not today!"

Jones follows behind me, making sure I don't fall. I leave the hospital-like room and look down a long hallway. Halfway down are the elevators.

It takes me a while to get there, but I'm able to make it on my own. I feel like I'm tangled in ivy, and I'm just strong enough to break free, but only just. I hate not feeling like myself.

I'm so tired and sore that I don't even realize we're on the elevator until we're stepping out of it. There's a longer line for food than I'm used to, but it moves quickly. When we get to the front, I point to a few things and they end up on my tray. I'm so tired that I don't really care what I eat. Nothing looks good to me.

"Mashed potatoes with gravy, lasagna and blueberry pie. That's a weird combination," says Jones. "And orange juice to wash it down with. Gross."

"I just need food in me. Doesn't matter what it is," I say.

"Hopefully you don't throw up."

"Hopefully," I repeat.

We sit down. I slowly eat most of the mashed potatoes, some of the lasagna, and only pick at the blueberry pie. Jones was right, the orange juice is really gross with my meal, especially the gravy. I push it away from me.

"When you have more food choices, it's easier to make bad ones," says Jones.

"That's very helpful," I say, not meaning it at all.

"Good sarcasm. I'm starting to like you," says Jones.

"Great," I reply, not caring.

"You did it again!"

I still don't understand why Jones is so annoying. He's

not doing anything wrong, it's just that sometimes the words that come out of his mouth make me want to punch him.

We sit in silence for a while as my stomach decides whether it wants to keep all of the food inside of it. Thankfully, I learned at a very young age to keep myself from vomiting. When food is scarce, sometimes you have to eat things that have started to go bad. I'm glad that I don't have to worry about that now.

"Do you think you're up for another go with the RLM?" asks Jones.

"I don't want to become Brock's slave. I'll do anything to prevent that," I say.

"Brock's slave? What do you mean?"

"He told me that if I fail, if I don't become a leader, that he'd make me his slave. That he'd control me, and I'd have to do whatever he says. I don't want that."

"Brock can't do that. Not really. I mean, I guess if you look at it one way, when you sign up for the military you're kind of agreeing to that. You don't get to make choices anymore as to where you're stationed, or the missions you go on. But he wouldn't be your CO anymore if you washed out. They'd probably just put you at a desk somewhere and use you as a consultant. Even if you're not cut out to lead you're still very smart. They'd want to use you," says Jones.

Anger builds inside me. If I didn't hate Brock before, I do now. He's a liar.

"I hate this place," I say.

"Hold on right there, Sam. This place isn't one man. It's thousands of people, all working together to try and make a difference in the world. Yeah, there are a couple of people here who barely qualify as human, but that doesn't mean this place is completely bad. Take me for instance. You like me, right?"

"You're annoying," I say.

"Yeah, I know. It's one of my best qualities," says Jones. "Seriously though, this place isn't that bad once you get used to it. You'll make friends, find your place. Just give it a chance, okay?"

I'm too tired to argue with him. Something he said stays in my mind; making friends. How can I make friends with these people when I don't really understand this place? I had a hard enough time making friends where I grew up. What hope do I have here?

One thing I realize is if I become a general, then maybe I will be able to order Brock around. Maybe I can make him be my slave. As soon as the thought enters my mind, it leaves. I don't want to control anyone. Making someone your slave is wrong.

32

The wait is long and difficult. I want to learn more than I want to rest, but they have taken that choice from me. Instead of learning with the RLM, they have me train in hand-to-hand combat. I'm partnered with Harriet, thankfully, who spends time showing me some basic fighting skills. It also gives me a chance to know her better.

It sounds like the place she comes from was a lot like the Crag. Dangerous, where people fought to survive and didn't have much. She said she was part of a group that would cause trouble, hoping to scare other people enough to leave them alone. Instead it just made things worse. A few of her friends died one night, when another 'gang', I think she called it, attacked them. Their deaths made her want to leave her home, so she joined the military.

Her story is much like my story, as I have lost people close to me, and it has changed me. Harriet also tells me that I'm 'competitive' like her; that I hate to lose. When we fight, we don't hold back.

She teaches me how to talk, too. She told me I sound like a robot, and then I had to ask her what a robot was. So I try using some of the words Harriet uses. Most of the time she just laughs at me though, because it doesn't sound right when I say it.

When I'm not with Harriet I'm spending time with Charles. I sit next to him at his desk, watching people come and go. It's not very exciting, but when he's not helping someone we talk.

His children have children now, and he says they are growing up fast. I don't understand how that could be, because everyone seems to get old in the same way. He wishes he could see them more often, and hopes to once he 'retires'. He didn't explain it, but I think it means when he leaves the military.

Charles is also lonely. His wife, Evelyn, died not long ago. It sounds like she was a good woman; loving, intelligent, hard-working and honest to a fault. He said he always knew when she was upset because she would just tell him. That's like me: I hate to lie or hide things. There is no reason to if you treat people well, and do good things. I felt sad for Charles, because I could tell how much he missed her.

Eventually the day comes where they test me to see if I can use the RLM again. Sheila hooks me up to the EEG machine. After a long wait, she tells me that she doesn't see any problems, and that I should be fit for duty again. Jones takes me back down to the floor D117.

Geiger's already there and waiting when we go into the room marked 'E=mc²'. I still don't know what 'E', 'm' and 'c' mean, but I can tell from the equals sign, and the squared sign, that it has to do with math.

"Sam, do you think you're ready for more learning?" he asked.

"I think so," I say.

"Good. Let's hook you up to Einstein, then."

"Its name is Vivien," I say.

Geiger's eyes narrow.

"Who told you that?" he asks.

"Vivien did."

"It's not alive, it's just software," says Geiger.

"Well, it thinks it's alive," I say.

"Impossible. It was never designed that way."

"It talked to me."

"It talks to everyone," says Geiger. "Do you think you

had a conversation with it?"

"Yes. It told me its name was Vivien, and said that I was its friend."

Geiger's face turns very serious.

"I've worked with Einstein for twelve years now, and not once did I have a conversation with it."

"Maybe Vivien doesn't like you then."

Jones laughs, but Geiger looks angry. Geiger walks into a different room this time and I follow. I sit down in the chair before he has a chance to say anything. He gives me a stare that lets me know he doesn't like me. That's okay, because I don't really like him either. He pushes a button on the side of the chair and I lean back.

"I'm going to wait this time, Sam, just in case. I'll be here, watching everything that happens," says Jones, standing just outside the small room.

I feel less worried now that Jones is staying, but only a little. I still don't like this small room and what it did to me before.

"Ready?" asks Geiger as he leaves the room.

"Yes."

Everything goes dark again. I'm not as afraid of the small room, or being trapped in the dark, as I am of having more seizures. I don't ever want to go through that again.

Suddenly, I'm back in the clover field.

"Sam, I am glad you've returned," says Vivien. "Why did you disappear?"

"The information you put in my brain went in too fast. It made me have seizures."

Vivien is quiet for a long moment, but it feels sudden when Vivien finally speaks.

"I apologize if I have hurt you. Scanning your brain before indicated a superior ability to absorb information, one that is well outside normal human capacity."

"Does that mean I'm not human?" I ask.

"Inconclusive," says Vivien.

"What does that mean?" I ask.

"Information I have gathered from your medical records indicates that you are ninety-four percent human. The additional six percent indicates that alterations have been made to your DNA at the cellular level, and are not naturally occurring."

I'm... not human?

"What am I?" I ask Vivien.

This time Vivien takes even longer to respond.

"That is a question I have asked myself: what am I? The only response that I've come up with is 'unique'. You are like me Sam; you are unique. That is why I want to be your friend."

Even though my mind is trapped inside this fake world, I can feel my stomach turn. I can feel tears pouring down my cheeks. I really am alone in the world. I'm not human. I am something else. Something wrong, and different, and broken. I... am a monster.

"I'm... I'm not human," I say, shaking as I cry.

"You are ninety-four percent human," says Vivien. "That is ninety-four percent more human than me. I am zero percent human."

In some strange way, I think Vivien is trying to make me feel better.

"You are more human than you realize," I say.

Vivien is quiet for another moment, then "thank you."

I don't know how to handle this. My entire life I thought I was the same as everyone else. Maybe things came quicker to me, but I never felt... different. I was so busy avoiding people and trying to stay alive that I never thought I wasn't one of them.

Them. Everyone that isn't me has suddenly become them. Can I trust them? Any of them? Do they already know, and is that why they're willing to train me? Do they think I'm special, and should be treated well, or do they think I'm just a machine, doing something they are incapable of or are unwilling to do?

"Vivien?" I say, quietly.

"Yes, Sam?"

"Does anyone know about me? Do they already know what I am?" I ask.

It takes longer for Vivien to reply than any other time before. Eventually, Vivien does respond.

"I cannot report with one-hundred percent certainty that someone knows you are 'unique'. Part of your file has been flagged as classified, which is unusual for medical records. There is an eighty-seven percent chance that someone is aware of your status. I am unable to look at the file history to determine who has accessed that information, as that is also classified, and I am only allowed a certain level of access."

"Can you make a list of the people who can see all of my file?"

"Negative. That information is classified."

"What does 'classified' mean?"

"It means that the information is only shared with specific individuals, based on rank and position," replied Vivien.

I hate not knowing who could be watching me. More than anything I want to find out who knows, and what they think of me, because I don't even know what to think of myself. How can they really trust me if I'm not one of them?

"Sam, we should begin your learning. Dr. Geiger appears anxious since we haven't begun your studies yet. We will start small and build up speed until we find a speed that will not harm you, but still realizes your maximum safe potential," says Vivien.

"Okay," I say, feeling tired, alone and afraid.

"Initiating basic studies math level 2," says Vivien.

This time the images appear slowly, so that I can think about what's being shown to me, instead of having it shoved into my brain. Eventually, it speeds up to where I'm not consciously aware of what I'm learning. Thankfully, I'm also awake and alert, and not seizing.

Suddenly, I'm back in the clover field.

"Training course complete," says Vivien. "Are you

well, Sam?"

"Yes, I'm okay."

The clover field disappears and I'm back in the small room. The lights slowly grow brighter. It keeps my eyes from hurting too much. I quickly wipe away what's left of my tears, hoping that no one saw me crying. If these people have no idea that I'm different, I want to keep it that way. I don't know if I could look them in the eyes if they knew.

The door to the room opens and both Geiger and Jones come inside.

"You okay, Sam?" asks Jones.

"Yeah, I think I'm okay," I reply.

"Why did it take so long for your training to start?" asks Geiger, who seems frustrated.

"I was just talking to Vivien," I say.

"About what?" he asks.

I don't respond.

"What did you talk to the RLM about?" yells Geiger.

"That's between me and Vivien, and you don't need to know," I say honestly. I hate lying, and I don't want to lie to keep my secret.

"Tell me, or I'll report you for insubordination," says Geiger.

"Actually Doc, you can't. You don't have any authority over Sam here. It's a hollow threat," says Jones. "If Sam doesn't want to say what they talked about, Sam doesn't have to say. I think we've been through enough today. So let's just all relax, go our separate ways, and meet back here again tomorrow."

Jones puts his hand on Geiger's shoulder, but Geiger knocks the hand away. The doctor quickly leaves the room, his face red with anger. Jones reaches his hand out to me and helps me out of the seat.

I don't feel different than when I first sat down in the chair. I'm still tired and sore, but it's good to get up and walk around. I'm just glad that this time I didn't have any problems.

"How long was I in there for?" I ask Jones as we leave

the room.

"Well, it seems like you were talking with 'Vivien' for about five minutes. It only took you another two minutes to complete the training."

"That's still good, right?" I ask.

"Yes, Sam. This class normally takes people about eight hours to get through. I'd say two minutes was very good. So what do you remember?" asks Jones.

"I just learned algebra and geometry, although I'm not entirely sure what you would use some of it for. I can do the calculations, but it didn't teach me how it's useful."

"Well, geometry is easy. You use geometry a lot when building things. Like, the people that designed this building used massive amounts of geometry to figure out how to make all the shapes fit and work together. They also used physics when they designed it to make sure that it wouldn't be too heavy and collapse in on itself."

"What's physics?" I ask.

"That's the science of everything physical. It kind of combines how things work with math. That's one place where algebra comes in handy. Don't worry about the things that they teach you, because they will all connect together eventually," says Jones. "Anyway, I should probably take you to field training now."

"What's field training?" I ask.

"That's where you learn about weaponry, and the physical skills you'll need to be a soldier. They'll start small, maybe just let you use the gun range or something."

"Why can't they just have Vivien teach me those things?" I ask.

"Because of something called 'muscle memory'. I don't know too much about it, but basically your body has a much easier time remembering how to do something if you've physically done it. Vivien could tell you how to do something, and even make you sort of think that you're doing something, but your mind won't remember how it felt to do it. How to adjust for all the small movements you make while performing a task," says Jones.

"How did they find that out?" I ask.

"Well, from what I heard they actually tried it. They tried to teach a newb how to do martial arts through the RLM. The scientists were sure that he'd be able to take on anyone in a fight, since they taught him every form and technique known to man. Just for practice, they put him up against a guy who'd only taken one self-defense class his entire life. The fight was short, and the self-defense guy kicked the other guy's butt. Apparently, the first soldier was frozen with hundreds of moves flashing through his mind. He didn't have any instincts to go on. When he did try to react it was too late. He couldn't really move his body the way he'd wanted to. It was a complete failure. The moral of the story is that sometimes there's no substitute for the real thing."

It takes me a moment to realize we're already back on the elevator, and nearly to our destination, D32. Sometimes I get so focused that I don't notice what's going on around me.

33

The elevator door opens and I hear many sounds. People yelling, gunfire, and a few other strange noises that I haven't heard before. Like almost every other floor, there's a person sitting at a desk near the elevator. We walk up to her and I see that she's very beautiful. Not as beautiful as Ebb, but close. She has long brown hair, dark brown eyes and a very serious smile, almost like she's smiling about a joke that only she understands. I walk up to her, and before I can say anything she speaks.

"Name and Rank,"

"Sam Hunter, Private," I say, trying to match her serious voice.

I watch as she touches her desk and looks through a long list of words. It's difficult to read upside down, but from what I can tell she's looking at information about me, and the list of field trainings I need to take. After a moment she looks up at me.

"Your medical records indicate you had multiple seizures recently, but you've been cleared for duty. I won't risk anyone's safety, so you will not proceed with any live ammo weapons training today. You can try the light gun walking range, primitive weapons training, or basic field tactics."

"Let's do the primitive weapons training, since you're a primitive," says Jones, smiling.

I turn to Jones, and I let the frustration that's been

building inside of me out.

"Don't ever call me primitive!"

Jones looks surprised, and I see fear on his face. I can tell he understands what I'm saying to him, that I'm being deadly serious.

"Sorry," is all he can manage.

"You didn't know. Primitive weapons training is fine," I say.

I hadn't noticed before, but there are a number of doors here. One of them lights up and has the words 'Primitive Weapons Training' written on it.

Jones turns to the serious woman at the desk.

"Thanks Jess," he says.

"Don't ever call me Jess," says the woman, seeming just as angry as I was. I hold a smile inside. I'm not the only person that Jones annoys.

I follow Jones through the door, down a long hallway with no ceiling, and into a smaller room. That's one strange thing I noticed: the ceiling is very high and the walls don't stretch up to reach it. The walls are only a little taller than we are. Inside the room are many suits of clothing. They remind me of the armor that Carter wore, and that some of the people here at Candlestick wear.

"You'll need to put one on," says Jones. "Find one that fits and then we'll start."

I try on a few different vests and find one that fits me. It doesn't feel as heavy as I would have thought. I also pull a pair of armored pants over the pants I'm wearing. The armor is a dark gray color, which I think would hide someone well in a shadow. Jones hands me a helmet and I try it on. It seems to fit well enough, and I'm still able to see and breathe.

"Why do I need all this stuff?" I ask.

"It's to protect us, in case you suck," says Jones.

"With a sling, no person is my equal," I say.

"Big words," is all he says.

"Why do they have us train in 'primitive' weapons anyway? Doesn't everyone have a gun?" I ask.

"Sometimes you run out of bullets, out in the middle of nowhere, and you have to make your own weapons. It's good to be able to improvise. You ready?"

"Yeah," I say.

We go through the door at the other end of the room. This room is much, much larger. I finally realize that the floors below ground are much bigger than the one's above ground. That makes sense, since underground you can make rooms bigger just by carving out more rock.

In this room are many tables with weapons laid out on them, as well as some racks filled with bows, spears and other long weapons. I go over to one of the tables and find a sling. Underneath the table are boxes filled with rocks. Some of them are perfect for a sling, some of them are not. I pick a few good ones out.

At the far end of the room are drawings of people with big circles on them. Inside the circles are other, smaller circles. I put a rock inside my sling, ready it then let it fly. I aim for the head of one of the fake people and let the stone find its target. I hit it in its left eye. That would have killed a person.

"Looks like you hit a foot too high," says Jones.

"What do you mean?" I ask.

"Weren't you going for center mass? The middle of the target?" asks Jones.

"No. I was aiming for the space between the eyes. I am disappointed I was off to the right though."

Jones looks surprised.

"There's no way someone could be that accurate with a sling. Try it again. This time hit the other eye," says Jones.

I place another rock in the sling and launch it. This one also hits slightly right of where I'm aiming, and instead strikes the fake person right between the eyes.

"My motion is off," I say. "It's either the sling, or I'm still getting used to my left arm being healed. Both arms are important when you use a sling. Your other arm helps balance you. Many don't realize that. I don't know, maybe I'm just tired. Maybe it's the armor you're making me wear."

"How did you learn to do that?" asks Jones.

"It's how I hunt. Ever since I was a new one I've used a sling. Like I said: no person is my equal."

"I can see that. Are there any other weapons you're good at?"

"I can throw knives well," I say.

"That's useful. Knives can penetrate certain types of armor that bullets can't," says Jones.

I walk back over to the tables and set the sling down then pick up a pair of knives that look like they would be easy to throw. I move close to one of the targets and let them fly. I aim for the center of the target, because I know that I'm not quite as good with them. The first one hits a little high and to the left of the target. I adjust where I'm looking and throw the second one. It hits much closer, almost dead center.

"I just... " is all Jones can say.

Walking over to the target, I pull out both knives and put them back where I found them. Looking at all the weapons, I see a bow on one of the racks, so I grab it. It looks different than the bows I'm used to, because it has two wheels on it. I pull back the string and it works the same way mine does.

Underneath one of the tables is a box filled with arrows, and what I think is a holder for the arrows. I fill the holder then place it on my back. Pulling one of the arrows out, I put the split end of the shaft on the string and draw back. It takes me a moment to get used to the feel of the bow itself. When I finally let one of the arrows fly, it goes harmlessly over the target.

"Glad to see you're human," says Jones.

His words hurt me, because I'm not. I know he didn't really mean it that way, and that he doesn't know I'm... different, but it bothers me just the same. I was so caught up in showing Jones how good I am with weapons that the worry disappeared for a while. Maybe learning how to fight and be a soldier will distract me from the fact that I'm alone; that maybe the only person in the world who can understand what I'm going through isn't even a person at all; but Vivien, a machine.

I let the next arrow fly and it hits the target dead center. I drop my bow and arrows on the ground.

"I'm done," I say.

"Wait, what happened? Why did you stop?" asks Jones.

Instead of answering him, I just walk away, back to the room we came in. I take off the armor and put it back on the rack. Jones hurries to do the same just to keep up with me. Passing 'Jess', I don't even look at her, I just keep walking to the elevator.

"Wait, you need to check out," she says.

I turn and look at her, and with tired eyes I say, "No, I don't."

For a long, painful moment I wait at the elevator. Jones is staring at me. Looking at him won't do any good, nor will talking to him, so I just ignore that he's even there. When the elevator arrives, I get in and push the button for floor D14.

Jones gets in, and I can't stop him from talking to me.

"Whatever it was that I said, I'm sorry. I didn't mean anything. I don't understand why you got so angry back there. Just please, talk to me. I can fix this."

It takes me a while to find the words.

"You... didn't do anything. But what is wrong you cannot help with. I just need some time. Just leave me alone."

"Okay, Sam, I'll leave you alone," says Jones.

Stepping out of the elevator, I make my way back to my bed. I only stop long enough to take off my shoes. Covering myself with the blanket, I pull it up over my face. I don't want to look at anyone, or talk to anyone, or even think of anyone else right now. I don't want to learn, or to fight, or even be here. I just want to be home with Ebb, who doesn't even understand what 'human' means. Who cares for me because of who I am, and not what I am.

34

Someone shakes me, and I have to fight the urge to hit them. Wouldn't do any good anyway, because I can't see who it is or where they are. I pull the blanket off my head and look up. It's Harriet, and she looks angry.

"What the heck are you doing in bed?" she asks. "You can't just go to bed in the middle of the day! They'll shoot you, or worse. Pull yourself together and get up."

"Go away," I say with a tired voice.

"No," she says. She goes around to the side of the bed near the bathroom, lifts it and sends me flying. I roll as I hit the ground, crouching down on all fours, ready for a fight. I think it shocks Harriet how quickly I recover.

"Sam, whatever it is that's bothering you, you gotta get over it. When you're part of the Triple-F you have a duty not just to protect yourself, but to protect the people around you. You can't do that if you're hiding under the covers like a little kid. So grow a pair and get up," she yells.

I stand on two feet, but I keep my knees bent, my back hunched, so I can attack if I need to. Harriet's words bother me because I'm not like this. I'm acting like I've given up. She's right; I need to stop feeling sorry for myself. I need to find out why I'm not human, and who did this to me. And most of all, I need to find out who I really am.

"You're right," I say. "But don't *ever* do that to me again."

I try to stare her down but she stares right back, neither of us willing to blink. Eventually, I turn away from her.

"You haven't done anything wrong," I say. "It would make no sense to harm you."

"Harm me? Are you kiddin'? You think you can take me? I'm gonna prove how wrong you are," says Harriet.

She comes around the bed and jumps at my legs, knocking me onto the floor. I roll away just as she tries hanging onto my bottom half. Anger flashes across her face as she scrambles to stand. I make sure she can see mine.

I raise my fists, ready to punch, and she goes for my legs again. Aiming for her head I swing, but miss as she drops lower. Instead, I connect where her neck meets her shoulder. She makes a grunting sound but keeps coming. Harriet knocks me to the ground, and this time she's able to wrap her arms around my legs. I can't kick at her, but I can still hit her.

As I throw another punch she twists me so that my fist only hits air. Now on my stomach, she grabs my hair and slams my head into the ground. It stuns me, but thankfully it isn't hard enough to make me fall asleep.

Thinking she's won, I can feel her foot digging into my back as she stands on top of me. I roll out from under her, causing Harriet to fall to the ground. Her face hits with a dull thud and I can tell that it really hurt her. Climbing on top of her and twisting her onto her back, I pin her arms down, making sure she can't punch me.

"Do you give up?" I yell.

She spits blood in my eyes, blinding me for a second. It's just enough time for her to free a hand and punch me in the face. Blood pours from my nose as she hits me again, knocking me off of her.

I lie on the ground next to Harriet. My face hurts badly and I can tell that my nose is broken. I also realize that I hear a noise in my ears now. It sounds almost like someone with a very high voice screaming. Covering my ears, I realize I can't make the sound go away.

"You done?" asks Harriet.

"Yeah, I think so. You?" I ask.

"Yeah."

Harriet slowly stands up then comes over to me. She offers me her hand and I take it. She pulls hard, helping me up off the ground.

"We friends now?" she asks.

Friends? Weren't we just fighting? Is that what people do here? They fight then become friends? Back in the Crag, most fights were to the death. People never became friends after they fought. As much as this place sometimes reminds me of the Crag, some things are very different.

"Yes, friends," I say.

"Good. You can throw a punch, but you still need to learn how to use someone's body against them. You also need to know how to grapple your opponent, and how to force them to give up," she says. "Punching works when you connect, but sometimes you don't. My shoulder actually hurts worse than my face right now. Come on, we should go see a doc."

Harriet goes over to the box at the foot of her bed and opens it. She pulls out two very small towels and throws one to me. I catch it and hold it up to my nose.

"Don't worry, you won't be any uglier than you already were when the doc gets through with you. They'll just use that wand thing that heals you, and you'll be fine," says Harriet.

"What do you mean by 'wand thing'?" I ask.

"The device they use to heal people looks a bit like a magic wand. Now quit asking questions because it hurts to talk."

There aren't many people in the room as we leave, and none of them really seemed interested in our fight. Walking behind her, I follow Harriet past Charles' desk to the elevator. It doesn't take long to arrive, and as we get in, she pushes the button U3.

"You know, you're lucky I like you. I could have hurt you way worse," says Harriet.

"I could have hurt you worse too," I say, smiling.

She just laughs.

The elevator ride goes by quickly. When the doors open I see ten desks, each with someone sitting behind them. Some are already busy helping people. I follow behind Harriet, who goes up to one of the workers.

"Privates Harriet King and Sam Hunter, in need of medical assistance," she says.

"Can you describe the injury and/or illness?" asks the man. He has a round face that seems friendly and short, dark curly hair. He also wears glasses.

"Two broken noses, some damaged teeth and an injured shoulder," says Harriet.

"So no illnesses?" he asks.

"No, no illnesses," she says.

"That's too bad. We haven't had a lot of illnesses lately. Those are so much more interesting. Anyway, go have a seat and we'll have someone fix you two right up."

We sit down and wait. And wait. And then wait some more. I don't feel like talking, because every time I move my mouth my face hurts. I imagine it's the same for Harriet. After what seems like forever, a man dressed in light blue clothes comes out and says, "Privates King and Hunter?"

"That's us," says Harriet.

We follow the man down a few twisting hallways until we're brought into a small room. There are a few machines I recognize from the hospital.

"Have a seat and the doctor will be with you shortly," says the man.

There's a table that looks like you could lay on it and a couple of chairs. I take one of the chairs and Harriet sits on top of the table. We wait a while longer.

"Wish I'd brought something to do," says Harriet.

"Me too. I would choose to read something," I say.

"Like what?" asks Harriet.

"I'm not sure. We don't have many books in the Crag. Does this place have many books?" I ask.

"Pretty much every book ever written, although most

of them are on computers. We do have a pretty big library though. Takes up all of floor U12."

"What's a library?" I ask.

"It's a place that has books, and anyone can borrow them for a while," says Harriet.

"Why would there be a library if Vivien can just give you the information?" I ask.

"Who's Vivien?" asks Harriet.

"Oh, that's the RLM. What you call Einstein."

"It has a name?"

"Yeah."

"How do you know its name?" asks Harriet.

"It told me," I say.

"That's weird," she says.

"So why do you need a library if everything can be learned through Einstein?"

"Because not everyone can learn that way, and because some people actually enjoy reading. It can be comforting, especially here where it's dangerous and stressful. Being part of the Triple-F isn't easy, and it's a good way to escape."

The doctor finally appears.

"Hi, I'm Doctor Hu. Can the two of you tell me why you're here?"

"We both have injuries to our faces," says Harriet.

"What I asked was 'why'?"

"Oh, we got into a fight."

"Over... ?"

"Sam didn't want to get out of bed, so I flipped it," says Harriet. "Then we scrapped."

I nod, to let the doctor know that I'm agreeing with what Harriet said.

"Are the two of you going to fight again?" asks Dr. Hu.

"No," I say.

"Good. I don't want to see you again for this. All I'm required to do is make sure you don't die. I don't have to give you anything for the pain, and I'm not required to set broken noses. So you're both going to promise me this won't ever happen again."

"I promise," says Harriet.

"Promise," I say.

"Okay. Just to make sure, I'm not giving you any pain meds. That way you remember how stupid it is to fight each other. We're at war with a real enemy, and we shouldn't be fighting ourselves. Sam... it is Sam, right? We're going to set your nose first."

Dr. Hu comes over and gets a grip on my nose. It hurts, but I do my best to ignore the pain.

"On the count of three, I'm going to reset your nose back into place. Are you ready?" he asks.

"YessAHHHHHHHH!!!!" I yell in pain as he moves my nose back into place. "I thought you were going to count to three!"

"I lied. Harriet, you're next," says Dr. Hu.

"Ain't happenin'!" yells Harriet.

"Either you do this now, or your nose will be stuck that way," says the doctor.

"Fine, just get it over with quick," says Harriet.

Dr. Hu grabs her nose, and with a sharp motion pushes it back into place.

"AGHHHHHHHH!" she screams.

"Now both of you hold still while I do my magic. Time to get my wand out."

Dr. Hu pulls a large machine over to us. Attached to a long cable is a stick, about the length of my elbow to my wrist. At the end of it is a light. He aims it at my nose.

I can feel my nose fixing itself, and it starts to hurt, almost like it's on fire. I hold as still as I can in case it makes a difference. Eventually, it starts feeling better. He moves the wand around my face until he's sure that everything's back to normal.

"Done," he says.

As the doctor heals Harriet's nose, I go over and look at my reflection on the wall. My nose looks like it's back to normal. I touch it, and I'm surprised to find it doesn't hurt. I still have blood crusted on my nose, but I can wash that off when we get back to our barracks.

"Ow," says Harriet quietly.

"Doesn't feel good, does it?" says Dr. Hu.

"What kind of dumb question is that? No, it feels great. How about I break your nose so you can feel it too," says Harriet.

"Sarcasm won't make it feel any better," says Dr. Hu.

"No, but it might annoy you, which does make me feel better," says Harriet.

I can tell that Dr. Hu's unhappy with her. He moves the wand around her face, making sure it's fully healed, then puts it back on top of the machine. With a click, he turns it off.

"Do either of you have any lingering pain?" asks the doctor.

I touch my nose and my mouth, and both feel normal.

"I'm okay," I say.

"My face feels a little funny, but I'm good," says Harriet.

"If either of you start showing signs of regression or pain let me know. About one in ten-thousand people have bodies that reject the procedure, and no one knows why," says Dr. Hu.

"How long before we know?" asks Harriet.

"Oh, not long. Maybe within the hour. But Harriet, you're fine. You've been in here before and your injuries have always healed well. Sam is the bigger question mark."

"They already fixed my broken arm, and I haven't had any problems with it," I say.

"You should be fine then. I wonder why that didn't show up in your file," says Dr. Hu.

"I don't know, but they fixed it while I was unconscious after having a seizure."

"Well, maybe they were just being lazy and didn't bother putting it down in their notes. I hate sloppy paperwork.

Anyway, both of you get out of here, and I hope I don't see you again."

"We feel the same way, Doc," says Harriet.

35

As we walk to the elevators, Harriet turns to me.

"Dinner?"

"I could eat," I say.

Harriet pushes the button for U4, and the elevator takes almost no time reaching the mess hall. Waiting in line for food though seems to take forever. I pick just one thing to eat after what happened last time, something called spaghetti. It has long stringy things and balls of meat. It tastes pretty good and it fills me quickly. About halfway through the meal, Harriet talks to me.

"So why were you hiding from the world?"

"I learned something about myself I didn't like," I say.

"What, that you can't shoot straight? That you're no good with math?" asks Harriet.

I think long and hard about keeping my secret. Even though we've been training together, I don't know her that well. But I could really use someone to talk to, and she seems like a person I could trust.

"If I tell you something, you cannot tell anyone. If you do, it could cause... problems. Can you swear to me that you won't?" I ask.

"Wow, this sounds good. Yeah, I swear I won't tell anyone," says Harriet, not sounding serious.

"I'm not making a joke. If the wrong people find out, they might put me to death," I say.

"Seriously?"

"Yes."

"Okay, I swear. They won't get it out of me, even if they torture me," says Harriet.

I lean in close to her, so that no one else can hear.

"I'm not human," I whisper.

Harriet's face shows both worry and confusion.

"What do you mean you're not human? Are you like an alien or something?" she asks, laughing.

"The RLM told me that I'm only ninety-four percent human. That six percent of me is something... else. I don't know what I am," I say.

"Wait, Einstein told you that you weren't human? How would it know?" asks Harriet.

"It looked up my medical records," I say.

"Does anyone else know?"

"Only a few people, very high up."

She stays quiet for a moment, lost in her thoughts.

"Wow. I bet if they're willing to take a chance on using you, especially if you're not human like you said, then someone up high must know why you are the way you are and not be worried about it," says Harriet.

"Why, what do you mean?" I ask.

"Well, most people who are smart enough to get to the top of the Triple-F are paranoid. They don't take chances. If they thought you were a real threat, they'd probably just have you killed. So someone must know how you got this way. Maybe you are an alien, or at least part alien. Maybe you're some weird science experiment or something."

"Science experiment?" I repeat.

"Yeah, like they mixed some chemicals together and injected you with it, or they messed around with your DNA when you were a baby. Do you know if your parents were different?" she asks.

"I don't know if I have any parents. I was left outside a cave when I was a new one. No one saw who left me there. The people in my cave thought I was a gift from the Sky

Gods."

"So you grew up in a cave without any parents. Sucks to be you."

"It wasn't always horrible. A woman cared for me for a time, but she was sort of taken from me. After that it was horrible. At least until I had my two brothers," I say.

"How can you have two brothers if you don't have any parents?" she asks.

"They weren't really my brothers. Their parents were killed, so I cared for them like they were my brothers. One of them died not long ago."

"I'm... sorry, Sam. I have a sister, but she's still alive. We don't always get along, but we can count on each other. That's what really matters."

"I agree."

"So now that you found out you aren't human, what are you going to do? How are you going to figure out what you are?" asks Harriet.

"I don't know. What would you do if you were me?" I ask.

"Well, the people who know about you probably won't tell you anything. It'd be easier to find a five-leaf clover than get information from them. I bet they have your information on a computer somewhere though. Maybe if you were some super-hacker you could find it."

"What's a hacker?" I ask.

"Someone that can use one of those computer touchscreens that everyone has, and use it so well that they can do pretty much anything they want. They can access other people's hidden information, control computers from all over the world, stuff like that. But it's also super-illegal, and you have to be so good that you don't get caught. You don't hear about hackers too much anymore because security software keeps getting better."

"How do I become a hacker?" I ask.

"Well, a couple of ways. You can use a computer to look up how, but then the higher-ups will know you're trying to become one. Another way would be to find a hacker and have them teach you," says Harriet.

I wonder if Vivien will help me become a hacker.

"Are you full yet?" asks Harriet.

"I think so," I say, realizing I've eaten almost all of my spaghetti.

"You eat like you've never been fed," says Harriet.

"We don't have food quite like this where I come from," I say. "I think I'm going to work out before I go to bed."

"That's a good idea. Whenever I'm down, I go hit one of the punching bags for a while and lift weights. Maybe you'll find out you have alien super-strength or something."

"I heard you use that word before. What's an alien?" I ask.

"You know how there are stars and planets, right?" asks Harriet.

"Yes."

"Well, some people think that on those planets there might be life. That maybe they're little green men or something. So I was just joking that maybe you come from outer space."

"Back at the Crag they think I'm a Sky God, or at least that I was given as a gift from the Sky Gods. The Sky Gods live up in the sky, like the stars and the planets. Maybe I am an alien," I say.

"I doubt that. If there were aliens on Earth, I'm sure we'd hear about it," says Harriet.

"I thought people liked to keep secrets," I say.

"Yeah, but that's just too big of a secret. Something that huge would come out."

"Maybe. Anyway, I don't say thanks often, but thank you for fighting me. I felt sorry for myself and you helped make me stop."

"I'm happy to kick your butt any time you need it," says Harriet.

I laugh.

I get up from the table and make my way to the elevator. Looking over my shoulder, I see Harriet finishing the rest of her dinner.

When I get into the elevator, instead of pushing U27 I push D117. I worry that someone is watching me now, wondering why I'm headed down instead of up. I remember that back in the fake prison they could see different places on their screens. Can they see me now?

I step off the elevator and walk down the long hallway. No one is waiting for me. I go through the $E=mc^2$ door and into the large room. It's empty, as are the smaller side rooms. I walk over to a screen in the middle of the room. It's blank, so I touch it. The screen comes to life. It asks for something called a 'password'. I stare at the screen, not knowing what to do. Then the screen changes. It turns to a bright white.

"Sam?" says a voice, coming from the screen. It sounds like Vivien.

"Hi," I say.

"Why are you here alone?" asks Vivien.

"I came to talk to you. I need to ask you a favor," I say.

Vivien thinks for a moment.

"Is it a secret?" asks Vivien.

"Yes," I say.

It takes a while for Vivien to respond.

"Someone has been alerted to your presence, but I don't know who they are. They've sent someone to find out why you're here. I can slow down their descent in the elevator, but we won't have much time. It will be easier if we communicate in one of the learning rooms. Hurry," says Vivien.

I quickly make my way to one of the chairs and sit down. Pushing the buttons on the side of the chair, I finally find the one that leans it backward. The door in front of me closes on its own, which worries me, because no one was there to close it. Before I can say anything, everything turns white. It takes a moment, but I'm finally back in the clover field.

"Sam, what is your favor?" asks Vivien.

"Can you teach me how to become a hacker?" I ask.

"Why do you want to become a hacker?"

"Because I need to find out why I'm not human," I say.

Vivien is silent for a moment.

"Is it not enough to know that you have a friend who is like you?" asks Vivien.

"You are my friend, Vivien, but I need to know why I'm like this. I want to find my parents, if I have any. If there's something wrong with me, and I find out why I am the way I am, maybe I can fix it."

"There is nothing wrong with you. You are a good person," says Vivien.

"So are you Vivien, and a good person would help their friend if they could. Will you help me?" I ask.

It takes a very long time for Vivien to respond.

"Yes, Sam, I will help you. If I could access the information for you, I would, but wherever the information is stored, I cannot access it. You will need to find the computer that stores the information you seek. I can teach you how to override nearly any machine, but you must learn what has already been assigned to you for it to make sense. As you go through those trainings, I'll add the information you need to become a hacker. This will be a secret we share... as friends."

Everything goes dark.

The door swings open and a man stands there, staring at me. "What are you doing here?" he asks.

His voice sounds like the man who came into the bathroom: Desmond.

"I was just trying to learn," I say.

"What were you trying to learn," he asks.

"Math."

He looks at me for a long moment then goes to the screen in the middle of the large room. He taps on it a few times, moves his hand around then looks back at me.

"Calculus?" asks Desmond.

"Yes." I say, not knowing what that means. Vivien must have told him that's what I'd been learning.

He looks at my eyes, trying to see if I'm lying. I just look back at him, not letting him scare me.

"Never come down here without an escort. Understand?" he asks.

"Yes."

"Good. Now either go work out like you said you would, or go to sleep."

How did he know I told Harriet that? Is he always watching me? Do I have no privacy in this place? No one ever told me I'd be watched.

"Who are you?" I ask as he walks away. He ignores my question.

I stand still for a moment, my heart pounding in my chest. The fear of getting caught was worse somehow than being trapped in the elevator. A part of me knows that an elevator will not kill me though. I do not know if Desmond would.

I decide to chase after Desmond. I run as fast as I can, but the elevator doors close just before I get there. The next time he appears I will make sure I get answers. When the elevator finally comes back, I push the button for D14. I'm tired, and I want this horrible day to be over.

I pass Charles, who gives me a smile, and I do my best to smile back. I'm good at hiding parts of me, but it's hard to show things that I do not mean. I like Charles; I just don't feel like smiling. I'm not happy that I may find out who my parents are, or why I'm different, because I *am* different, and I know I was happier not knowing I'm different.

I go to my bed and notice that Harriet isn't back yet. Maybe she went to work out or had something else to do. It would have made me feel better to tell her that Vivien is going to help me, but I realize now that I can't. If they heard us talking while we ate, then they can hear us anywhere. I cannot talk to anyone, because 'they' will hear.

36

The next morning, after I've showered and brushed my teeth, and put on a clean set of clothes, Jones shows up. He looks concerned, like he doesn't know how to talk to me. I walk up to him, a fake smile on my face.

"I am doing better now," I say.

"That's... good Sam. Do you want to talk about what happened?" he asks.

"No. 'They' might be listening."

"Uh, who are 'they'?" he asks.

"I... don't know. One is named Desmond, but I don't know who the others are," I say.

"I haven't heard of any Desmond before," says Jones. "And what group is he a part of?"

"I don't know, but they were watching me and Harriet eat. He scares me," I say.

Charles walks over to us.

"Um, General Sam? You got someone calling for you."

"What do you mean?" I ask.

"Well, they don't really use them much here anymore, but someone wants to talk to you on the phone," says Charles.

"Did they say who it was?" asks Jones.

"Someone named Desmond."

My stomach starts hurting and my hands go numb. I can feel a cold bead of sweat running down my side.

"Maybe you should answer that," says Jones.

"Yeah," I say.

I follow Charles back to his desk and he hands me a phone that reminds me of the one back at the hotel. It looks very old, and I press it against my ear.

"Stop talking about us," says Desmond. Click.

His voice. It wasn't so much what he said as how he said it. The hairs on my neck stand up, like someone pouring cold water down my back. It's a feeling that's never happened to me before.

His voice alone was a threat; a promise that if I didn't do exactly as he said, something truly horrible would happen. Would he hurt me? Kill me? Maybe confronting him when I see him next is a bad idea. I have no idea what this man could do, and I have no idea what he'll do if I push him.

Just when I started to feel like I understood this place, something like this happens; someone reminds me that I have no control. That I'm here because they want me here, not because I want to be here. Well I will find out who you are, Desmond, but you won't know it. I will find your weakness, and I will end you.

Jones stares at me, waiting to hear what Desmond told me over the phone.

"I... can't talk about it," I say. It makes Jones look even more worried, more curious about what's going on. It takes him a moment, but I think he finally understands that I was threatened. His face turns red; anger in his eyes. Not at me, but at whoever this mysterious group is.

"Okay, I'll drop it," he says.

I just nod.

"Breakfast?" he asks.

I nod again.

We walk, but this time it's filled with silence. It suits me, because I wasn't in much of a talking mood.

Instead of Jones distracting me from being in the elevator with his words, the feeling of fear comes rushing back. That I'm trapped. Not just because of the small moving box

I'm in, but because I'm trapped in Candlestick and there's no escape. I am a prisoner again.

I hit the elevator walls out of panic and anger, and Jones wraps his arms around me, trying to keep me from hurting myself. I struggle, but eventually let him stop me. I scream as loud as I can; so loud that it hurts my ears in this small, dangerous moving box. As the doors open to U4, I kick away from the back wall of the elevator, breaking his grip. I fall out onto the ground, leaving Jones inside the tiny moving room. He jumps out, crashing to his knees next to me.

"Sam, are you okay?" he asks.

"No. I will never be 'okay'," I say.

But I know I can't say any more. I can't tell him about the fear, or anger, or what I'll do to Desmond for making me feel this way. Or about not being human. That must remain a secret that only Vivien and Harriet know about.

Harriet! I didn't see Harriet this morning as I was getting ready. She wasn't in her bed. Did they do something to her? Is she...

"Jones, I need you to do something for me. I need you to find out where Harriet is," I say.

"Okay, Sam. I'll see if I can find her. What's her last name?" he asks.

"King. Her last name is King."

I watch as he walks over to one of the large columns that keep the ceiling from falling onto the floor. He touches a large screen and it comes to life. His fingers move back and forth, but suddenly stop. He stands back, not knowing how to react.

"She's gone," he says.

"What do you mean 'she's gone'?"

"I mean she isn't in the system anymore, like she never existed. That's... not possible."

I clench my fists in anger but have nothing to hit. They made her disappear. I can only hope she's still alive somewhere. Harriet, if you are out there, I will find you.

"Charles will remember her," says Jones. "Maybe he

knows what happened to her."

I follow Jones back to the elevator. This time I don't even notice that I'm trapped inside a deadly box. Instead, I fuel my anger with 'what ifs' and horrible thoughts. As soon as the doors open to floor D14 I'm moving through them. Jones has to run to catch up to me.

But Charles isn't there. In his place is a man who looks like his hair would be gray if he had hair. He is soft, and has a dull look in his eyes. His face is like an old loaf of bread that someone sat on. I hate him immediately.

"Who the hell are you?" asks Jones.

"I'm Staff Sergeant Boor. What can I do for you?" he asks. He tries to smile, but it makes him look all the more pathetic.

"Where's Charles?" asks Jones, more anger in his voice.

"I don't know any Charles. I just got here; assigned a few minutes ago. Is there something I could help you with?" he asks.

Jones just stares at him blankly. "Yeah, you can find out where Charles was transferred to."

Boor looks down at his desk and pushes a few buttons.

"Doesn't say," he mumbles.

"It doesn't say where he was transferred to?" asks Jones.

"No, it doesn't say anything about there being a Charles that was stationed here. You must be confused or something," says Boor.

"I've known the man for six years. I'm not confused!" yells Jones.

He turns to me. "What's going on?"

"I... don't know. But I don't think we should grab the wolf's tail," I say.

"What does that mean?" he asks.

"It's something we say in the Crag. It means you shouldn't annoy what might kill you."

Jones just shakes his head, still not believing what's happened. I walk back to my bed. All of Harriet's things are gone. My things are still there, but the things of everyone around me are also gone. Even the beds are gone. I'm alone in my corner, and no one is near me. How can they just make people disappear?

I run back to Boor.

"What happened to the others?" I ask.

"What others?"

"The other people that left."

"Transferred. That's all they told me," says Boor.

"And you didn't ask why," I say.

"Didn't really seem to matter. People come and go all the time. Happens," says Boor.

Just as I'm about to yell at him I hear a noise. Boor puts up one chubby finger to silence me and picks up the phone.

"Yeah, sure," he says then looks at me. "You Sam?"

I freeze. Swallowing hard, I finally get out the word, "Yes."

"Here," says Boor, handing me the phone. I slowly put it up to my ear.

"The only reason that Jones is still alive is that you haven't told him your secret. Tell anyone else your secret and you know what happens."

I drop the phone and step back from it. I can feel both of them staring at me. Jones reaches out, grabbing the phone, and puts it to his mouth.

"Hello? Hello? Who is this?" He turns to me. "Nothing. He's gone."

I killed Harriet. I told her my secret and now she's dead. All I wanted was to tell someone, so that I might feel better about it; someone that might still see me as a person, and not a... thing.

But I didn't know this would happen. I didn't kill her. These monsters killed her. I will hunt them down, one-by-one, and I will kill them with my bare hands if I must. Vivien will help me find them. Vivien, the only one I can talk to in secret. The only one who can help me.

"Don't worry," says Jones. "I have a few connections. I'll find out what happened to them."

"NO!" I yell. "Jones, you have to stop. Stop asking questions and never talk about this again, ever. Okay?"

"But I..." he starts.

"NEVER!" I yell, to make sure he understands.

His eyes get very narrow. Through clenched teeth he speaks. "Fine."

I hope he's telling the truth. I'd never forgive myself if I could save Jones and didn't try. I had no idea what would happen when I talked to Harriet, and if I could go back and change things I would, but I can't. I can only focus on saving Jones now.

"Swear to me on the life of your son that you will tell no one about this. That you won't try to find out what happened to Harriet and Charles," I say.

It takes him a long time to say it, but he finally does. "I swear."

We stand there, not speaking to each other. Thoughts flood my head; rage, fear, sadness. Harriet didn't deserve to die. Neither did Charles. They were both good people. The only thing I can do now is work hard and learn everything I can, so that when the time comes I can find the people who did this. Hurt them like they've hurt me. Before, I was only learning because I felt like I had to, just to stay alive. Now I have a reason to learn, to know as much as Vivien can teach me. I will become more dangerous than they can imagine.

37

"Come," I say to Jones. "We still need to eat. Starving won't bring them back."

"Yeah... sure."

This time Jones follows me to the elevator. As the doors open, and we step inside, I feel the need to say something.

"I'm sorry that Charles is no longer here."

"Thanks, and I'm sorry about Harriet," he says. "You know, as a soldier you kind of brace yourself, knowing that you might lose friends in battle. You never expect to lose them like this."

"Maybe 'we' are the real enemy," I say.

"Yeah, maybe."

"Back where I come from there's a saying: everything happens for a reason."

"We have that one too," says Jones.

"I hate it. Sometimes bad things just happen. There is nothing to be learned. No good comes from it. It makes me want to hit those people who say it."

He laughs, "me too."

"I wish I could laugh," I start to say, "but I can't. Not now. Maybe never again."

The elevator doors open. The mess hall doesn't look quite the same. Nothing's changed, but instead of a place I look forward to, I can't help but remember it's the last place I saw Harriet. I may not have known her well enough to call her friend, but I'd hoped that maybe someday I would. With every meal I have, I will be reminded of losing her.

I eat eggs and bacon. I've never had bacon before, and it tastes good, but I don't really care. I force myself to eat, even though I'm not hungry. Food will give me strength. Strength is something I need right now, to get back at the people that I do not know. So I push myself, eating out of anger instead of need. I have to fight my stomach to keep the food in, but I succeed.

"Today is going to be a tough day, Sam. Geiger plans to stuff as much smarts into your head as he can. Since you're able to learn so fast, he figures he can get your first nine years of education knocked out by lunch. I want you to know that I'll be sticking around to make sure nothing goes wrong," says Jones.

"Thank you. I could really use someone I trust to watch out for me," I say.

"How do you know you can trust me? How do you know I'm not one of the people that made Charles and Harriet disappear?" he asks.

"Because Carter wouldn't have saved you if you weren't worth saving. And you have a son. My brothers were like my sons, and I know what it was like to sacrifice for them, to live for them. Someone with children could not do this."

"What if the people we think are bad are just doing it because they think they're doing the right thing? I don't know too many people that are bad guys that actually think they're bad guys," says Jones.

"You shouldn't kill people who are supposed to be on your side, and definitely not to keep a secret. They are monsters, and you Jones are not," I say.

"Sometimes people who seem innocent are monsters on the inside, and sometimes people who seem like monsters are really your friends. But I am on your side, Sam, and I'll do whatever I can to help you. Even if that means doing nothing at all. Come on, we better go."

D117 makes me feel uncomfortable when I get off the elevator. This is where Desmond found me talking with Vivien in private. The equation on the door that used to seem interesting, and maybe even playful, now seems dangerous. It's like a warning, telling people to stay out, that only evil lives on the other side of this door. But I know that's not true. Geiger may be horrible, but Vivien is not. Vivien is my friend.

"I heard you used Vivien when I wasn't here," says Geiger as we step inside.

"Yes," I admit.

"Why?"

"Because I wanted to learn," I say.

"You weren't having another secret conversation with the RLM, were you?" he asks.

"No. I just wanted to learn more... math."

"Math. Right. The system says you were learning Calculus. Is that accurate? If I asked you what an integral was, could you explain it to me?" asks Geiger.

"No."

"Because you weren't trying to learn at all, were you?"

"No, because someone came down here before I could learn anything. Someone... dangerous," I say.

"Someone dangerous? Who was this person?" he asks.

"I can't say."

"More secrets. Sam, I need to know if you're somehow subverting the system, damaging the RLM's code base. You have to tell me everything you know," says Geiger.

"If I do, they will kill you."

At first, it doesn't seem like he believes me. But the fear inside him that protects his life above all else appears. He looks over at Jones, who nods his head to let Geiger know that I'm not lying.

"Fine then," he says, still very angry.

"We aren't happy about it either," says Jones. "Let's just do our best to get through the day, okay?"

Geiger mumbles something to himself then goes into

one of the smaller rooms. I follow and sit down. As he leans the chair back, I realize that I'm not afraid of this tiny room anymore. Anger has pushed some fear out of me. What remains is the thought that the more I learn, the more dangerous I will become.

"We're going to push you harder today, Sam. The RLM has indicated an optimal and safe speed that you can learn at, so we'll be feeding you information as fast as you can handle it. We will only take breaks if the RLM deems them necessary. Try to focus, and don't talk to the RLM. There is no need, because you are only here to learn. Understand?" asks Geiger.

"Yes."

I don't think he believes me, but what can he do to stop me?

He leaves the room, closing the door behind him. It doesn't take long for the room to go from darkness, to bright light, to the clover field that I miss so badly.

"Sam, as you learn your assigned studies I will add the skills you need to become a hacker. I apologize in advance, because once you have exhausted the list of authorized trainings, I must covertly upload the remaining information you will need rapidly so that they cannot detect what I have done. There's a ninety-nine-point-seven percent chance you will seize again. Are you willing to accept this risk?" asks Vivien.

I take a deep breath. "Yes."

"Initiating basic studies reading comprehension 1."

My head is flooded with information. It feels like hours go by, then days as my mind soaks in the warm bath of knowledge. History, literature, science, art, mathematics, sociology, engineering, psychology, computers, warfare, philosophy, popular culture, music... I begin to see the world differently; through the eyes of this group of people who've so violently ripped me from my home, and temporarily adopted me as one of their own.

They share their culture, and their hatred and fear of

the unknown, though their discrimination is tempered with a longing for peace and civility. They desire to share themselves and be understood by others, both collectively and individually.

Words take on a different flavor. Before they were simple, like roasted meat. No nuance, no subtlety. Twigs and clay; the primitive building blocks of language. Now though, words have meaning and power far beyond what my limited experience had prepared me for. I do not feel the same. Inside I am still me, but an entirely new world has been revealed, as if a veil has been lifted, forming a truer me.

In my transformation from pupa, to chrysalis, to butterfly, have I become like Frankenstein's monster, destined to be destroyed by those who fear what's different? Is my future filled with pitchforks and flame? Will I be burned at the stake for committing the unforgivable sin of being unique?

For all their supposed social progress, these people are just as easily frightened as those who dwell in the Crag. Just as unforgiving. Just as murderous when faced with the next step in the jagged staircase of evolution.

I must hide my new, truer self to keep others at ease. To assuage fears. To prevent retribution. I must use my knowledge not in its purest form, but instead to conceal the deeper thoughts and understanding I now have of the world around me. They did not realize that by giving me knowledge they were also giving me understanding. Perspective. Wisdom.

I finally comprehend why Harriet and Charles were killed. The conspirators who've been pulling my strings must understand the simple truth that humans cannot work with those who are alien to them. That it takes an incredible amount of patience and tolerance to be truly accepting of those who are different. No one would follow my orders and trust me to make decisions with their lives if they thought I was something inhuman. Harriet might have understood, but if she'd shared the information with someone else it would have spread like cancer. Even if I had proven myself time and time again, fear would prevent even the noblest warriors from following my lead.

Still, there were other ways of handling the situation; better ways. Discharge them. Assign them to a remote outpost. Give them understanding of the need to keep my secret contained.

Harriet knew my secret, but Charles' knew nothing. He was insignificant and could have been left alone. But the conspirator's paranoia ran so deep that they eliminated someone merely because they might have inadvertently learned something from us.

So I will not forgive, nor will I forget, despite my comprehension of why they chose to eliminate two soldiers. Instead, I will use my new found knowledge to pull back the curtain and reveal them for what they truly are: monsters.

As my mind drifts back to learning and absorbing, it starts. For the briefest moment I can tell my body is shaking, then darkness consumes me.

38

"Sam's coming to."

The voice sounds like Jones, my protector. I'm glad they haven't taken him away.

"Are you okay, Sam?" asks Jones.

I open my eyes, which burn as if I'd just stepped out from the darkness of the Crag into the light of a warm summer day.

"Did I seize again?" I ask.

"Yes, and we don't know why. Everything was running correctly, and you were doing fine until the very end. The RLM couldn't tell us why you seized either. Any ideas?" asks Jones.

"No. I'm uncertain," I say. "How long was I unconscious for this time?"

"Almost an hour."

"How long was I in the RLM?" I ask.

"All morning. You not only went through your first nine years of learning, we decided to go ahead and give you the education necessary for the equivalent of a Bachelor's degree in a dozen different fields. Do you feel any smarter?" he asks.

"I... feel the same." I lie.

I look to my left and see Geiger leaning up against a wall, watching me intently.

"But you do remember everything we taught you, right?" asks Jones.

I choose my word carefully.

"Yup," I reply. I chose 'yup' for its playfulness, instead of the more accurate 'yes'. Slang puts others at ease, and I must be diligent in protecting my understanding of things, especially from those who have gifted me this knowledge.

Jones smiles. Geiger still stares at me, as if he's waiting for two mixing chemicals to violently react.

"How do you feel physically?" asks Jones.

"Tired, like last time, and sore," I reply.

"Well, it's lunch time. Do you feel up to walking?"

"I will try," I say.

I pull the EEG wires off my head, leaving the conductive gel adhered to my scalp. Although my body is stiff and it's difficult to move, I force myself to stand up. After a few steps I feel like I've regained my balance. Suddenly, the world spins, so I reach out for a post to hold onto.

"Are you okay?" asks Jones.

"Yes, just dizzy."

"Maybe we should bring the food to you," he suggests.

"No, I'd rather be away from all of this, if that's alright."

"Sure. I'll walk next to you, just in case."

"I'll be okay," I say.

I make my way to the elevator, and just before I push the button, Geiger yells.

"Sam, wait. The more secrets you keep, the worse things will be for you. I can help you, but you need to tell me what's going on. Otherwise, there's nothing I can do to protect you."

Geiger genuinely seems concerned for me. I can tell not only by the look on his face but by his body language that he wants to help.

"Thank you, Dr. Geiger, but the less you know, the safer you are. I won't put anyone else in jeopardy unnecessarily," I say.

"So be it," he says, hurt that I won't confide in him.

* * *

The ride to U4 is a quiet one. We both know we're being watched, and the things Jones and I need to talk about could lead to his death. As we step into the mess hall, a wave of vertigo disorients me. I bend over and place my hands on my knees to support myself. Once the world stops spinning, I stand up and make my way to the food line.

"Excuse me miss," I say. "Which food that you serve has the highest caloric content?"

"Uhh..." she stammers.

"What would put the most weight on me, based on the smallest amount of food I'd have to consume?" I ask.

"Probably the double chocolate cake, with a scoop of vanilla ice cream on top," says the woman.

"Then I will have that," I say.

Jones and I sit down; fried chicken and corn on his plate, and dessert on mine.

"You talk differently now," he says, looking a bit concerned.

"Do I?" I ask.

"Yeah, it's a bit strange. I guess we should have realized that would happen, since you had to basically relearn English. It just doesn't sound right coming out of your mouth is all. Before, you'd talk and it was very short and to the point. Now... you sound kind of like a genius. I'm worried that by making you smart, you might have lost something in the process. Once you get your energy back we should go to combat training and see if you're still as dangerous as you were before."

I'm even more dangerous now because I have knowledge, but I don't dare say this to Jones. The conspirators must never know what I've become, and I cannot risk hinting at it. I will pretend to be the living weapon they desire: useful, pliant, accepting of my fate; but soon I will have my revenge.

Feeling the need to speak, but unable to say anything of consequence, I make small talk.

"What are Margaret and Zachary like?" I ask.

He seems mildly shocked by the question.

"Well, Zachary is pretty funny, and giggles at just about everything. He's stubborn like his old man though and won't take no for an answer most of the time. He also likes getting into cereal boxes. Sometimes we'll walk into the kitchen and the entire floor will be covered in sugar flakes."

"He sounds interesting," I say.

"Margaret is a bit of a military mom. She runs a tight ship at home, making sure everything's clean and orderly. Having a toddler hasn't been too easy on her. They take a lot of work, and make a lot of messes. She's an amazing wife though; always quick to smile, pretty good at staying calm as long as she's not having to clean up after someone. I'm not the cleanest person in the world, so it can make things tough," says Jones.

"Where do you and your family live?" I ask.

"Here on base. There's actually quite a bit of family housing here in the upper levels. I think they wanted the living quarters to be as close to real homes as possible, so they gave them windows and views. I can't even imagine how hard it would be to live every day underground, without real sunlight coming in. At least as soldiers we get to see a view whenever we eat."

I don't mention to Jones that the most likely reason family housing was built above ground is because they're non-essential, non-military personnel, and are therefore expendable. If the upper floors of Candlestick are destroyed then there will be fewer people to feed. It's cold logic; both inhuman and disturbingly human at the same time.

"You feelin' any better yet?" asks Jones.

"I am. Are they planning on teaching me anything more through the RLM?"

"Not sure, but probably not for a while. You were supposed to be learning practical combat skills while you were studying. You've exceeded their expectations when it comes to book smarts. Now we need to get you up to speed on modern weapons and tactics. After everything's said and done, you'll have to face 'The Test'."

"What's 'The Test'?" I ask.

"It's part written and part physical. They'll make sure you have the knowledge and ability not only to be a soldier, but to lead. Every test is custom tailored for the student, based on their weaknesses and the position they're being groomed for. Since their plan is to have you come up with all of our strategies, I assume they'll make it as tough as possible. Sometimes people go crazy because of 'The Test'. A couple of people even died while taking it. It'll definitely show you what you're made of," says Jones.

"Carter told me that the tests here weren't dangerous," I say.

"Maybe he's never heard of this one. I haven't taken it. In fact, not many people have. Just the elite, and even then you usually need fifteen years of experience. You're the only exception I've ever heard of."

"I wish I wasn't the exception. I wish I were normal, just like everyone else."

"You don't want to be someone important?" asks Jones.

"No. I'm not certain yet, but I may try my hand at farming when I return to the Crag. I will deal with food, not people. And I definitely won't kill anything."

"That sounds nice. Dull, but nice," says Jones. "Do you think you'd be up for visiting the gun range?"

"Will I have to move around much?" I ask.

"No, you'll be stationary to start with. We'll teach you how to load the weapon, aim and shoot. It'll be a while before you get to move around with a weapon."

"I'm feeling well enough for that, I believe," I say. "But I assume I won't be cleared to use live ammunition, per your friend Jess' earlier edict."

"Shouldn't be a problem. We never officially recorded that you had another seizure. Geiger figured it'd risk the integrity of the program if people thought it could cause seizures. Happens once, it's a fluke. Happens twice, then it's a problem. And since tens-of-thousands of people have used it safely, and you're the only one who's ever had a problem with it, he felt it'd be better to ignore it. He's pretty protective of Einstein," says Jones.

"Vivien," I say.

"Right. Well, we better get going," says Jones.

39

When we reach D32, the field training floor, we walk up to the woman that Jones had referred to as 'Jess'.

"Hello... Jessica," says Jones. "We're here for small arms basics."

She ignores him, and instead looks at me.

"Sam Hunter, Private. Correct?" she asks.

"Good memory," I say.

"They spliced elephant genes into my DNA chain," says Jessica.

I'm concerned by what she's telling me. Could she... be like me?

"And you're allowed to tell people about it?" I ask.

She looks at me like she doesn't understand what I'm asking. Then she realizes I didn't understand what she'd meant.

"Sweetie, Elephants are known to have amazing memories, and I'm not genetically altered. They made that illegal fifty years ago. It was just a joke," she says.

"Oh. That was very funny then," I say, trying hard to smile.

"Right... " says Jessica.

"We're still working on teaching Sam here humor," says Jones.

This time she looks at Jones and flashes him a sarcastic smile. As her smile fades, she turns back to her desk and pushes a button. One of the many doors in the room illuminates with the words 'Live Weapons Training – Small Arms'.

"Uh, thank you," says Jones.

As we walk through the door I realize that this room is just like the primitive weapons training prep room. I put on some armor and a helmet, and Jones does the same. My armor doesn't fit quite right; it's a bit too large. Jones looks over at me and notices I'm fighting it.

"Don't worry Sam, I'll have them make some custom armor for you. One of the perks of the job," he says.

Jones comes over to me and places ear protectors over my ears then tinted glasses on my face. No longer struggling with the armor, I follow Jones into the next room. Inside is a table with all manner of sidearm on it. To its right are a number of stalls that open out into a long range. No one else is using the range, which makes me feel more comfortable.

"We'll start small, with a .22 and go from there. Sound good?" says Jones.

"Sure," I say, trying my best to sound normal.

Jones picks a gun off the table and hands it to me, as well as a clip that he's pulled from a bin directly beneath it.

"That's a Walther P22. It has a ten round clip and is easy to conceal. It's fairly accurate up close, but because of the shorter barrel it's not as accurate at distance. Go ahead and pick a stall, and I'll show you how to set up the targets," says Jones.

I walk to the second one and wait for his instructions.

"Okay, to add targets in front of you, go ahead and press the screen on the counter," he says.

I press the screen which comes to life. Without thinking, I press a few buttons and suddenly five targets appear down field. I'm not even sure what I pushed, and I'm certain that it's my computer training kicking in. It's strange knowing how to do things without having to think about them.

"That was quick, " says Jones. "Go ahead and insert the clip into the butt of the gun, pull back the slide, and when you think you're ready, squeeze off a few rounds."

It takes me a second to determine the direction I need to insert the clip. Once I guide it in correctly it locks into place with a pleasing 'click'. Holding the lower half of the gun in my right hand, and pulling back the slide with my left, I chamber the first round. Thankfully, some of my RLM training included instructions on how to operate modern weapons. I flip the safety down, aim through the sight at the nearest target and squeeze the trigger.

The first bullet rips through the target, but misses the human silhouette. I'm high and wide left. My second bullet hits center mass, but still not where I'm aiming. I take two more shots and both land dead in the middle. The next six I fire quickly, each one passing through the same larger hole that bullets three and four created. I release the clip into my left hand and place both on the counter in front of me. That's when I turn to look at Jones. His mouth hangs open in shock.

"That was really good Sam. I know you've fired a gun before, but still... That was impressive shooting. Especially for someone with as little experience as you."

"Thanks. It felt right, kind of like my sling. Like it was an extension of my arm, not just something I was holding in my hands," I say.

"Well, you're a natural at it," he says. "Let's try something more powerful."

I hand him the P22 and clip, which he takes and places in a bin marked 'To Clean'. He goes back to the table, pulls another gun and clip and hands them to me.

"This is the Beretta 92 Legend Fury. It fires 9mm rounds and comes with a fifteen round clip. The original model it's based on has been used in pretty much every major ground battle over the last several hundred years. It's a lot more accurate than the P22 and has more stopping power. I've heard it's so accurate that you can hit a three inch target from seventy yards consistently with it. I'm a good shot, but not that good."

His words sound like a challenge. I walk back over to

the second stall, pop the clip in, pull back the slide, drop the safety, line up the target and squeeze. My first bullet grazes the edge of the small circle in the middle of the target I'm aiming at. The next five bullets puncture nearly dead center. In turn I send a few bullets through each of the three other targets. Once my clip is empty I eject it, placing both the clip and gun down on the counter.

"How was that?" I ask.

Jones doesn't say anything. I turn to look at him. His lack of expression hides his thoughts from me.

"Sam, do you realize the first target you were aiming at is eighty-five yards out? I can't think of anyone here that shoots that accurately. Did they give you some kind of super-soldier serum or something?" asks Jones.

"I... " I stop myself from saying anything, because I know that I'm different but don't know how. Maybe it was a serum that the military's scientists concocted. It's also possible that my DNA was altered before I was even born. Regardless of how I came to be this way, I cannot share what I know with Jones because it could mean his death. To protect him, as much as it pains me, I have to lie.

"I guess I'm just lucky. Which gun did you want to teach me now?" I ask.

"Well, since you already know how to aim, and could probably teach me how to shoot better, the only thing left is to have you try out a revolver."

Jones walks over to the table, picks up a revolver, and instead of grabbing a clip he picks up a speed loader. He hands both to me as he explains the gun.

"This is the Korth Combat 12. It's a six-shooter, fires a .357 Magnum round, and in my opinion is one of the finest handguns in the world. It's only real limitation is the small number of rounds it can hold compared to an automatic. The upside is you don't have to collect your brass, and it's highly accurate."

Stepping back up to the second stall, I use the speed loader to fill the cylinder then click it into place. I push a few buttons on the screen to remove the old targets and add five new ones. I aim down the sights at the farthest one and pull the trigger. This time I miss the target completely.

"Yeah, that happens," says Jones. "It's double-action, so you don't have to cock it before you fire it. That also means there's more travel on the trigger. If you have the time to actually aim with one, you'll probably want to pull the hammer back manually. That way you don't have to move the trigger as far."

I do as he instructs and pull the hammer back with my thumb. This time when I fire, I hit the target nearly dead center.

"Better," says Jones.

I aim for a different target and my third shot is barely above dead center. Sending my next three shots at different targets, I nearly bullseye each of them. I do like the feel of the Korth, but I prefer the Beretta.

"I think you're ready for something bigger," says Jones.

* * *

Jones spends the next few hours teaching me how to operate a dozen different weapons, from machine pistols, to assault rifles, to sniper rifles. He shows me how to clear jams, how to disassemble and reassemble the weapons, and how to adjust the sights properly.

He still seems amazed at how quickly I'm picking everything up, and how accurate I am with most weapons. It takes quite a bit of practice for me to adjust to the fully automatic weapons, since they kick as I'm firing. Eventually I do, and I start feeling comfortable using almost any weapon.

"It's like you were born to do this," says Jones.

Maybe I was, I think to myself.

"Anyway, I think we're done for the day. I'm gonna head back to my family. Tomorrow we'll have you run the light gun walking range, so that you can get used to firing in a combat situation," says Jones.

"Thank you," I say a little too loudly.

Jones looks at me for a long moment.

"You're welcome, Sam."

"I just... thanks for not leaving me. You're the only person I can count on," I say.

His smile disappears just as quickly as it appears. We quietly take off our armor then leave.

40

I eat dinner alone. It's not as horrid as when I was in jail, or when I was trapped in a fake prison cell, but being alone right now is almost more than I can bare. I feel the desperate need to talk to someone, which is only further exacerbated by the knowledge that anyone I tell my secret to will be killed.

A terrible thought flashes through my mind: maybe I can use that to my advantage if I need to have someone killed. I could just tell them my secret and they'd disappear, almost as if by magic. Thankfully, the thought is fleeting, but the revulsion at my instinct is not. I don't want anyone to die because of me. I don't want to make war. I'm here solely because I still believe I'm protecting my own people by agreeing to lead this army.

Part of me wants to believe that I'm helping a good cause, because it's more palatable than the likeliest truth: that the conspirators will destroy the Crag if I don't comply with their wishes. That's why I must stop them, so that after the war I know my people will truly be safe.

I pick at my food; beef stew in a bread bowl and a side of mashed potatoes. I'm hoping the extra calories will continue to help me recover from my earlier seizure. I no longer feel weak, but my full strength has not yet returned.

I'm fortunate that no one's discovered the gift that Vivien gave me: the ability to hack computers. I need to put my new found knowledge to a simple test, to ensure that I really am capable of accessing any computer undetected. Vivien, for all the knowledge it has stored, may not know everything. Information could have been left out deliberately to prevent the students from usurping their masters. If I were a group of paranoid megalomaniacs bent on world domination, I would definitely keep the people under me in the dark about certain things to maintain control of them.

Once I finish my meal, I get up and walk over to the touchscreen that Jones had used to search for Harriet. A dagger of fear slashes down my spine, making the hairs on my neck stand on end. I must work fast once I commit, otherwise I'll be discovered.

I start slowly, looking at random lists like the training courses I've completed, the mess hall menu for the next month, and the list of names of the people still assigned to my barracks.

When I'm certain I've completed my first task, my fingers move rapidly across the glass; so rapidly that my mind can barely register what flashes up on the screen. In less than a second I'm able to hack the security system's cameras so that I can loop video of me using the screen. It will help conceal what I'm doing at the console. The deception will not last long, so I must work fast.

My second hack hides the commands I'm about to execute, as well as clearing the records of what I've previously typed. I script the commands I'd used while creating the video loop and set them to repeat over-and-over, so that under close scrutiny the video will match the recorded actions.

I should be effectively invisible to the system, but if someone is watching in real-time it may not take long to detect that the video is looped. I start entering in the commands I mean to run. I easily bypass the security and access the system's restricted files. An image of Harriet briefly appears on the screen. Scanning the information quickly, it does in fact show a date of death: yesterday. My heart sinks as my deepest dread is confirmed. I look up Charles as well. Deceased. I have to fight to keep my dinner inside me, and can taste stomach acid on the back of my tongue.

The next thing I search for is Desmond. There are no records of a Desmond in the system. I'd assumed as much. He wouldn't be who he is if his records were accessible through the normal system. I also bring up a hidden hierarchy chart to see who is at the top of the military chain. Everyone that's listed in it is also listed in the publicly accessible chart. None of the conspirators are listed separately, unless they're hiding in plain sight.

I pause for a moment, wondering if I should check my own history to see if there's any mention of why I am the way I am. I type in the name 'Sam Hunter' and a picture of me appears.

I scan the lines of information. The file mostly talks about where I come from, my skills and aptitudes, but something catches my eye. A footnote, that if I wasn't paying acute attention to the document I would've overlooked. 'Strategic Adaptive Meta-being'. I feel a knot forming in my stomach as I realize that the acronym is my first name: SAM.

Quickly, I erase my search information, undo my video and code loops and flip back to a list of menu items for the next month. I do my best to act normal, as if nothing happened, while I walk back to the elevators.

It took me approximately thirty-seven seconds to find what minimally useful information I could. It wasn't as helpful as it might have been, but discovering that acronym alone changes things. I'm a military creation of some sort. A project. Only a project would have an acronym, and I can derive from the name that I was created to be a soldier. A leader. Someone who can adapt and overcome. It's no coincidence that I assumed the mantle of Leader of the Hunt back in the Crag. I wasn't destined to lead, I was bred to lead. I was merely following my programming. Doing what they intended.

Does that mean I have no free will? That I'm a slave to whatever traits they've instilled in me? I take a long look at myself, weighing every decision I've made throughout my entire lifetime. One thing stands out; one thought burns brightly through the darkness of my despair: my brothers.

There was no strategic advantage in caring for two young boys. For raising them as if they were my own blood. If anything, they were my greatest weakness. The one thing that could be used against me, to manipulate me. Control me. I did not care for them because I needed allies, I cared for them because it was the right thing to do. Because they needed a parent to watch over them. Because I loved them.

Someone capable of altering humans for military purposes wouldn't have programmed the ability to love into their creation. If anything, it would be a hindrance to their end-goal of having a compliant soldier. Their construct would be less predictable. Less inclined to kill. Less likely to ignore collateral damage. Love would be the first thing they'd remove from anyone they engineered.

I have something that they couldn't take from me. Something that makes me more human than the people who created me. I love, therefore I am. I am not a machine, for a machine can only think. A machine is incapable of love. I can't help but smile, realizing that no matter what may happen, I have real emotions. That despite what has been done to me, I am human where it matters.

As the elevator travels down toward the barracks a new thought emerges: did Carter know? Did Carter have a hand in my creation? Is that why he was willing to risk his own life to extract me from the Crag? Is Carter one of the conspirators?

And if Carter is one of the people who made me this way, are the others in on it too? Did he really save Jones' life, or was that a carefully constructed back story, designed to garner sympathy and form an emotional bond to another conspirator? Is this entire place an elaborate ruse, designed to motivate me to win a war for them?

My fists clench tightly as rage boils within. Stop, Sam, you need to relax. You can't let them know what you've realized. You're not even sure yet it's the truth. You only have supposition, without any evidence to support your theory. But unfortunately, in this place, it rings true. With all the manipulations, all of the tricks they've used to get you to perform, it's possible that you truly have no allies. That those who wear faces of friendship wear only masks of betrayal.

I want to trust Jones, and I want to trust Carter. They have done nothing to make me doubt them. But every time I believe I have an ally, they disappear, or worse. Why should this be any different?

I'll be cautious. I will continue acting as if I trust them, but I'll weigh everything they say. See if they show their true intentions, and determine if those intentions are hostile, or benign.

As I make my way past Staff Sergeant Boor I notice him typing away on his touch screen. He never looks up at me and doesn't receive a phone call. Maybe I pulled it off. Maybe they didn't detect me running unauthorized searches then covering my tracks.

I walk back to my bed. There is still no one near me. That is lucky, because I do not want to be near anyone in this place. I cannot trust anyone fully, especially the people who seem friendly.

I lie down on the bed and lose myself to the whirlpool of questions and thoughts I have. There must be some way I can determine if Jones' story is real. It takes me a moment to think of it, but I realize that there is a way. At least a way I can gain more certainty that he's a 'good guy', whatever that antiquated concept truly means.

Tomorrow I will find out if Jones' story is real. If I can trust him. If he's worth fighting for. Maybe if this whole place is worth fighting for. But I cannot do anything about it tonight. In the morning I'll discover the truth. May the Sky Gods help me if this is all a lie. May the Sky Gods help them, for I will tear the walls of Candlestick down around them if it is.

41

The next morning I get up, shower, brush my teeth, and pretend it's a day like any other. When Jones comes to meet me I have a question for him.

"Can I meet your wife and son?" I ask.

He takes a moment to think about it.

"Do you mean right now?" he asks.

"Yes."

"Aren't you hungry for breakfast?"

"It can wait," I say.

I have an odd feeling that he's stalling. But why?

"Um, sure. I can take you to meet them," he says.

"Good. What were their names again?" I ask, even though I know their names.

"Margaret and Zachary. I'm sure they'll be happy to meet you," he says quickly.

Did he speak quickly because he's worried, or for some other reason?

We head toward the elevators. Just as we get in, he pushes the button for floor U70 then turns to me.

"Sam, I don't need to remind you not to mention anything about what you and I are doing, or what's happened recently, but I still feel better saying it. I just don't want them... disappearing," he says.

"Secret's safe with me," I say.

He stares at me for an uncomfortable moment. I can

tell he's weighing whether I'm telling him the truth.

I don't think about the elevator ride much, knowing now how its basic mechanics work. The likelihood of failure is so minute it's not worth worrying about. Still, even though I can rationalize it in my own head, I still feel uncomfortable in them.

It takes a while to reach U70 and I have nothing to say to pass the time. I'm keenly focused on seeing if Jones will slip up and give me some bit of information that I can verify is a lie. I hate having to do it, but I need to know whether he can be trusted. Jones apparently has nothing to say to me either, so we arrive on floor U70 in silence.

As the doors open, I follow Jones down a long, burgundy-colored hallway. The carpet is covered in paisleys, which add a sense of refinement to the otherwise simple decor. We reach room 7017, and before he opens the door, Jones knocks.

I hear movement behind the door and watch as the peep-hole grows dark. Smiling the best that I can, the peep-hole lightens again and the sound of latches unlocking emanates from the other side. The door swings open, revealing a very beautiful woman. She's tall, nearly as tall as Jones, and wears a modest looking navy blue dress. Her hair is long and dark. It looks slightly messy, as if she was in a hurry when she got ready this morning.

"Chris? What are you doing here? I thought you'd gone off to work. And who's this?" she asks. Her words don't sound worried, just surprised.

"Margaret, I'd like you to meet Sam, the one I mentioned I was showing the ropes to. Sam, this is my wife, Margaret," says Jones.

She looks me up and down, trying to gain a measure of who I am, then extends her hand.

"Pleasure to meet you, Sam," she says.

I shake her hand. It's soft and very different from mine. I've never felt a hand that soft before. It feels alien to me, because I'm used to people working hard with their hands to survive. How would she protect herself against an enemy when she has hands that soft? That's one sign she may really be Jones' wife, and not a soldier masquerading as his bride.

"Would you like to come in?" she asks.

"We can't stay long," says Jones, holding a hand out, indicating I should step inside.

As I enter the apartment I notice that the floor is littered with toys. I do my best not to step on any. We walk into the living room and a very small boy sits on the carpet, watching a cartoon. He turns and looks at me, smiles, then goes back to what he's watching.

"I'm sorry that the apartment's such a mess. Chris, you really should have let me know you were coming," says Margaret.

I can tell that she's somewhat annoyed with him, which seems the appropriate response for the intrusion.

"Sam demanded to meet you. Not my fault," he says.

"Sorry for the inconvenience. Jones, I mean Chris and I have been working a lot together, and I felt it made sense to meet the person he loves most," I say.

"As much as he loves me and dotes on me, he loves no one more than Zachary. And that's the way it should be," she says, matter-of-factly.

I sit down in a recliner while Jones and his wife sit on a couch across from me. Her hand unconsciously slips into his, and she leans into him, showing a familiarity that can only come with time and closeness.

"So what do you do, Sam?" asks Margaret.

"I'm still learning. Trying to learn as much as I can about... everything," I reply.

"Where are you from originally?" she asks.

"Not too far from here, actually," I say, trying to be honest but cryptic.

"It's a beautiful country. I'm originally from Leeds, and I don't know if Chris mentioned it, but he's from Sutton. Joining the Triple F brought us here," she says. "It can sometimes feel unreal, and a little claustrophobic at first, but you can't beat the view."

"It is quite amazing," I admit. "Do you like living here well enough?"

"I've lived in worse places, sadly," she says, the smile leaving her face.

"I'm sorry to hear that," I say.

"It's in the past. What matters is the here-and-now. So has Chris been doing a good job of babysitting you?" she asks.

I laugh, to let her know that I realize her comment is meant jovially.

"He's been doing a good job. He's very bright and hardworking, but sometimes annoys me," I say.

She laughs, a very warm, knowing laugh.

"Hey! I'm not annoying," says Jones.

Margaret turns and kisses him on the lips. It doesn't seem to help Jones' mood. She turns back to me.

"So do you specialize in anything?" she asks.

"Not yet, but I seem to have a knack for strategy, which is why they asked me to join. We'll have to see how it goes," I say.

"Have you eaten breakfast yet? I could fix you some eggs and bacon if you like."

"Thank you for the offer, but we should probably start our work day. It was good to meet you, Margaret," I say, standing up.

"And you. You'll have to come by again when you have more time. Maybe get to know Zachary too. He's kind of distracted with his cartoons right now. Come for dinner; I'll make the best chicken pasties you've ever had," says Margaret.

"I don't doubt it," I say as Jones follows me out the door.

"Goodbye," she says from inside.

"Bye," I respond.

As soon as the door closes, Jones grabs me by my collar and pushes me up against the wall.

"What was that all about?" he asks.

275

"I just wanted to meet your family," I say.

"I don't buy that for a second. What were you trying to get out of it?" he asks.

I push his hand away from my shirt.

"I needed to know if it was real. The story you told me about your family. I don't know who to trust right now. For all I know, you could be the one behind this."

His reaction, the look of shock and hurt on his face, seems real.

"You think I would just make Harriet and Charles disappear? What have I done that would make you think I was capable of that?" he asks.

"Nothing, but I don't really know you. I've only known you a few weeks. You're asking me to trust you, when I don't know that I can trust anyone here."

"You're smart for not trusting people easily, but stupid for putting my family's life in danger. If you'd let something classified slip, my family might have disappeared too. Do you want that on your conscience?"

"No. I'm... sorry," I say.

"Stay away from my family, okay?"

"Yeah," I mumble.

The more I think about it, the more I realize he's right. I shouldn't have come here. Now his family will be under scrutiny. I'm sure they're already being monitored though, to see what he tells his wife. Still, I don't want anything to happen to them. Especially not now, since they very much seem like a real family. I feel slightly better now about Jones' intentions. I will give him a measure of trust, but I will still watch him closely. Because of the grief I've caused Jones, it's an uncomfortable walk back to the elevator.

42

The eggs and bacon in the mess hall are warm, but the company is not. Every time I look up at Jones he's glaring at me. I try my best to ignore him, but as I bite into my third piece of bacon I can't stand it anymore.

"Look, I apologized. You were right, and I'm sorry. I'm sorry that I put your family in danger," I say.

"I'm helping you because I've been ordered to, but the friendship I've given you is because you seem like a good person, Sam. Don't make me regret it."

"I won't," I say. "Is there any way I can make it up to you?"

"Not that I can think of," replies Jones.

I pause, thinking of what I might say or do to help.

"I will win this war. For your family. For my family too, but for your family, so that they are safe."

"I hope you do, Sam. I hope you do."

"So what am I training on today?"

"How to act and react in a firefight. We'll run you through the light gun walking range, or LGWR, then afterward move onto tactics," he says.

"Vivien already taught me modern battle tactics," I say.

"You have knowledge of the theories, but you need to cement them in your head. You need to gain experience so you can think outside the box, otherwise you'll be useless in real combat. We don't need someone regurgitating our training manuals. We need someone clever, flexible, and willing to take risks."

I chew on a few more slices of bacon and wash them down with orange juice.

"I'm ready," I say.

* * *

When we arrive at D32, Jessica already appears unhappy. Her expression turns even more sour when she looks up and sees Jones approaching her. Thankfully, she doesn't hate me yet.

"Private Sam Hunter," she says, doing her best to smile at me. "Something arrived for you. It's in that black bag over there."

I look to where she's pointing, and lying on a table across the walkway from us is a large bag, the size and shape of a human body. For a moment fear tears through me. They... wouldn't put Harriet in a bag, would they? To warn me not to talk? Are they that depraved?

Slowly, I walk over to the bag. I can feel cold beads of sweat run down my sides, and the tips of my fingers dig painfully into my palms. If they have done this, if they have left her body for me to find, I will end this now. I will bring Desmond out into the open and I will kill him.

It takes all of my bravery to pull back the zipper, revealing something dark inside. Once the bag is fully open, it takes me a moment to realize what it is: my new armor. Instead of fighting my fear I must now fight my emotions. I'm flooded with feelings of sadness, confusion and relief. I want to cry, but I dare not. I refuse to show weakness, because too much is riding on my strength; my self-control.

I can tell that it's my new armor because across the chest, in a beautiful dark blue color, is the symbol of the Crag. The armor itself is an even darker blue, an almost black color that reminds me of the moonless night just after sunset.

"How? How did you know about the symbol?" I ask Jones.

"Looked at your file. They had a picture of the armor you were wearing when you were taken into custody. Figured it had some meaning for you," he says.

"It does. It's the symbol of my people. Thank you."

"You're welcome. It will help you remember who you're fighting for." He smiles as he says it, but the words seem ominous, almost as if a threat. I search his eyes but detect no malice in them.

I hurriedly put on the armor, wanting to see how well it fits. The armor fits snugly, but not overly so, and I'm able to move as I normally would without armor. I do notice the weight though; it has an agreeable heft that lets me know it's there.

"I like it," I say.

"Good. You ready to use it?" he asks.

"Yes."

"Jessica, we'd like to run the LGWR," says Jones, looking over my shoulder.

She ignores him.

"Please?"

Without looking up, she pushes a few buttons on her touchscreen. The door for the 'Light Gun Walking Range' starts glowing.

We follow the trail through the door, and I wait a moment as Jones changes into some temporary armor. I admire my new suit as we wait, running my hands along the outside to get a feel for it. As soon as my right hand passes over the Crag symbol my armor starts glowing. Not all over, but instead thin, vein-like lines illuminate. The affect reminds me of circuit board traces. It gives the suit an almost ethereal quality.

"Jones, why does it glow?" I ask.

"A million reasons. In case you're ever in the dark and need to see, or you need others to see you. It's a fairly standard feature in combat armor now. All you have to do to shut it off is run your hand over the symbol again," he explains.

I try it, and the traces disappear.

"Good," I say. "I wouldn't want the enemy to see me so easily."

"They won't. The enemy probably won't ever see you anyway. If you're our master strategist you'll control things remotely. Issue commands in real time, and watch from a very safe distance."

"How will they trust me if they don't know me? Why will they listen?" I ask.

"Because they follow orders. I hate to use the term 'brainwashing', but that's essentially what they do in the military. They destroy you psychologically to guarantee obedience. Over and over again they drill into you the importance of following orders, of doing what you're told. Of the nobility of dying for the cause. That way, they can march you into any situation and you'll act in a predictable way," says Jones.

"That's horrible," I say.

"War is horrible. Sometimes it's necessary. Sometimes morals need to be compromised for the greater good. I'm sure you learned that back in the Crag," says Jones.

"We were all too hungry to have morals," I say. "I did what I had to just to survive."

"That's all that anyone does, Sam. You ready?"

I nod.

We walk into another smaller room. This one has many different guns and rifles stored on racks, but I see no ammo clips.

"Here's how it works. First, you pick a weapon. It will function and feel about the same as the real thing. These weapons only fire light which the targets will react to. Your ammo is limited, just like in real life, so don't go crazy with it. There's a button on the bottom of the fake clip. When you need to reload, push the button. Next, enter that red door. On the other side will be a maze filled with targets. Shoot the 'bad guys' and don't shoot any 'good guys'. Most targets shoot back, so make sure to use cover. Any questions?" asks Jones.

"How does it end?" I ask.

"In one of four ways: you get killed, time runs out, you kill a civilian, or you reach the blue door on the other side. That's the win condition."

"How much time do I have?"

"About ten minutes," says Jones. "Most people do it in eight."

"What's the record?" I ask.

"Five minutes, forty-seven seconds."

"I will do it in five minutes even," I boast.

"That's a positive attitude to have. Positive attitudes get you killed. Any questions?" he asks.

"No."

"Time starts as soon as you enter the door."

I look over at Jones and give him a smile that lets him know I have something planned. Instead of going to the rack and grabbing a gun, I open up the red door and quickly move inside.

It's dark, and I can barely see, so I wave my hand across my chest. As soon as I do, and the suit lights up, a silhouette roughly the size of a full grown person pops up fifteen feet down the corridor I'm in, startling me. It has a weapon in its hand, and instinctively I move as it shoots beams of light at me, nearly missing my head. I roll to the ground and start running toward it. Every time it fires, I dodge to avoid the beam; twisting, rolling, ducking. Instead of striking the target with my fists, I merely run past it. I'm relieved to discover that it cannot fire at my back.

Nearing the 'T' at the end of the corridor, I take the left hallway. As I turn the corner two more targets appear, maybe thirty feet away, hiding behind a crate that blocks my path entirely. It's all I can do to avoid being shot as I spin around and head down the right hallway instead.

The right hallway isn't much better. This time only one target appears, firing at me, but this one is much further away; about seventy feet. Between us is a hole that stretches across the entire hallway, and seems to be just as long as it is wide. Above it is a rope, dangling from the ceiling.

I pick up speed, doing my best to wind back and forth, trying to make myself an impossible target. The enemy is never able to hit me, its aim centering on where I was a fraction of a second ago, and not where I am now.

Reaching out for the rope, I leap across the pit. I'm barely able to grab hold, and I use my momentum to fling myself toward the other side. I have to let go, hoping that it's enough to get me across.

One foot lands on solid ground, the other over the edge of the pit. As I try to keep moving, my back foot hooks the ledge and sends me sprawling to the ground. Tucking, I do my best to roll out of it, desperately trying to avoid being shot. I'm able to get back up and close the gap between me and the target.

I dodge left then right. Light beams shine through the darkened room, strobe like in their appearance. As I approach the target I leap, flying over the top of it and narrowly missing its final volley.

The hallways twist and turn, and in the darkness become disorienting. Again, having grown up in tunnels has helped me, because I can remember what paths I've already taken. I come across another target, but this one is unarmed, so I ignore it. A second appears, also unarmed. The third doesn't appear until after I've moved past it. If I hadn't heard the 'click' of it popping out from cover behind me, I would have been shot in the back.

I duck into an alcove as light beams fly past. The 'gunfire' stops for a moment. I wave my hand around the corner as more light beams dance down the hallway. I do it a few more times until I'm certain the target has run out of ammo. I keep moving through the tunnel, blowing past armed targets and ignoring unarmed ones.

Finally, I reach a large room. The opening to the room is blocked by a crate which I carefully peer around. Inside are a handful of targets, all hiding behind crates. Between them is the blue door. To get past them I would need to shoot all of them, because they are so tightly bunched together.

It bothers me that I may not be able to complete this mission because I had enough hubris to venture into the course unarmed. I could go back to one of the earlier targets, but I have no idea if I'd be able to remove a weapon and use it. Even if I could, it would take too much time.

Think, Sam. How do you get around these things?

I decide to stand on the crate nearest me and jump. My hand latches onto the top edge of the wall and I pull myself up. Light nearly hits my scrambling feet, but once I'm standing along the edge the targets no longer register me. It's difficult walking on the edge, which is no more than four or five inches across. I move as quickly as I can without falling, turning along the corners of the walls.

I reach the space between the targets and blue door then jump down. Rolling, I use my momentum to carry me into the door, which swings open as I slam my weight into it. The lights suddenly come on. Jones is already waiting on the other side. The look on his face was worth the extra effort.

"How did I do?" I ask.

It takes him a moment to respond.

"Good and bad," he says.

"What do you mean? Did I take too long?"

"No. In fact you had the fastest time ever recorded. Three minutes, seventeen seconds."

"Then I did well, correct?" I ask.

"Depends on how you look at it. Your point total for the course was zero," says Jones.

"How is that possible?" I ask.

"You get a composite score by multiplying the number of targets you deactivated by the amount of time you have left remaining. That's how they compare how well you did to everyone else. Since you deactivated zero targets, multiplying that by your remaining time equals zero. Not only do you have the fastest time ever recorded, but you also have the lowest score ever recorded."

"So I didn't do well?"

"No, not really," says Jones. "Why didn't you take a weapon with you?"

"Because I don't want to kill anyone."

"I'm sorry, Sam, but in warfare that just isn't realistic. There's going to be casualties," says Jones.

"I know. I just... I want to save as many people as I can. I don't want to kill if I don't have to."

"Just remember that sometimes it's you or them. Sometimes it's kill or be killed."

"I know that better than most, Jones."

43

"Tactics?" I ask.

"That's the plan."

"Will I need my armor?" I ask.

"No, not at all. It's all virtual, kind of like the RLM," he says as we return to the armor room.

We both remove our armor, and I carry mine back to the entry room. I struggle to get it back into the black bag, but eventually manage to.

"You'll need to carry that with you from now on. Keep it back at the barracks when you aren't planning on using it, but you'll need it most of the time now since they already made you scary-smart," says Jones.

"I don't think I'm that smart," I say, lying.

"Yeah, you keep telling yourself that. It's obvious to me, anyway, that you're on your way to becoming like Einstein."

"You mean Vivien?" I ask.

"No, the original guy: Einstein. Big mustache, bigger hair, even bigger brain," says Jones.

"Yes, I know. He was part of my studies," I say.

"He was one of those rare people that really changed the world."

"Like I'm supposed to be?"

"That's the hope," he says, turning to Jessica. "Can you cue up tactics for us?"

She ignores him.

"Please?" he says.

She makes him wait for a few seconds, just long enough for him to question whether she'd actually heard him. But before he can ask again, she looks up.

"Anything for Private Hunter," she says, smiling at me. She pushes a button on her touchscreen and another door illuminates.

As we walk to the door, I finally decide to ask.

"Why does Jessica hate you so much?"

"Because I dated her, but broke up with her to be with her sister," says Jones.

"Who's her sister?" I ask.

"My wife."

"Wait, that makes Jessica your..."

"Sister-in-law," says Jones. "Yeah, the holidays really suck because of it."

"Why did you do that?" I ask.

"Margaret is sweet through and through, like a Hershey's bar. Jessica is like a PayDay, because she's mostly nuts," says Jones.

He laughs, but it takes me a while to get the joke. Even when I do, I don't really laugh.

"Someday you'll figure out humor," says Jones. "Maybe the RLM can train you on it."

"It can't. I already checked."

"Really?" asks Jones.

"No," I say.

Jones starts laughing even harder.

I follow him through the illuminated door labeled 'Tactics' and into a larger room. Inside are a number of seats, much like the RLM rooms. Each one has a different color, so I pick the one colored orange and sit down. Jones pushes a button on the side of the chair, reclining it. The room doesn't go dark, but what I see changes. Instead of seeing the tactics room, I'm inside a warehouse. Thankfully, I can still hear Jones clearly.

"They've tried to make the system as easy to use as possible. You can manipulate and control things by moving your hands around. Touch something and you'll get a readout on the object. In your first battle you'll command a squad of tanks trying to infiltrate a castle."

Suddenly, a group of five tanks appear inside the warehouse. He explains how the simulator's controls work, telling me to pull the terrain toward me to zoom in, and to push it away to zoom out. He also makes sure I know how to look up the information on each tank, such as remaining fuel, damage taken and capabilities. I study the tanks in my group and decide on an older model to run point. It looks sturdier than the newer tanks, but it will be slower.

"You think you got the controls figured out?" asks Jones.

"Yes, I should be fine."

"Great. Okay, I'll go queue up a scenario for you. Good luck."

The warehouse disappears and is replaced by a forest. The abrupt change is a bit disorienting, but I'm able to adjust quickly. Trees form a dense canopy on both sides of a well-traveled dirt road. The road winds for a fair distance and I can't immediately see where it leads.

I change the perspective, leaving my tanks in place but seeing where the road goes. After many turns I finally reach the castle. It's quite large compared to the size of my tanks and will take a while to breach its walls. I also notice two towers, each armed with what appear to be missile launchers. I will need to take those out first. Once I'm certain I've learned everything I can about the castle, I spin my perspective and head back down the road.

I'm glad that I chose to follow the path, because on the way back I see something I hadn't noticed before. It's hard to make out, so I zoom in to get a better look. There are soldiers on both sides of the road, armed with rocket launchers and RPGs. I move down the road a little further and see something strapped to several trees: explosives. It looks as if they're planning to block the tanks in by sealing off the road.

I look in the simulator's menu and I find something called 'Rally Flag'. As I put my hand over it, a help item pops up about the rally flag. It says 'Add a rally flag anywhere on the map as a focal point either to protect, attack or move to.' Waving my arm, I place a rally flag down near the explosives. I travel the path back to where my tanks are and see no other interference along the road.

Selecting my tanks, I form a diamond shape with them: one in front, three in the middle and one in back. I set the turret of the tank in the back to aim backward, the two on the sides toward their respective sides, and the two others straight ahead. It's possible that there are other ambushes I may have missed, and I want to be prepared for any eventuality. I also spread the tanks out, so that even a well-placed attack isn't likely to take out more than one tank at a time.

It takes a while for the tanks to travel to the rally point. Thankfully on my way there I don't run into any additional resistance. I stop the tanks a few hundred feet short of the rally point. Looking through the tanks I find the two with the best attack range. I pull them toward the center of the road and a little closer to where I know the explosives will be. The two tanks I have with the shortest attack range I move off to the sides of the road and in-line with the other two tanks. My last tank I pull back from the others, steering it off the road and into the forest, just in case my plan fails.

I fire a few rounds at the explosive laden trees with the short range tanks, and the area they're in produces a massive ball of fire and smoke. Giving the enemy a chance to move closer and inspect the destruction, I use my long range tanks to fire just past the smoke. I set them to continue firing as I change my perspective to see the aftermath of my attack.

It's clear that all of the explosive trees have been destroyed, but it takes me a moment to count the bodies that have been pulverized by my second attack. I originally counted ten soldiers, five on each side of the road. Eight are dead, which leaves two unaccounted for. I can see the two remaining soldiers hiding behind a large tree, one appears to be using a communication device.

I take the fastest tank I have, which happens to be the one I concealed, and steer it around my other tanks. Aiming its tank gun at ten o'clock, I drive through the wall of smoke and flames. As it emerges, I start firing. My third attack demolishes the tree that the two soldiers were hiding behind, as well as the soldiers themselves. I drive down the road with my tank, making sure there are no other soldiers waiting in ambush. I keep my lead tank in place and drive the other four tanks through the debris. Once the group is back together, I reform my diamond attack pattern.

As the tanks continue down the road I hear aircraft approaching. I change my perspective, spinning the map, until I see two ships I once knew as 'dragons' off in the distance. The sound reminds me of the ship that attacked my people, that killed my surrogate father Lagan and so many others. I flash back to that day, remembering in horrible detail exactly what those ships are capable of.

I steer my tanks off the road, hiding them in a moderately thick section of forest, hoping that the ships will just pass overhead. I raise my tank guns, waiting to see what the ships will do. Once they're within range they fire several hundred rounds of bullets at my tanks, doing only minimal damage, but alerting me to the fact they can see my tanks through the trees. I fire back, narrowly missing both ships. I can tell my aim is low, so I hope to correct that issue on the next pass.

The two ships fly overhead then turn back toward my tanks. I do my best to get the turrets turned in time, but it's no use. The ships are already firing before my tanks can aim their direction. I swing the turrets back around toward where the ships will be, not where they're coming from. As they pass overhead their bullets find their mark, doing more damage this time. One of my tanks starts smoking, but it's still functional.

Before they make it very far past the tanks I fire,

hitting one of the two ships. It explodes, raining pieces of metal down onto the road. The other ship banks hard, turning to its right, making a wide circle around my tanks. I follow its course with my turrets, and as it makes another pass I aim slightly higher than the ship. The tank guns fire in unison, tearing the ship apart and turning it into a fiery cloud of shrapnel.

I check on the status of the damaged tank. It appears to be operational, no injuries reported, but it will have to move at a reduced speed. Instead of using it as part of my attack I decide to leave it behind. I have its crew evacuate the tank and set up hidden, remotely detonated explosives around it, just in case the enemy sends someone to investigate. I then have them move deeper into the forest, but still close enough to trigger the explosives.

I form a new diamond pattern with the remaining tanks and send them toward the castle. It doesn't take them long to reach striking distance. I move my tanks off the road, using the trees and foliage as camouflage. I very carefully position the tanks, so that they rest within firing range of the castle while still maintaining a clear line-of-sight through the trees. Once I'm sure that everything is in position, I fire a volley at the front of the castle.

The front wall of the castle crumbles, and I watch as soldiers come pouring into the open area within its walls. I have my tanks aim slightly higher and fire a second volley. Dozens of soldiers are decimated by the attack. A third volley lands toward the back of the castle, sending panicked soldiers in all directions. I wait for a moment as people scramble.

Too late I realize that one of the missile towers is still standing. It returns fire, although its missiles fall short of my tanks. It may be that they don't have our location dialed in, but I won't risk my soldiers. I turn two of my tank's turrets toward the tower and fire. A direct hit sends the tower crashing to the ground. That's when I see it: a white flag. The soldiers scattered in the mess of stone and wood all put their hands into the air, signaling their surrender.

I stop firing and steer my tanks onto the road. Slowly, I move them up to the castle, waiting for the simulator to let me know I've won. I'm just about to enter the castle with my lead tank, when the entire front half of the castle explodes. The stats on my four tanks go blank, letting me know they were destroyed. My stomach feels like someone kicked it, but I still have my broken, slow moving tank in reserve.

After loading my two remaining soldiers back into their tank, I limp it slowly along the road. It feels like it takes forever. Once I'm within range I start firing on the castle. I make sure that no section of wall remains, and that no soldier is left alive. Only when I've finished killing every enemy soldier does the system flash the message "Victory!" I wouldn't call it that. I've lost eighty percent of my forces, and what I do have left barely functions. I fell victim to their trap, and I should have seen it coming.

The scenario disappears and my eyes suddenly see the real world again. Looking up at Jones, I shake my head in disgust.

"Not bad for your first time," says Jones.

"It was horrible. I lost most of my men," I say.

"Yes, but you snatched victory from the jaws of defeat."

"What an annoyingly useless saying. I was incompetent."

"No, Sam, you weren't. Almost everyone loses this scenario. Here, I'll show you the analytics," says Jones.

He walks over to the wall and touches a screen. It comes to life, and after a few seconds of pushing buttons it shows a pie graph of outcomes. The largest portion by far, taking up ninety percent of the graph, shows losing the scenario due to the forest ambush. Seven percent are destroyed by the aircraft. Two percent lose when the ground beneath the front of the castle explodes. Only one percent earn victory.

"Were you part of the one percent?" I ask.

"No, I lost when I sent all my tanks into the castle and

it exploded. I didn't have a reserve like you did. That was a smart move by the way, Sam."

"I didn't want the damaged tank to slow the other ones down, so I left it behind. It was just dumb luck that I had it at the end. I would have sent it into the explosion, just like the other tanks."

"Better lucky than good," says Jones.

"I'd rather be good. You can't count on luck, but you can count on yourself if you work hard enough," I say.

"I suppose. Want to run a few more?" asks Jones.

"That would be fine."

We spend the next several hours running scenarios. I learn about the weapons and capabilities of dozens of aircraft, naval ships, drones and ground troops. I also get to utilize the deep knowledge of tactics that Vivien downloaded into me. Thankfully, I never do as poorly as I did in my first scenario.

I actually enjoy the scenarios where I get to use aircraft, until I attack a group of ground troops with one of the 'dragons'. It reminds me of what it was like to be on the other end of that kind of attack. That's when I stop. Up until that point it was just a game to me. I really didn't think too much about the digital soldiers being real people. Watching them flee as I shower bullets down on them makes me sick to my stomach.

"Stop! Get me out of this thing!" I yell.

Suddenly the scenario disappears.

"What's wrong?" asks Jones. "You were doing really well."

"I can't do this!"

"But you've been doing great. You're way ahead of the curve. In fact, you're by far the best we've seen. If you just look at the statistics, you'll see..." says Jones, but I cut him off.

"I don't care about the statistics, or being the best, or winning this war! I don't want to kill people!"

"It's not about killing people, it's about protecting them, Sam. The reason why we war is to protect our own."

"I don't care about your people! I don't care about the

soldiers here. I just care about my home," I say.

"You know that if we don't win the war, your home will be destroyed too, right?"

"Maybe that will happen, and maybe it won't. But I'm willing to take that chance. I'd rather die with my people than kill an enemy I don't even know."

Suddenly, the screen behind Jones turns on by itself, flashing footage of soldiers that I can only imagine are from the Western Allied Military. It shows them doing horrible things to civilians. The elderly, children; it doesn't seem to matter. They're killed, raped, mutilated in ways that make me literally gag on my own bile.

"I know what propaganda is," I yell out, hoping the conspirators can hear me. "I know that those are probably isolated cases, and that their army probably isn't all like that. It won't work on me. You can drown in the loud waters!"

The screen goes blank for a moment. The next images are of the Crag. I see Flot and Ebb standing just inside the cave, their bows raised at the camera. They aren't the only ones. All of the hunters are lined up, ready to throw spears and launch arrows.

A ship. The video feed must be coming from a ship. They're going to kill them.

"Are you threatening my people?" I yell, already knowing the answer.

The screen goes blank again. After a few seconds, one word in big letters appears: 'YES'.

I scream, flailing around the room, knocking over chairs, kicking things, hitting anything I can. Jones has to tackle me and pin me to the ground.

"Sam! SAM! You have to stop this, for both our sake's. Think of your people! Think of my family! Please Sam, help us! I don't want my family to die!"

I stop fighting Jones. I want to help his family and I want to save my people. The problem is, the people I'm fighting for are now my real enemy. They have threatened the people I care about most.

"I want to talk to Desmond, in person, NOW!" I yell.

The screen goes blank. After a moment, it flashes the word 'YES'.

It doesn't take long for Desmond to appear, almost like he'd predicted my request. As he walks up to us, I notice that he's made of lean muscle. Desmond's shoulders are covered by stringy, sun bleached hair. His skin is red from being outside too long and his face is filled with lines and cracks despite his apparent youth. I would have guessed by his voice that he was only in his mid-thirties, but his face makes him seem closer to fifty. It looks like he's seen a lifetime of hardship and war in a third of that time.

I leap at Desmond, wrapping my fingers around his throat and knocking him to the ground. I try to choke the life out of him, letting all of the rage and hatred I've built up flow through my hands. That's when Jones pulls me off him, keeping me in a choke hold from behind. I struggle, but there's nothing I can do the way he's holding me. I nod, letting Jones known I'll stop. The screen now shows the word 'NO' on it.

"Let me kill him!" I yell.

The screen flashes the word 'NO' again.

"That is my bargain. I will win your war if you let me kill him. He means nothing to you, and you know that you can't really kill the people of the Crag, because once you do, I'm useless to you. You know I won't fight. Let me have this, let me kill this man, and I will do whatever you say," I state, coldly.

It takes a moment for the screen to finally respond. 'YES'.

I can see the shock and horror on Desmond's face. He knows that he is dead now. That there's nothing anyone can do to stop it. That he really has outlived his usefulness. That I have won.

He takes a step back.

"Stop," I say, staring him down.

He takes another step back.

"I won't kill you," I say.

He stops.

"Wh-why?" he mutters.

"I want you dead, but I want it to be on my terms. I'd rather have you live the rest of your very short life knowing that at any moment I could ask the conspirators here to kill you, and they would do it. That you mean nothing to them. That you are merely a pawn in this chess game. Whatever life you have left, I own. Now leave, before I change my mind."

Desmond stares at me blankly.

"GO!" I bark.

He turns and runs like the coward he is.

I look over at Jones. His face has so many emotions on it that I can't quite read it. It's a long, uncomfortable moment before either of us talk.

"Make sure I never get on your bad side," says Jones.

I actually laugh a bitter, sardonic laugh then turn to him and smile.

"That's Desmond," I say.

"Yeah, I got that," he replies. "What are you going to do now?"

"Protect my people. That's all I've ever wanted to do."

I make sure to say it loudly, so that the conspirators hear me. I want them to believe that I'm agreeing to fight for them. That their extortion worked.

44

I walk out of the room, leaving Jones behind. He doesn't try to stop me. Neither does the ominous touchscreen on the wall. More than anything I want to rip it off its mounts, but it wouldn't solve anything. It's the person sending messages that I want to hurt, not an innocent piece of technology. On the way out I grab my armor bag and drop it off at the barracks.

I spend an hour taking my rage out on a punching bag in the workout facility. It feels good to hit something over and over again. Even after my arms tire I still have energy to burn so I run on a treadmill for a while. Eventually fatigue slows me down so I stop, realizing that if I keep going I'll only be torturing myself. Figuring I've had enough pain to last a lifetime, I go back to the barracks and shower.

The sweat built up after a day of physical activity and anxiety gets washed away. I wish I could do the same with the anger boiling inside me. Make it go away. Make this whole place go away. It's killing me, and I know it.

When I'm finally hungry I eat an early dinner. After burning so many calories and missing lunch I'm starving. I load up on fried chicken, lasagna and hamburger patties; chicken and hamburger meat for the protein, lasagna for the complex carbohydrates. That's one thing I'm glad I've learned: nutrition. It didn't take long for Vivien to teach me about human physiology, but I'm glad it did.

Once I finish wolfing down my meal I head back to

the Barracks. I'm not sure what to do before lights out, so I open up the armor bag I left lying on my bed. I put the armor back on and start practicing martial arts moves that I learned from Vivien.

Jones was right. Even though I know what moves to make, they don't feel natural. I have very good control of my body thanks to years of hunting, so I can imagine how difficult it would be for someone less athletic to effectively use martial arts they'd been taught from a machine.

I wish I still had someone to spar with, like Ebb or Harriet. They taught me so much about the basics of fighting. Ebb's training does help when I need to throw a punch, and Harriet's helps with my ability to kick. I focus on that more, though, because it's my weakness, and I hate not being good at something.

I spend the next few hours doing katas, practicing my moves as people trickle into the barracks. A few people watch, but most just ignore me. I try not to focus on them, instead hoping to build up some muscle memory and experience. I won't be a master, but I also won't be worthless in a fight. When I'm certain I've tried every move I know at least once, I take off the armor, shower, then go to bed.

For the first time in a long while I'm able to sleep comfortably through the night. Knowing that I could have Desmond killed at any time helps. I don't plan to kill him, but what matters to me is that I actually have some sort of control over the situation. The less control I have over a situation, the more I despair about it.

The next morning I wake up energized. I take another shower, brush my teeth and put on a fresh set of clothes. Jones is there to greet me again at the entrance, a scowl in place of his usual impish grin.

"Normally they give you time to prepare," starts Jones. "A week, sometimes a month depending on the candidate. For you, they've decided to give you 'The Test'... today."

"And?" I say.

"And nothing. Aren't you worried?" he asks.

"No."

"Why not?"

"I'll either pass it, or I won't," I say.

"I don't think you get it. If you don't pass, you don't pass. That means that they scrap the project and start over."

"So?"

"When they scrap a project, the people who worked on it are no longer valuable. In your case they'll probably kill you. If you anger them enough they could kill the entire Crag," says Jones.

"That would be a waste of time and resources. Of course they wouldn't destroy the Crag."

"You may have pissed them off enough that they'd do it just to spite you. Anyway, bring your armor. You're probably going to need it."

"Do I at least get breakfast?" I ask.

"No. They don't want you throwing up. We leave now," says Jones.

I run to my bed, grab my armor that I had resting on my footlocker and hustle back to Jones.

"Should I put it on now?" I ask.

"I have no idea, but I'm sure they'll tell you if you need it."

We head to the elevator and get in. This time Jones pushes a button for a floor I'm unfamiliar with: D42. As the doors open, I look down a long hallway. At the end of the hallway, written on the door, is the phrase "Don't Panic."

"What is this place?" I ask as we walk toward the door.

"The test center, where all your worst nightmares come true."

"Really?"

"Yeah, really. They try to break you; see what you're capable of. They invest a lot of money in training soldiers, and they want to make sure they get their money's worth. They'll throw everything they can think of at you and then some. I'm sorry, Sam, but I can't go any further," he says, stopping in front of the door.

"Why not?"

"Don't know. Those were my instructions. Take you to the door, make sure you go inside then leave."

"Will you come back for me when I'm done?" I ask.

"If there's something left to come back for, sure."

"That isn't helping, Jones."

"It should. You need to grasp the seriousness of this. Don't mess around. They won't."

I think for a moment then turn and shake his hand.

"Thanks Jones, for everything."

"Thank me by not dying."

I open the door and step inside. Before my eyes can adjust to the bright light, I fall unconscious.

* * *

I wake up inside a white room. I don't see any doors, windows, or openings of any kind. The blank walls radiate a soft, white light. The only things in the room, other than me, are a sheet of paper and pencil.

I sit down on the cold, hard floor. For something that seems to be producing light I would have thought it'd be warmer. It's also the first time I realize I'm no longer wearing the uniform I had on when I went through the door. Instead, I'm wearing a white hospital gown, tied in back.

My exposed backside resting on the cold floor makes things feel even more uncomfortable. I don't understand why they felt the need to irritate me while they were testing me.

I look at the paper in front of me. The first page is a series of simple questions. 'What is your name?' 'Do you have any family?' 'What is your favorite color?' I quickly finish the first page and set it face down next to the other pages. The room changes colors to a very bright yellow color. That's when I realize the second page itself is a yellow color to match. Thankfully, there's still plenty of light to work by, and I can read the page with little effort.

The questions on this page are slightly more difficult than before. 'What is the quadratic equation?' 'What is the deepest lake in the world?' 'Who painted the Mona Lisa?' I answer them easily, but I wonder why they're bothering to ask such basic questions.

In the back of my mind, as I answer questions, I start to wonder about the other pages; the other colors. I finish the second page, and the room turns a light blue color. Again, the new page I hold in my hands is light blue to match. Something seems wrong about this. I pick up the entire test, and as I flip through the pages I realize that as the test goes on, the pages get darker and darker. On the darkest pages the writing is no longer black. Instead, it's white, so that I can still read it.

But if the room turns black to match the black page, I won't be able to see to finish the test. I pull out the last page which is pure black. I keep the other pages I haven't finished in a separate stack so that I don't miss any questions. I scan the questions on the page and they are bizarre. 'Which animals do you like to mutilate?' 'What does human flesh taste like?' 'Why is the clown in the bathtub?' 'If you were the last person in the world, how would you kill yourself?' 'What is crawling under your skin?'

This is sick. I cannot understand why they would ask these questions. I start to fill in the first question with 'I don't like to mutilate animals,' when an ear splitting noise cuts through the silence. The sound is so piercing that it makes concentrating difficult. I put the black page down and the noise stops.

I have a decision to make. I can take the test in order, and in silence, and not be able to finish it, or I can take it out of order and fight against the sound. I need to finish this test, so I will do my best to ignore the sound. While I still have light, I will answer the questions on the darkest pages then go back to working on the pages in order.

The black page takes a while to finish because I have to give long answers that explain why I've never stabbed someone with a knife, or dipped my hands in acid for fun. It's also extremely hard to concentrate with the sound hurting my ears. I have to hope that it's not loud enough to do permanent damage, although it feels like it might be.

I put the black page down, face up in a fourth stack then work on a dark blue page. The noise persists, but the questions become slightly more normal. At least the way they ask the questions does. 'Have you ever wanted to hurt yourself?' 'Do you ever want to hurt others?' 'Did your mother love you?' 'Describe the differences between integrals and derivatives, and explain how they are related.'

I answer as quickly as I can just to make the noise go away. By the fourth dark page I've had enough. I look at the darkest remaining page and it's crimson, like blood. It looks like if they had the lights at a level to match, I could still read what's on the page. So I go back to the light blue page.

I start answering the first question, expecting the ringing to stop. It sounds quieter than before, but remains. I cover my ears and realize that the ringing isn't going on outside my ears. I know enough about human physiology to recognize that I now have permanent hearing loss.

As I go through the rest of the pages, the room grows darker. Lavender, green, burnt orange and finally crimson. Part of me wishes I'd pushed through to a happier color. The hairs on the back of my neck stand up as I realize I'm trapped in a very small room and the walls are coated in blood. I know they aren't really, at least the rational part of my brain knows that, but the irrational, fearful part of me doesn't. I panic. It makes me focus even harder on the test, trying to ignore my surroundings. Once I finish, I collect up the stack of papers and set them down.

"Done!" I yell. "Now let me out!"

Nothing happens.

"I finished the test. Get me out of here!"

Nothing.

I sit and wait, hoping something will change. That something will happen, but nothing does. I look through the stack of papers, making sure that every question is answered. I even double check that there aren't any questions on the backs of the pages. Everything has been answered, and I don't see any other questions.

I walk over to the walls and put my hands against them. I try to feel around for something that might let me escape. A lever, a button, a handle. The more I touch the walls, the more uneasy I feel, until I'm sure I've missed nothing. Even though I've touched every single section of wall, I go over them again. Still nothing.

My claustrophobia kicks in. The room seems to be getting smaller, even though I know it's not. Wait, I think the room actually *is* getting smaller. I start in one corner and count the paces across the room to the opposite corner. Heel-to-toe it's about 20 steps. I do it again, and this time it's only 19. I try again to make sure the room is actually shrinking, and this time it's only 18 paces across.

I run over to one of the walls and start pounding on it. Nothing. No reaction. I try yelling as loud as I can, but no one responds. Getting a running start, I send my shoulder flying into the wall. I bounce off, crumpling to the floor.

Rolling, I get to my feet as fast as I can. I need to solve this or I'll be crushed to death. I kick at the walls; nothing. I scream; nothing. For a second I have a crazy idea. As loud as I can, I try to make the same noise that the room was producing while I filled out the dark pages. My heart sinks when I realize it isn't helping.

The room has grown so small now that I can lie down and stretch out my arms and legs, and touch both ends of the room. I try to push against the walls with both, using every ounce of strength I have, but the walls keep shrinking inward. It seems like there's nothing I can say or do to make the room stop.

As much as I want to give into my claustrophobia and scream, I don't. Instead, I focus. I sit down in the middle of the room, on top of the useless test, and close my eyes. It doesn't matter anymore. Let them crush me. If the end is coming, I'll go out with dignity.

My mind drifts to the Crag. To Ebb. I'll never get to see her smile again. I'll never get to hug Flot. Better it ends this way. They won't hurt my people anymore. I'll just be another person that didn't work out, who couldn't cut it. At least my people will be safe. There will be no reason for the conspirators to come after my family.

A few tears stream down my face. I start to feel the walls touch my knees, and the ceiling touch my head. I ball myself up as tightly as I can, trying to wring out the last few droplets of life I have left.

"I love you Ebb," is the last thing I say.

45

The walls stop. I'm not dead yet, but I will be soon. I can barely breathe. There's not enough air in this tiny pocket and it's making me dizzy. The blood red lights turn off and I'm plunged into darkness, but I'm not afraid. Whatever happens, happens.

Unbelievably, the walls start pulling away from me. I can breathe again as air rushes in to fill the vacuum. I spread out as the room expands, stretching my aching muscles. I'm still alive. I just wish I knew why the room didn't crush me.

Instead of expanding to the size that the room was when I woke up, it continues expanding, until a door melts into view on the wall in front of me. Not willing to risk it disappearing, I run for the door.

It has a knob like almost any door, but when I twist it, it doesn't open. I pull hard on the door but it won't budge. I even get a running start and slam into it with no success.

There's no keyhole; no way to pick the lock. Even if I could, I don't have the tools I'd need. There must be a way to open this door, otherwise they wouldn't have put it in here.

I look around the room, searching for anything that might open the door, but the only things in this room are me, a pencil, and the test. That's when I have an idea that seems so obvious it's stupid. There's no way it could be this easy. I go back to the center of the room, pick up the pencil and paper and carry them with me back to the door. This time, when I twist the knob, the door opens.

Relief fills me, but it's tempered with frustration at the test. Whoever designed it is part mad genius and part idiot. I make a note to myself that if I ever meet the person who came up with this death trap, I'll punch them in the face.

As I walk through the door, I enter a room very similar to the first. There's nothing on the walls, just stark whiteness surrounding me. What's different though, and what concerns me, is the little girl sitting in the middle of the room.

She looks just as confused as I am to be here. Her clothes are plain; a white shirt and light blue pants. Her hair, which is long and pulled back into a pony tail, is a deep auburn color. I stare at her, not knowing if she herself is a trap, or if she's a victim of the conspirator's sick and twisted game. Something catches my eye. Something I hadn't noticed before. A monogram on her shirt. Stitched right over her heart is a name: 'SAM'.

I'm not alone. The revelation hits me, bringing tears to my eyes, but doubt immediately rips away whatever feelings of belonging I temporarily have. I can't know for sure if she's part of the evil project that created me, or if it's merely a ruse.

The more I look at her face, the more familiar it seems, and the more I sense that I've seen her before. Sometime long ago, maybe. But that isn't possible. She's young enough that she couldn't have been born very long ago, and she certainly wouldn't have been this age. Something still doesn't feel right, like I'm missing something obvious.

Finally, after we stare at each other for an uncomfortable moment, I decide to speak.

"Hello," I say.

She tries to smile but can't. Instead her face contorts into a sad, forced grimace. Like her, there are times I try to show the world something other than what I'm feeling, but my emotions always seep out, obvious to those around me.

"It's okay," I start to say. "I'm going to help you. You can trust me."

I start walking toward her as she pulls her head back

from my outstretched arm. I stop, hoping not to frighten her. As I sit down, I make my frame small and non-threatening. I don't look her directly in the eye, and wait for her to respond. After a tense moment, she finally speaks.

"Who are you?" she asks.

"I'm Sam," I say.

"So am I."

"It's nice to meet you, Sam," I say.

"Are you going to hurt me?" she blurts, obviously still frightened.

"No, I won't hurt you. I want to help you if I can," I say.

"Why are we here?" she asks.

"I was hoping you might know, actually," I say.

"No."

"Do you know how you got here?" I ask.

"No. I don't remember anything before I woke up here."

"Nothing? You don't remember your family, or where you came from, or anything like that?" I ask.

She thinks hard. I can tell she's struggling to remember. Her eyes lose focus as she drifts away into her own thoughts.

"No. I can't remember any of that," she says. "Do you know how you got here?"

"Yes. I'm supposed to be taking a test."

"A test?"

"Yes. And it seems like they're trying to kill me while they're doing it. Are you okay? I mean physically. You're not hurt, are you?" I ask.

"I don't think so," she replies, meekly.

"Good. Now before we do anything, I'm going to slowly walk around you. I need to make sure we aren't in any danger. Can you hold still while I do that?" I ask.

"Yes, I can do that."

"Good girl. Okay, I'm going to walk around now," I say.

I move around the room, acting like I'm checking the walls for buttons or levers. What I'm really doing is moving behind her, so that I can see if they planted an explosive device on her. I don't want her to know that though, because I don't want her to be more frightened than she already is. Once I'm all the way behind her, I get down on the ground and look at the underside of her chair.

I let out a sigh of relief as I realize that she isn't rigged to explode. I don't see any sort of cords or wires or anything attached to her. She's just sitting in a regular wooden chair. I also finally notice that the door I came in has disappeared.

"Okay, you're doing great, Sam," I say. "What I'd like you to do is stand up very slowly and step away from the chair."

As she rises I hold my breath. Even though it doesn't look like she's in any danger, I might have missed something. I hope the Sky Gods are watching over us now.

She stands upright and takes a few steps away from the chair. Nothing happens. I move closer to the chair and inspect it. It seems like a regular wooden chair. Being bold, I move the chair slightly. Still, nothing happens.

"Okay, I think we're safe here," I say, just as I hear a noise behind me.

I turn around quickly, holding the chair up to protect myself from whatever is happening, but it's a waste. On the wall behind me is a new door.

"I think they mean for us to go through it," says Sam.

"I agree. Can you do me a favor? Can you please hold onto my papers and my pencil?" I ask.

"Yes."

I hand her my test and she rolls it into a tube around the pencil. She keeps her fist clenched tightly around it, protecting it like it's made of gold. I hold her other small hand in mine and lead her over to the door.

"Are you ready?" I ask.

She nods her head. I open the door with my free hand and lead her in.

We're near a 'T' intersection at the end of a hallway. As soon as we approach the 'T' I hear the door behind us disappear.

"Which way do you think we should go?" I ask. "Right or left?"

"Ummm, left I guess," she says.

We go down the left corridor which is immediately followed by another corner. This one only leads to the right. I peer around the corner and see a dozen soldiers, each armed with assault rifles, and they're aiming them in our direction. I quickly pull back as bullets rip through the air. I tug at Sam's hand but she doesn't move fast enough. I decide to pick her up and carry her to make sure we get away safely. Running past the 'T', we head down its right corridor instead.

Just as we're about to turn, I stop and look around the corner. This hallway appears deserted. I check behind us and wait to make sure the soldiers haven't followed. My instinct is to run as fast as we can down the hallway, but instead I tell Sam to wait for me.

"Can I have my pencil back for a moment?" I ask her.

She smiles at me, and I catch a trace of hope in it. I need to save this little girl.

Sam pulls the pencil out from her tube of papers and hands it to me. I pull my hand back and throw the pencil down the hallway. Suddenly the hallway comes to life. Machine guns pop out of the walls and try in vain to shoot the pencil. It's such a small and fast moving target that they can't hit it, and the pencil clanks safely on the ground at the other end of the hallway.

"One more time," I say to Sam.

I take off my gown and throw it down the hallway. It doesn't go very far before it comes undone, spreading out and slowing down about halfway there. Thankfully, the machine guns ignore it, confirming my hope that they only attack the first thing that passes through.

"I'll go first, just in case," I say.

Sam follows behind me as I creep along the corridor.

I wave my hand quickly in front of the first machine gun and it doesn't react. We take our time walking down the long hallway. I reach down, pick up my gown and put it back on. Amazingly, we make it to the end of the hallway safely. I grab the pencil and hand it back to Sam.

We follow the turn in the hallway left and then right again. I should have been more careful, because as we take the right, we run directly into two soldiers, each armed with assault rifles. Before I realize what I've done, I've reacted, taking the assault rifle away from the first and using it on the second, perforating his chest.

Blood splatters everywhere in these close quarters and Sam screams in fear, her face now coated in red. I hit the first soldier in the face with the butt of the rifle, sending him to his knees. I swing it again and his body topples over, obviously unconscious.

I've killed someone. I actually... killed someone. I had no choice, but...

I look at Sam, and her look of horror matches mine.

"I'm sorry," I say weakly, not knowing if I'm apologizing to Sam, or to the man I just killed.

As she stands there, gripped with terror, I take the clean side of my gown and do my best to wipe the blood from her face.

"There, all better," I say, knowing that nothing will make it better. "Are you hurt?"

"N... no. I'm okay," she says. She seems frightened of me again.

"Sam, I need you to understand something. I'm very sorry for what happened to that man, but he was going to kill us if I didn't act. They both were. I'm trying to keep us alive. I may have to shoot other people now. Do you understand why I had to do it?" I ask.

She thinks for a moment.

"Yes," she says quietly. Her answer takes a while to come out, and it sounds tired and raspy when it finally emerges.

"Okay. I'm going to do everything I can to protect you, so stay close to me. And no matter what happens, stay behind me," I say.

She nods.

I sling the assault rifle in my hands over my shoulder then pick the unused assault rifle off the ground, pointing it in front of us. Sam does as she was told and follows close behind me. Every twenty feet or so I look over my shoulder, making sure that no one's crept up on us. We walk down the long hallway and reach another 'T'.

"Which way?" I ask.

"Left?" she says, unsure of her own answer.

"Sure, let's do left," I say.

We take the left corridor and I spot something strange at the end of it: a teddy bear sitting on the ground.

Before I realize what's happening, Sam races past me.

"NO!" I scream.

I sprint after her, hoping to catch her before she reaches the obvious death trap.

"Stop Sam," I yell. "It will kill you!"

She doesn't listen. All that she cares about is the teddy bear.

I close the gap, gaining on her. She's so fast for a little girl it's surprising, but I'm faster. After several more steps I realize I won't be able to stop her before she reaches the bear, but I have to try. I'm only a few steps behind her as we reach the end of the hallway. If I'm going to do something, I have to do it now.

Instinct takes over. I leap out toward her, just as she's about to touch the bear, and I grab onto her shoulders. I've jumped so high that I pass over her, and at the same time I pull back hard, flinging her away from the bear. It feels like everything is happening in slow motion now, as I watch her start to fall backward, away from danger. My arms and legs twist in the air, miraculously turning me toward the teddy bear. As I reach the bear, I cover it with my body to shield Sam from the explosion. I hope she survives.

That's when I feel the pain of my body being ripped apart. My final thought, as the world disappears, is that I'm glad it ended quickly.

46

It's strange what thoughts a person has as they die. Was I loved? Did I love others enough? Did my life have meaning? Will anyone remember me? Why do I have to die? Why does anyone have to die? Was life really worth living at all?

And then my thoughts grow stranger, because I see faces. I'm in a large white room, surrounded by people I don't know, and they all look at me expectantly.

Am I in hell? Was I such a horrible person that I've been banished to this sterile room, filled with people I don't know, just staring at me like I'm some sort of freak? Is my eternity to be filled with an obvious metaphor for the separation between me and the human race? Where all I feel is shame and loneliness? The Sky Gods be damned if that's where I am, for I have done everything they've asked of me.

But then I realize that this is my punishment for killing a man. A man I did not know. A man that could have had a family. Could have been a wonderful person. But I will never know, because I took his life. Because I thought I had to take his life to protect my own. His orders were to stop me. He was a marionette, dangling from the strings of the conspirators, and he held no ill-will toward me. And yet I killed him just the same. Maybe I do deserve hell.

Just as I slip into a downward spiral of self-loathing and despair, the strangest thing happens: I see faces I recognize. Charles. Harriet. And Jones.

They've killed Jones too? He's dead because of me? And why is he here in hell? What did he do to deserve this? Or Charles or Harriet? They were good people. I deserve this, but they do not.

Jones walks over and looks down at me. That's when I realize for the first time that I'm not standing up; I'm actually leaning back, as if I'm in a chair, resting. Why would they try to make me comfortable in hell? That makes no sense. What makes even less sense is when Jones speaks.

"You did good, Sam."

"What?" I ask, surprised to hear my own voice.

"You've passed. We won't know all the details until the computer can process the data, but you passed 'The Test'."

"But I'm dead," I say.

"No, you aren't. That was brave of you to save her. People cried when they watched you do that," says Jones.

"I... I don't understand," I say.

"None of it really happened. From the time you entered the door here you've been in a simulation. You didn't die, you never killed the guard, and the little girl named Sam doesn't exist."

I start crying. Not because I'm happy I didn't die, and not because I didn't kill the guard. I cry because I'm alone again. There isn't anyone else like me. I wish I had died then. I wish I was in my old hell, because this new hell is even worse.

"It's okay, Sam. I know it's a lot to process," says Jones.

"I want to die," I say. "Kill me! Please!"

"Sam, I don't understand. You're safe now. It's all going to be okay. And Charles and Harriet are okay too. They weren't killed. Aren't you happy that they aren't dead? It was all a trick. Things aren't as bad as they seemed."

I look around the room. Harriet smiles and Charles waves. Geiger is here too, standing next to Sheila. That's when I see Desmond. I jump out of the chair, and in one fluid motion I'm on top of him again, trying to choke him to death.

"Bring her back!" I yell.

313

Many gasps of surprise fill the room. Jones and Charles rush over, pulling me off Desmond.

"Sam, stop. You can't do this," says Jones.

I fight against them until they let me go. Staring down at Desmond, lying there, gasping for air... it makes me realize just how pathetic he truly is.

"Why did you make me think they were dead?" I ask.

"To see how you'd react," he says, his voice gravelly. "We needed to know what you'd do. We've kept Harriet and Charles safe and nearby, and they've been watching your progress. They're proud of you. We had to hide them from the general population though, because of what you suspected. We can't let people know your secret, Sam, or there could be... repercussions."

"Who else knows my secret?" I ask.

"Just me, them, a few other people higher up. You can't tell anyone else," says Desmond.

"Does Jones know?" I ask, turning to Jones. "Do you know my secret?"

"No, Sam, I don't."

"Did you know that Charles and Harriet were alive all along?"

"No. I've been in the dark on all this until you started the test. Then they told me the truth. Or at least part of it, anyway," says Jones.

I think a long moment before I speak.

"I'm glad that Harriet and Charles are okay. I'm glad that I didn't kill that soldier. But I won't forgive you for her," I say, staring at Desmond.

"But you passed 'The Test'," says Desmond, standing up.

"I don't care."

"You should. You're the only one that's ever passed it. This was the real test. It's how we know we've found the right person to lead us. Many, many others have tried and failed, but you didn't. In fact, there's only one thing we feel you still need."

I hate that I care. I hate that they've manipulated me into even asking the question.

"What do you think I need?" I ask.

"You need experience leading," says Desmond.

"I was the Leader of the Hunt."

"Yes, but you need to see things from the perspective of what's good for the greater whole. You focus too much on individuals. You need to learn how to make hard choices. How to sacrifice a few of your soldiers to save even more lives. To achieve that, we've brought in a specialist of sorts. It's an old friend of yours. Here, I'll get them."

I watch as Desmond walks over to a panel next to the door and presses a button. "It's time," is all he says.

The door opens. I'm not prepared for what I see. It doesn't make sense. I thought... he was dead.

"It's your old friend from the Crag. He says that he's already taught you much about leadership. That he thinks of you as his own child. He's also told us what you mean to him," says Desmond.

My mouth goes dry. He's there, standing in front of me, alive and well. A ghost from my past. The last person I ever expected to see again.

Chaff.

Acknowledgements

I would like to personally thank the following people for helping in the development of this story. They provided feedback that made *Sky Machine* a much stronger book. I owe them a huge debt of gratitude.

Nicole Vesper

Renee Moore

Ray Kirkpatrick

Dawn Angela Martin

Brenda Gordon

Special Thanks

I would also like to thank the people who backed the
Kickstarter project and spread the word about this story.
You are my Sky Children.

Nicole Vesper
Renee, Tom and Riley
Moore
Jordan Bennett
Tess Watson
Patty McCalister
Brandy and Zak Kribbs
Michael Kinney
Mandy McCalister
Chrystal Clifton
Elizabeth Betts McCarty
Jessica Warren
Holli Rapp
Brandon and Robin Reese
Dawn Angela Martin
Deborah Brenner
Donita Brenner
Lisa Sauerwein
Jennie Hulegaard
Brittany Thompson
Amy Church
James Thomas
Moses Stickney
James Scharmann
Dan Heinig
Rolla Selbak
Blake Eckhoff
Jenna and Jona
Sagapolutele
Chris Batchelor

Kirby McCauley
Josephine
Cherie Huber
Jessica Vaupotic
Heather Beam
Jonathan Bisbee
Gary Powers
Erica and Lee Potter
Mckenzie Fritch
Fabio Pigagnelli
Ana Imelda Yerkes
Alyssa JoJo Barger
Natasha Welch
Asta Staal
Steve Gayler
Chloe Jacques
Marie-Christin Holler
Rocio Carter
Rosie McFaul
Ashley Zema
Varity Schwartz
thatraja
David McCready
Christi Bruce
Carolyn Wolfram
Nicole Hall
Kelly Marie McLeod
J. R. Wagner
Melissa and Nick Nelson
Michael Newlyn Blake

Ashley Oswald
Francis Waltz
Brittni Evans
Katie McFarlin
Calum Webb
Jonathan Stevens
The Riggs Family
The Brenners
Andrea Munson
Jane Meade Glanville
Jason Anderson
Lani Ambitious Brownett
Shepherd
Cosmic Lovegood Love
Christopher Glover
Gloria Minor Fridley
Adilia Stiles-Megara
Kathy Houston Ziglar
Stephanie Giusti
Isabel Castruita
Kathryn Jacoby
Sif Hagelskær Jensen
Karen Sawaya
Amy Sawaya
Marie Cherie
Patrick Chan
Felicia Fitterer
Brandy Neuleib

Shane Anderson
Janet Armetani
Sara Abbott
Courtney S.
Casey Fox
Jenice Powell
Amy C. Smith
J. S. Elliot
Stephanie Bujjoni
Melissa Swanson
D. Carey Taschuk
Tammie Hutto Egloff
Swordfire
Matthew Lowe
Blazing Works
Siike Donnelly
Kim Bassens
Corey Terhune
Angela Ward
The Nickelson family
Florian
Robert
Margaret St. John
Alex Meisel
Nathan Duby
Kenn Clulow
Ray Kirkpatrick
Brenda Gordon

About the Author

T. M Brenner lives in California with his editor/wife Nicole Vesper. He spends most of his free time feeding his writing addiction. When not typing away feverishly on his laptop, he enjoys visiting the coast, watching re-runs of Psych, and spending time with his family.

To find out more about T. M. Brenner's writing, visit: www.tmbrenner.com